"So are you saying I'm better or worse than your ex-fiancé?" Larry asked.

"Worse, from a woman's perspective. I bet every woman who's dated you thought she might be the one who makes you fall in love," she said. "You are the worst sort of man. A challenge with just enough charm to make women not hate you."

"You know me so well," he said, and she couldn't be certain whether he was being sarcastic or not. "And not every one was trying to marry me," he said slowly, as if he were tallying them all up in his head.

Kat let out a snort. "Someday, it'll happen to you. You'll fall in love, and then you'll find out what it feels like to be me and all the other women who were dumb enough to fall in love."

He raised his eyebrows. "Are you saying you're in love with me?"

"You *are* hopeless," she said blandly. "I wouldn't fall in love with you if you were the last man on earth." She meant every word.

"All the more reason to sleep with me," he said.

Also by Jane Blackwood from Zebra Books

THE SEXIEST DEAD MAN ALIVE

A HARD MAN IS GOOD TO FIND

You Had Me At
Me At
Goodbye

Jane Blackwood

ZEBRA BOOKS

Kensington Publishing Corp.

www.kensingtonbooks.com

Chapter 1

Kat Taylor always stood at the bow of the Martha's Vineyard ferry, no matter what the sea was doing that day. She loved the sea air, the way it felt against her face, the way it made her hair move in a wild way—as if *she* were wild, as if she could still fly off and be . . . something. She was a girl from New Hampshire who only made it to the seaside maybe twice a summer, so she'd come to appreciate that buffeting wind. It was cleansing, somehow, and God knew, she needed to be cleansed.

It was a brilliantly sunny day, and the Atlantic between Woods Hole and Oak Bluffs was unusually calm. Kat wished it was raining, storming, gusts lashing at her, stinging her skin. Instead, a seagull followed the ferry on the gentle breeze as if somehow suspended from the sky on an invisible string. She could take that, too. Kat knew she could take anything but what she had left behind her in Keene. Heck, she supposed she could even take that, too.

Just not right now.

She squeezed her dark brown eyes shut and pictured the house in Oak Bluffs that she hoped was her savior. The house was built in 1880, complete with the ornate gingerbread details that made Oak Bluffs such a unique New England town. A huge wrap-around porch hugged the white house: two large rockers, also white, always sat on the porch's wide-planked floor. At the top of a roof filled with peaks and dormers was a widow's walk that had one of the most spectacular views of the island. Like many homes on the island, it had a name—Sunrise—because it faced the east and the rising sun. Kat figured it wasn't the most original name, but it fit the romantic nature of the home and the island. The story was that a sea captain built the house, but then again, most people who owned old Victorians on the waterfront claimed that a sea captain built their house. Kat could believe it though, because the house had a tower and widow's walk and because she wanted with all her heart to believe in something.

The house was hers for the summer, a respite from a life that had somehow taken a wrong turn when she was about ten and her mother finally told her the identity of her father. Her mother had never married, but that certainly hadn't meant she'd been lonely. "Cal, your father, was a good man. Good in bed, anyway." Betty Taylor had laughed because nothing was so serious that you couldn't laugh about it. And that's how Kat found out her father was Cal the water meter reader. Good in bed. Gotcha, Mom.

The ferry plowed through the wake of a cruise ship heading to New York, and a bit of sea spray splashed on the group of ferry passengers who liked the bite of the Atlantic as much as she did. She licked her lips and tasted the salt and smiled for the first time in weeks. God, she needed this holiday. She'd have to call her Aunt Lila and tell her again how she'd saved her niece's sanity. Two months in Sunrise. Two months with nothing to do but sit on that huge wraparound front porch and sip cheap wine, pretending it was something fancy and French, and gaze out at the cold Atlantic.

Long before the ferry docked, she could see the house, looking lost and forlorn. Kat had a terrible and dangerous habit of putting human emotions to inanimate objects, particularly houses. She loved houses, loved to imagine what they looked like inside. She wondered who lived there, who had died there. When they were filled with kids, they were happy or at least content in their mission. And when they were left empty like Sunrise had been this season, they were tragic. A house left empty always seemed so sad to Kat.

"I'm coming, girl," she said softly and found her smile again.

Twenty minutes later, Kat stood in front of the house, two huge rolling suitcases beside her. She felt a sudden pang for Carl, Lila's late husband. If it hadn't been for his generosity, she never would have known how wonderful the Vineyard was. She certainly could never have afforded a month-long vacation on the island, never mind in a waterfront house.

Of all her aunts—Kat had six of them—she loved Lila best. She was more like a sister than an aunt because they were so close in age. Lila had a heart as big as her double-D breasts, and she had a particular soft spot for older men. Much older, rich men. Kat's mother claimed because their father was so old when Lila was born, Lila had simply been looking for a replacement ever since. Lila was a miracle baby, born when her mother was forty-eight and her closest sister was already in her twenties. She had been her father's particular favorite, and the two of them were inseparable. But Tony was sixty-five when Lila was born, and even though he lived to the ripe old age of eighty-three, their time together was far too short.

Lila's first husband, who she married when she was twenty, was seventy-two years old. She loved him until his death two years later. When she was twenty-five, she married Harold. He was eighty. He died six months after their wedding. Lila was alone for two years before she met and married Carl, whom she claimed was the love of her life. Unfortunately, he was seventy-six. Still, they had five wonderful years together before he died, leaving Lila heartbroken once again.

No one ever suggested to Lila that perhaps she ought to look for someone younger, maybe a man in his sixties, for Lila truly loved older men. "They're so appreciative of everything I do," she said. "They make me feel like a queen. Queen Lila."

No one was more different from Lila than Kat, but somehow they loved each other and understood one another. When Kat needed it most, Lila was there for her. "Go to our cottage on Martha's Vineyard. Go and *heal*. I'd go there myself, but it's just too painful right now," Lila said, her soft voice breaking. "It's a shame for the cottage to be closed up all summer. It makes me so sad to think of it like that. Please go, Kat. It will be good for you and good for the cottage. Carl loved that old place, and I know he'd want you to use it. Please."

And so here she was, standing outside the house she loved, savoring the moment, the anticipation of the beginning of an end—the end of failure, the end of the girl whose father was the water meter reader.

She grabbed her suitcases and waited for a clear spot in the summer traffic on *Sea View Avenue* and ... stopped. Someone or *something* had moved in the tower room. The window was shut, but she could have sworn the curtain had moved a bit, that a shadow had crossed by. Lila and Carl had never mentioned a ghost, Kat thought, half excited and half frightened by the idea. She stared a good while longer before convincing herself she was a complete idiot.

The house had virtually no front yard to speak of, so Kat heaved her bags up the porch steps, reached inside a fish-shaped wind chime, and smiled when she found the key. Roy, who ran a bed and breakfast next door, had a spare key, but Kat was glad not to have to bother him. She let herself in and stared at the abandoned house, furniture still covered with dust sheets. For a moment, she felt a tingle of fear and listened for a sound from the tower, but there was nothing but the noise of the traffic and, beyond that, the surf pounding the beach. Then she saw it: the large portrait of her aunt lying nude on a pile of what looked like polar bear rugs and covered with discreetly placed white feather boas. This was definitely not a sad house, not a haunted house. And for the next eight weeks, it was going to be her house.

Immediately, Kat went around the first floor and opened every window. Then she made short work of the dust covers, smiling in satisfaction when the living room began to look more lived in. She decided to take the bedroom on the first floor, which had absolutely nothing to do with the ghost walking around the tower room. Besides, it was the guest room, and she still was a guest in this house, and it happened to be one of her favorite rooms.

A large wrought-iron bed dominated the room, which contained only an antique wardrobe and two shabby-chic bedside tables with chipped white paint. Kat pulled out linens that felt and looked expensive and a cheerful yellow and white comforter and made the bed, feeling happier than she'd felt in weeks. She sat down on the bed and watched as the sheer white curtain surrounding a window that faced the sea blew gently, bringing with it the unmistakable scents of summer: mowed grass, ocean air, and a hint of honeysuckle. *I could be happy here*, she thought even as her heart squeezed painfully in her chest.

After a quick walk to the small grocery store in the town's center for essentials—some frozen burritos and coffee for the morning—Kat did something she hadn't done in years: she took a nap, idly hoping her ghost stayed put in the tower room while she was sleeping.

It was dusk when Kat awoke, feeling slightly groggy but immensely happy. The only thing she had planned for that evening was curling up on the living room couch and reading a book. Tomorrow she'd go over to see Roy and reminisce about Carl and their summers together, but tonight was hers and hers alone.

She got up, stretching, loving the feel of the cool hardwood floors beneath her feet. She'd have to remind her aunt never to put carpeting in this house. Scruffing up her matted hair, she headed hungrily toward the kitchen, knowing a frozen chicken burrito awaited her. Frozen chicken burritos were one of several weaknesses Kat was willing to admit to. Her friends wrinkled their noses every time she bit into the gooey mass that held some unknown but delicious filling. She didn't want to know what was in the thing; she only knew it tasted good.

Feeling wonderfully sleepy, she padded into the dark kitchen and directly into something tall and hard and hairy. They both screamed—Kat and whatever it was that was backing away from her—three times. In unison. And then, "Bloody hell," followed by a succession of swears, all uttered in a cultured male, British accent.

"I have a gun," Kat said, staring at the shadow of what was obviously a man, a tall, half-naked, hairy man standing in the middle of the kitchen. This was no ghost. He was way too big and solid for a ghost.

"You do not," he said, sounding far more calm than she did. He almost sounded . . . amused.

"A knife, then."

And he laughed, letting out a low chuckle that Kat found slightly comforting. A madman or rapist wouldn't laugh like that, would he?

"I know karate," she said, knowing she was being ridiculous. She was rewarded with another chuckle.

"I'm turning on the light," he said with a voice a person uses when approaching a snarling dog. He did, putting the room into such instant brightness Kat was momentarily blinded, and she backed into a corner as if that would save her if he were indeed a madman.

"Now do you mind telling me what you are doing in my house?" he asked with utter calm.

Kat squinted toward him and wished she hadn't. He

was, indeed, half naked and tall; beefy arms folded over his hairy chest. Out of a face filled with dark facial hair glinted two brown eyes that looked at her as if she were the one trespassing. He wasn't exactly hostile; his expression was more curious than angry.

"This is my house. My aunt promised it to me," she said, sounding about as assertive as a three-year-old.

"The aunt of the picture?" he asked, raising his eyebrows in a way Kat didn't at all appreciate. Sure, the portrait was ridiculous, but Lila was her aunt, and Kat was fiercely loyal to her. She couldn't count the number of times people had either hinted at or blatantly suggested Lila was nothing but a gold digger. And this guy's eyebrows seemed to be saying just that.

"Who are you?" Kat asked, suddenly more angry than afraid.

"I am Lawrence Kendall." He paused as if his name should mean something to her. Maybe he was a duke; he sure sounded like one. She stared at him hard and wondered if he was some British actor she was supposed to recognize. "And you are?" he asked, raising his bearded chin a bit.

"Kat Taylor."

He stared at her as if searching some inner data bank to see if he could place her. "Kat?"

"Short for Katherine," she said.

"Well, Katherine, it seems as if we've both been promised the same house."

Oh, God, no. No. No. "My aunt said I could stay here until Labor Day."

"Ah." He made a funny little clicking noise with his tongue. "I'm very sorry, but Carl promised the place to me months ago."

"You know Carl?" she asked suspiciously, knowing that if someone truly knew Carl, they'd also know he'd been dead for more than a month.

"He was much more my father's friend, but yes, of course I knew Carl. He knew he was ill and wouldn't be using the place and said he wouldn't mind if I used it. So you see, I was promised first."

Kat blinked. Was this guy actually suggesting that she leave? "I'm sorry, too. But Lila owns this house now, and she promised it to me."

He rubbed his jaw in what seemed a practiced way. "Quite a quandary," he said, and somehow, with his accent, that didn't come out sounding ridiculous. He stood in front her wearing nothing but a pair of rolled up khakis and seemed completely at ease. Maybe he was a male stripper; he certainly had the body for one, Kat thought, and she was faintly shocked when she realized she'd let her mind wander like that.

"I have a copy of an e-mail Carl sent me giving me details on how to get here. It's dated in April. I hadn't planned on taking him up on his offer, but here I am."

"And here I am," Kat said miserably, feeling her summer dissolving beneath her feet. She would not give this up. She needed this house more than he did. She'd spent time here; she wasn't some stranger camping out for a few months. She had emotion invested in this house, a history. Memories. "I'm not leaving," she said firmly.

"I'm afraid you've no choice. I have to be alone."

"So. Do. I."

"You're angry," he said, sounding like one of those Discovery Channel narrators describing with no emotion a lion eating a gazelle. *Note how the lion tears into the still living beast. It has no chance to survive this killer of the jungle.*

"I'm not angry," she said through gritted teeth in a tone that, even to her own ears, sounded angry. Kat let out a puff of air. "Okay, I am angry. I've been looking forward to this vacation for a long time. I'm sorry that Carl promised it to you, but he's dead. My aunt owns this house. I'm a blood relative, so I should get the house."

He raised one eyebrow. "That's your argument? I take it you're not a lawyer," he said lightly.

If she was a cartoon character, steam would have been whistling out of her ears. He must have sensed it because he put his hands out as if to ward her off. "This is a difficult situation, and we're not going to resolve it tonight." He put on what looked like a fake smile and clapped his hands together like a person who's used to being obeyed without question.

"I've resolved it," Kat said stubbornly.

He set his jaw. "I'm afraid you'll have to leave in the morning. I won't be so callous as to send you out alone at night. I'm certain you'll find other accommodations on the island."

"If I can, so can you."

He looked at her as if she were a strange species, something he didn't quite understand. "The house is mine," he said, slightly exasperated. "I've been living here for nearly two weeks already. You're going to have to leave in the morning." He really was an awfully intimidating-looking guy with all that beef and dark hair—a cultured mountain man.

Kat quickly weighed her options, factoring in the fact he was a big guy, probably more than six feet, who didn't look very happy at the moment, and decided, foolishly she was sure, that she wasn't going anywhere. "Make me," she said, crossing her arms over her own chest and not meaning a single syllable.

He stared at her for a moment, then let out a laugh so sudden and violent it nearly frightened her. His booming laughter filled the silent house, and Kat watched through narrowed eyes as he bent at the waist as if unable to stand due to his state of utter glee. "Oh, God," he said when he'd gotten control of himself. "You are funny. I have a feeling you're trying to look fierce, but I'm afraid you're failing miserably." He wiped at his eyes, and when he was finally able to focus on her, Kat tried very hard not to let him see she was fighting a smile.

He looked sheepish and charming all of a sudden, and in that moment, Kat realized that maybe he wasn't pretty but he certainly was handsome. In a scruffy, charming, English way. If he were cast in a movie, he'd be the villain, the gorgeous evil guy that you hope turns out to be a good guy in the end. But who usually didn't. "We'll resolve this in the morning. Maybe one of us will have a change of heart."

"Listen, Larry . . ."

"I prefer Lawrence," he said, smiling politely.

"I'm sorry, but I'm not leaving. Morning is not going to change my mind."

"Morning may not, but perhaps I can persuade you." He opened the refrigerator and pulled open the vegetable bin to retrieve what looked like one of those supermarket prepackaged sandwiches. She hadn't noticed it when she was putting her few items in the fridge because she'd been planning to go to the small farmer's market to get fresh vegetables and hadn't opened the bin.

"I'm dining in this evening," he said, shaking the sandwich toward her. "Good night."

"Good night," she mumbled. Then, "Wait a minute. If you've been here two weeks, why did the place look deserted? And why wasn't there any food in the fridge?"

"I eat out ninety percent of the time, and I haven't used the main floor. I've spent my time in the tower room and didn't see the point in uncovering the furniture down here. Anything else, madam?"

"I'll let you know," she said, smiling good-naturedly. When he disappeared up the stairs, Kat sagged to the kitchen floor. "Damn, damn, double damn," she said softly. Kat was pretty good at acting tough, even at telling herself she was tough, but she knew deep down inside she was a big ol' wimp. Standing up to Sir Larry had not come easy, though he'd never know it. All her life she'd heard people tell her she was tough, resilient, that she could take what life dished out. No one knew how scared she was half the time. Hell, most of the time.

Kat pushed herself up, sliding her back against the wall. She was not going to have this taken away. Kat pressed the heel of her hands against her eyes so hard it hurt. "Do not cry," she said low and fierce. "Don't you cry." When she pulled her hands down, she smiled because there wasn't a salty tear on them. Not even one.

Lawrence closed the door to his room with a soft snick. "Bloody, bloody hell," he said. All he needed was a woman skulking about the house, disturbing him, interrupting his work.

He stopped at that thought and stared at his laptop, a machine the devil himself had taken over. Work, he thought. What work? He hadn't written more than a few paragraphs in months. He'd heard of so-called writer's block and had always figured it was for other poor slobs, those writers who weren't very good and never would be. His editor said to write through it, that his gift would come back. But it hadn't, and Lawrence was terrified that it never would.

"There are no stories in my head," he'd told William Goodall, his editor at Thorpes Publishing, trying not to sound as desperate as he felt. "I don't know where the hell they went because I never know where the hell they come from."

"They'll come back, Lawrence. Trust me."

That had been when he'd still been in England, when Carl had still been alive. Carl was one of his father's favorite people . . . and one of Lawrence's, too. He hadn't thought much about his marrying a woman far less than half his age, and he'd never met the woman. His mother had called her trash, her nose so high in the air even Lawrence, a confirmed and self-proclaimed snob, had to laugh.

"If the old man got lucky enough to find a young wife, then good for him."

"Oh, really, Lawrence, he's making a fool of himself. I wish your father could have talked some sense into him."

Lawrence had bit his tongue, for he was fairly certain his father not only approved of the marriage, but he was also likely a bit envious. The old dog.

He'd talked to Carl about his difficulties getting started with his next novel, and the old man had offered him the cottage. A change of scenery might be just what he needed, he'd said.

Lawrence looked out the window and grimaced. Martha's Vineyard—at least this part of the island—was not what he had been expecting at all. He was expecting the Bill Clinton secret hideaway Martha's Vineyard where cultured people discussed world events and the literary scene and had charming lawn parties and enlightened conversation. Instead, he'd found himself in the middle of a tourist Mecca where fine art consisted of a painting of a lighthouse on a seashell and culture was watching men gut large sharks.

He hadn't realized he was such a snob until he came to this island. These Americans seemed to be fascinated by the strangest things. He'd actually become part of a large crowd of people gathered around a fisherman gutting fish. Their faces were rapt, as if they were watching great art or something thrilling that had never been done before. Frankly, the knife slicing into the fish's white belly had nearly made him ill, but for reasons he even refused to acknowledge. It was almost comical that watching a fish being gutted should bring back the moment of his worst failing.

Instead of escaping his life in this foreign place, he found himself with too much time to relive it, every agonizing, humiliating moment. Because he couldn't write, he could hardly even think. He couldn't return to England empty-handed, with nothing to show for the past weeks but a pathetic story about how he couldn't write. He'd already asked his brother for a loan, and he'd be damned if he did it again. His agent, very funny man, had also suggested he might have to get a real job. Writing *was* a real job—just not one that paid very well.

"Lawrence, if you're so worried about money, you've got to write and write quickly. And you've got to write something that appeals to a broader audience. I'm not saying sacrifice your ideals, not all of them, but if you want to make money in this business, you've got to sell more books. Way more. I'm hearing some rumblings from your house."

"Rumblings?"

"You're up for a new contract after this book. Rumblings, Lawrence. Think about it."

It was all he could think of. His agent was subtly telling him to write for the masses and he just couldn't do it. He didn't know the masses; didn't have the slightest idea how they ticked, what they thought, what they wanted to read. He'd been born with the proverbial silver spoon in his mouth, grown up in privilege, attended cricket and polo matches, and gone to England's finest private schools. He'd made his parents proud, then ended it all in a crushingly enduring way that left everyone in his family wounded. So what in God's name did he know about the huddled masses?

"They're the ones who buy books, Lawrence," his agent had said.

It wasn't enough to get published; he had to sell, and Lawrence just didn't know if he had it in him to write a book the so-called masses would want to read.

He knew what his older brother John would say then, could hear the disappointment, the pity. "Perhaps you should put aside your writing and do something more suited to a man with your education. Certainly, you can do something more than you're doing."

But he couldn't, and he didn't know if he ever would.

Lately though, his brother's pity and concern had turned to disapproval and resentment. Lawrence had found he wasn't very good at handling adversity. He'd always thought he would be. Hell, he'd been trained to handle the best God could throw at him. But he'd failed, and when he had, he'd wasted a very expensive education, then blown his inheritance in such a grand, mature way on beautiful women, expensive cars, and endless holidays at luxury resorts. At least he knew how to have fun. Before the money went dry, he'd take two or three months off and write something fabulous to keep his brother happy. Now the money was nearly gone, and he'd lost any real desire for expensive cars and luxury resorts. The women? Well, one couldn't get a gorgeous woman without money, could one?

He pushed his hair off his forehead and idly stroked his beard, wondering if he should shave and knowing the only reason he wondered that was because of the woman downstairs. He shouldn't care what she thought of him, but no matter how low his life had gotten—and God knew he'd been pretty damn low—he'd never let his appearance go.

Lawrence walked to the bathroom, flicked on the light, and looked at his reflection. "Good God," he muttered, taking in his rather fiendish look. Then he smiled. He was a big man in pretty good shape, an intimidating guy at any time. But she'd stood there in the dark and threatened him with imaginary weapons. And when she had gotten a look at him with his wild, uncombed hair and his dark, two-week unkempt beard, she had stood her ground, even challenged him.

"Damn," he said aloud, staring hard at his reflection. He knew she wasn't going anywhere.

Chapter 2

Lawrence made his way downstairs the next morning, bleary-eyed and unshowered, to the sound of someone humming cheerfully on the front porch. Good God, he thought, tough *and* perky. He stuck his head out the door, and she immediately smiled, stunning him for a moment before he remembered to at least try to frown.

"How is your search going for other accommodations?" he asked.

She put on a big show of frowning. "Not good. How's your search going?"

He gave her a level stare before slowly closing the door, fighting a grin until he was out of sight. She wasn't going to budge, and he couldn't bring himself to throw her out. If she had thrown a hissy fit or even if she had cried, it would have been easier to demand that she leave. Hysterics were the best way to irritate him. This girl, this Kat person was, he had to admit, entertaining. As he had predicted, she was also distracting. Just knowing she was in the house seething about his existence had been enough diversion to keep him from focusing on his writing.

Last night he'd tried, God knew he'd tried, to type something remotely interesting, never mind the riveting moneymaker his publisher was looking for. All he could think of, though, was the way she'd pretended not to be scared when she'd run into him in the kitchen. Any sane woman would have run from the house screaming.

He stuck his head out the door again, thinking of making peace and that maybe if he were nice, she'd leave the house to him. "You want to join me for breakfast? There's a diner down the street."

Kat looked at her watch and frowned. "It's almost eleven."

"Is it? I was up nearly all night."

She dropped her book and shifted in her wicker rocker so she faced him. She really was quite pretty, he realized, though definitely not his type. Most of the women he dated—in fact, *all* the women he dated—were tall, blonde, and busty. It was a sickness, a wonderful fixation.

"I didn't realize I frightened you that much," she said and smiled.

He couldn't help but smile back. "You really do have to leave, you know. I'm a writer and I didn't get any work done just knowing you were wandering about the house."

"I'm two stories below you," she pointed out. "I wasn't wandering, and I don't snore that loudly."

"I don't think you understand how vital it is that I'm alone."

She gave him the strangest look, and he almost

almost caved in right then and there. "I do understand," she said evenly. "That's why you need to go. I don't just need to be alone; I need to be alone here. In this house. Alone. You can go write anywhere."

Even though he knew she was right, he also knew he had inherited his father's stubborn streak. The man would argue that the sky was purple until you believed it, too. Besides, he didn't have the cash to go anywhere else. He didn't even have a home of his own to go to, and he refused to stay with his brother and their three children.

"I'm sorry, Katherine. I'm not leaving." Then he got what he thought was a brilliant idea, a sure way to get this tough nut to crack. "I've an idea," he said overly casually and watched as her guard was immediately lifted. "If neither of us is willing to leave, I suggest we make the best of it and have ourselves a good time. A summer fling, so to speak."

She looked up at him, her brows knitting just slightly. Then she turned back to her book, seemingly unconcerned. "Nice try, Larry. Though I must say your offer is tempting, now that you've shaven."

My God, he thought, he might as well accept defeat. And he probably would have if he hadn't been so bloody stubborn.

Kat watched the door close and stifled a laugh. This guy was an amateur, she thought, knowing she'd won that battle and that total victory was only a day or so away. Lawrence Kendall had met his match, she thought happily. It occurred to her she needed to know her enemy better if she was going to win this war of wills. Kat waited for Larry to leave for breakfast—it was noon before he made his way out the door—then grabbed her laptop, plunked herself down on the couch, plugged her computer into a phone jack, signed in to AOL, and then did a quick search on Amazon for Lawrence Kendall. There he was, or at least, there was Lawrence Kendall's latest book: *Visions of Solitude.*

"That's what I need," she whispered. "Solitude." He'd had five books published in all, and all were out of print but *Visions of Solitude.* She clicked on it and read some reviews, grimacing and beginning to feel a little bit sorry for Larry.

Then she decided to Google him.

Googling someone wasn't really spying, Kat told herself as she typed in Lawrence Kendall, then pressed "search."

She watched, amazed, as hit after hit came up . . . and hardly any had anything to do with his books. She clicked on one entry: "Playboy Kendall Runs Boat Aground."

"Must be the wrong Kendall," she said as she waited for the page to appear on her laptop. But no, there he was in all his glory, wearing a swimsuit and standing aboard what Kat would call a yacht, not a boat. "Whoa." The "whoa" was not for the boat but for the man standing on the boat. Of course she knew he had a nice body—she'd seen it firsthand last night—but this glistening Greek god she was staring at was a pumped up version. Kat had never thought of herself as an ogler, but here she was practically drooling at the man she saw smiling rakishly at the camera. He was beautiful, all lean muscle and tanned skin, his hair wind-tousled, his eyes sparkling with humor. Kat glanced at the date: it had been taken five years before, and she could see how time had changed him. He was bigger, more filled out, more man—less carefree, Kat supposed. Once Kat was able to, she dragged her eyes off his body and took in the beautiful blonde draped around him. He had one hand casually resting on her tiny, tanned waist, and Kat frowned.

"Lawrence Kendall, one of Europe's most eligible bachelors, got in another spot of trouble over the weekend when his sixty-foot yacht, "My Pleasure," ran aground on a small island near Crete."

Kat clicked back to Google and selected another item. "Lawrence Kendall has been selected chairman of the London Society for Literacy." It was a picture of Kendall wearing a tuxedo, standing next to a couple of elderly people. He looked stunning in formal wear, nearly as stunning as he had in his swimsuit.

Kat clicked to Google and selected item after item, most of which were newspaper articles of events where, inevitably, he had on his arm another beautiful blonde and he was described as one of Britain's most eligible bachelors.

He was rich, she realized. Someone who went to events like those described in the articles was the kind of filthy rich she'd seen only on television. And he wanted *her* to leave? He could probably buy ten houses like this one. Boy, did he have another thing coming to him—and it sure as hell wasn't a summer fling. Larry could afford to go anywhere; she could barely afford to buy herself the needed groceries for this summer hiatus.

Kat shut down her computer, more determined than

ever to make Larry go away. She went out on the porch
wishing Larry and his British charm would simply disappear. Roy was next door, sweeping his porch as he
did every day. He looked up and nodded, and Kat
could tell he didn't recognize her immediately.

"Hey, Roy. It's Kat, Lila's niece."

"You here for the summer?" he called over, prop-
ping his hand on the broom handle.

"You bet. 'Til Labor Day."

He paused a minute as if he was going to ask her
something, probably about Larry, but instead said,
"Why don't you come on over tonight at five."

"Just as long as you don't make me drink one of
your martinis," Kat said, wrinkling her nose. She'd
tried to like martinis because they seemed sophisticated, but Kat was a simple girl, and she always stuck
to cheap wine and beer.

"I'll see you later then," Roy said and disappeared
into his bed and breakfast.

At five o'clock, Roy Baxter carefully measured the
vodka and poured it into the shaker, then strained
enough for two martini glasses. He dropped a single
green olive into one and two olives and an onion
into the other. Every time he made martinis, he
thought of his wife, how she had enjoyed a good
martini as much as he did. Each evening at six o'-
clock, she'd make them both a drink, then bring it
to him out on their front porch facing the Atlantic
and curl up in the big rocker without a word and
take a sip. God, he loved to watch the way her mouth
touched the delicate rim, the way her tongue would

dart out, the relaxed sound she'd make when she tasted it. One drink each night, and man, did he enjoy that drink.

Twenty years after her death, he could still picture her sitting in the rocking chair next to him. She would tuck her bare feet under her and face him, never the sea, the glow of the late-day sun making her strawberry blond hair seem a soft, burnished gold. She had freckles and bright blue eyes, and he'd loved her to distraction and wondered how a small-town boy could have managed to make this beautiful woman fall in love with him. They would talk and laugh and sometimes argue and sometimes cry. It had been just the two of them for years, and that was not okay, not for Sara. And not for him either. By the time they figured out why Sara couldn't get pregnant, her cancer was so advanced all they could talk about was how to say goodbye. She'd only been thirty-two. He couldn't wrap his mind around that now, twenty years later, having lived all those years without her; she'd been so damned young.

Two years after she'd gone, he'd turned their house into a bed and breakfast because he couldn't bear to sell it and he couldn't bear to be alone all the time. Most people thought he rented out rooms because he had to financially, but Roy did it for the company. He couldn't stand to be alone for long stretches of time, wandering around the rambling seaside cottage his great grandfather had built. He'd made good friends over the years, people who'd stayed at his place every summer for years. They'd sit out on the porch with him and talk or not. But they were warm bodies moving about his old place, and he liked it that way.

As alone as he felt, Roy never remarried. He just couldn't find a way to fall in love with anyone the way he'd fallen in love with Sara. He wasn't a maudlin man with pictures of his dead wife in every room. He had no real objections to remarrying—God knew the local single women had tried for years to get him down the aisle. He just wanted to love someone, if not in the same way as Sara, at least as much. It never happened, and he figured it never would. He was fifty-five years old and not quite the looker he'd once been. He was starting to get a little bit of a belly, and his hair wasn't nearly as thick as it used to be. One long-ago girlfriend said he had Paul Newman eyes, so he supposed he wouldn't break any mirrors.

Roy picked up the martinis and headed out to the porch to the only other man he'd ever met who valued the taste of a good martini as much as he did.

"Here you go, Lawrence."

"Thank you, Roy. I need it."

Roy chuckled. "Another great day at the keyboard, I take it?"

Lawrence gave him a short nod. "Not that, though I still haven't written anything worth a damn. Apparently I've acquired a temporary roommate. Lila's niece."

"Ah, yes. I saw her on the porch today."

"Anyway, my hopes for any solitude or privacy have flown out the window." He took a sip of his martini, closing his eyes briefly to enjoy the moment.

"Tell her to leave."

"I did. She won't. Besides, Lila didn't know I'd be

here and promised the house to her. We're at a stalemate at the moment."

Roy nodded. "If she's like her aunt, she'll win." They sat in companionable silence for a minute. "I wonder if Lila is coming here this summer."

Lawrence, recalling the large portrait of Lila in the living room, gave Roy a shrewd look. "I don't believe so. At least, nothing was mentioned. But you can see a whole lot of her any time you want," he said, with obvious reference to the portrait.

"God, the picture. Still can't believe they put it in the living room," Roy said with a chuckle. "How long is—what's the niece's name again?"

"Katherine."

Roy frowned briefly, then his expression cleared. "Kat. She's come over every summer for a week or so since Lila and Carl married. She had a boyfriend." He leaned over, glancing at the house next door. "Boring as hell."

"Don't tell me he didn't appreciate your martinis," Lawrence joked.

"He drank beer," Roy said with disgust. "Budweiser."

The screen door opened next door, and Roy hoped Kat hadn't heard what he'd said. "Kat, why don't you join us?"

She looked over at the pair of them and smiled, lifting up what appeared to be a bottle of wine and a tall glass filled with ice. "Be right over."

Lawrence watched her bounce down the steps like a child, scuttle around a family walking by, and jog up to Roy's porch. She was as graceful as a puppy and seemed to have as much energy. She was wearing a white short-sleeve blouse and tan capris; her feet were bare, and her toenails were painted bright red. Two of her toes had small rings on them, and for some reason, Lawrence's gaze kept straying to those two rings.

"Hi, Roy. Glad to see you're keeping up with tradition," Kat said, motioning to the martinis. "I think I'll stick with this, though."

This was a bottle of wine, but it fizzed as she poured it into her glass, and the ice crackled.

"Fine vintage," Lawrence said dryly, eyeing the pinkish "wine" that chugged out of the bottle.

"Arbor Mist. And I like it. It tastes like Kool Aid."

"Fruit punch," Roy supplied when he saw Lawrence's confusion.

Katherine gave him a look that told him she didn't care what he thought of her choice of wine and took a deep sip. He watched, slightly distracted by how long and smooth her neck looked as she drank. She looked prettier than she had earlier, but he couldn't put his finger on why. She wore no makeup that he could see, and her short hair looked exactly the same as it had. Maybe it was the softening of the light, but for some reason, he found himself studying her and liking what he saw.

"Is your boyfriend coming to the island later?" Roy asked.

Katherine visibly stiffened and looked startled by the question, then shook her head and smiled. "Not this summer."

There was something a little off about that smile, Lawrence thought.

"I hear you two are engaged. When's the big date?"

The strangest thing happened then. Lawrence, who hardly knew this woman, found himself disappointed in a profound way that she was unattainable. He hadn't even thought of attaining her, at least not on any conscious level. The idea of a fling had been a challenge, not a recognition of any attraction. And yet here he was feeling bothered that she was taken, that he would never find out what it would be like to pursue her. It was as if a large red X had been painted over her.

She glanced down at her glass. "We actually won't be getting married."

Lawrence watched her as she stared at her bubbling wine, aware she was trying to hold it together and horribly afraid she would break down and cry in front of them. Instead, she smiled that strange smile and said, "It was a mutual thing. I think we dated too long and lost interest in each other." Lawrence studied her expression but found no hidden sadness, nothing to indicate she was suffering over the loss, and he was slightly amazed at how good an actress she was.

"He drank Budweiser," Roy said, as if that explained everything. Katherine laughed.

"And I drink strawberry wine. We were a perfect match for a while there."

She sounded much too chipper. Clearly, she was here to lick her wounds. The desperate need for solitude suddenly made perfect sense to Lawrence. Poor girl probably wanted to wail and moan into her pillow without any fear that she'd be overheard.

"If you'd like, I could let you have the house for, say, two days," Lawrence said, feeling overly generous.

"Two days? Gee, Larry, why this generous change of heart?"

She glared at him, and Lawrence had a sinking feeling he was about to lose another battle. "I thought you needed to lick your wounds. The broken engagement and all," he said, suddenly uncertain.

"No wounds to lick," Kat said with more confidence than she felt. She'd be damned if she admitted to Mr. Most Eligible Bachelor that she'd come to the island for the sole purpose of licking her wounds. "I just need a vacation."

"And what sort of work are you vacationing from?" Larry asked, and Kat could tell he was just being polite.

"I own . . . owned a housecleaning service. Taylor Maids," Kat said, wondering what God had against her to send her this man who was managing to sprinkle salt on her open cuts.

"You've retired?" Larry asked.

"If you must know, I got sued. One of my clients had a show dog, a little thing that looked more like a mop than a real dog, and it ran out into the street and got hit by a truck. I suppose I was to blame because I'm the one who opened the damn door."

"You killed her dog?"

She looked at him deadpan. "Frankly, given the dog's owner, I think it may have been suicide."

Larry let out a bark of laughter. Kat still couldn't bring herself to laugh about it, especially since that single moment had meant the end of Taylor Maids. She'd spent the last four years building her business, focusing on high end clients, only to lose everything when her most powerful client sued her. She'd made the mistake of building her customer base in a single large upscale development. The dog owner was president of the homeowner's association, so overnight, Kat lost eighty percent of her customer base. She'd had to lay off her two employees, which had broken her heart.

A week later, Brian finished her heart off by stepping on it.

"That's such a sad story I've half a mind to let you have the house for the summer."

"Really?" Kat asked hopefully, but with a large dose of skepticism.

"Unfortunately, the other half of my mind is in charge," Larry said, grinning.

"Ha ha," Kat said grumpily, pouring a little bit more wine into her glass. Then, partly to irritate him, she offered the bottle to Lawrence. "Try some. As long as you don't think of it as wine, you'll be fine. Drink right out of the bottle. It'll help you to know how the other half lives."

"Other half?" he asked, looking to Roy to see if he knew what she was talking about.

"I Googled you," she said, and she could tell he was momentarily confused. "The Internet. Most eligible bachelor running yachts aground, attending charity balls with Barbies."

"My God, that's all online?"

Kat took a sip. "You bet. Fascinating stuff."

After looking at Roy in mock horror, he took the bottle grimly. "Shouldn't this be in a paper bag for the full effect?"

"I'm not trying to make you look homeless, just like a real person."

"Do real people drink straight out of the bottle?"

he asked Roy, and Kat knew he was simply indulging her and having a bit of fun.

"I'm not a real person," Roy said dryly.

Lawrence upended the bottle and chugalugged it, making bubbles roll around the bottle. "Not bad," he said, grimacing only slightly.

Kat looked at her now half-empty bottle and frowned. "You're a quick study," she said.

"I aim to please." He looked at Kat, and even though she'd later swear it was an innocent look, innocent words, she felt the biggest rush of lust she'd felt in . . . well, ever.

She was going to have to make sure she got rid of him, and soon.

Chapter 3

Kat looked glumly out the living room window at the painfully blue Atlantic as she listened with not a small amount of resentment to Larry move about the kitchen on one of the rare occasions when he was actually preparing something to eat. Her vacation, she thought morosely, was not turning out at all the way she'd thought it would. She was about to turn back to the kitchen when she saw him. Brian. Walking along the boardwalk, dragging an overnight bag, his blond crew-cut hair glistening in the sun.

"Oh, God. Oh, God."

She couldn't keep her eyes off him; she couldn't move. She could only stare as he got closer and closer, her mouth gaping open.

"Katherine, what's wrong?"

She needed a paper bag to breathe into. She needed a semiautomatic rifle to shoot him with. "Brian," she managed to say.

"You don't seem very happy to see him," he said, clearly making a vast understatement. He craned his neck to look out the window at the approaching man.

"He broke my heart," she whispered.

And then for a reason she wouldn't understand until much later, Larry grabbed her and kissed her. Man, did he kiss her. It was like something out of a movie, Rhett ravaging Scarlett after he carried her up the stairs. It left her breathless and weak-kneed and happened so quickly she hardly had time to enjoy herself before it was over. Without her knowing it, he'd managed to unbutton her blouse slightly so she looked like a Victoria's Secret model, albeit a small-breasted one. He quickly untucked his shirt and mussed up his hair, then hers, and when the inevitable knock came on the door, he held her against him and counted to five. Slowly. Nothing had ever been as sexy to her as the sound of his voice, low and hot, near her ear, counting. One. Two. Three. Four. Five.

"Now, let's answer the door, shall we?"

"What the hell are you doing?" she said, finally finding her sanity.

He shrugged and smiled and moved slowly to the door and opened it.

There he was, the man she had thought she was going to marry, the future father of her children, the man whose gnarled, veiny hand she'd thought she'd be holding when they were eighty. The man who'd gotten engaged to another woman while sleeping with her.

"Hi, Brian," she said, and she was amazed how it came out all breathy.

"Kat." Brian stood uncertainly in the doorway looking handsome and wonderful and hateful and weak, and Kat wondered what the hell was stopping her from launching herself at him and choking the living daylights out of him. Oh, it was Larry, holding her arm firmly but gently. Possessively.

"Who's he?" Brian asked, jerking his head at Larry.

"Lawrence Kendall," Larry supplied, and damn if he didn't even nod at Brian like the perfect English gentleman.

Kat felt a warm hand on her shoulder, a small caress on her clavicle, and she had to suppress a shiver. Now she got it. Duh!

"He's my roommate," she said and leaned back into Larry.

"Roommate's a bit tame, isn't it, love?"

Kat felt like kissing Larry right then and there because she would have given every nickel she had left to capture the look on Brian's face for perpetuity. She leaned back a bit more and smiled up at Larry, a thank you in her eyes that to Brian, very probably looked like something else entirely.

Brian pressed his lips together, his eyes darting from one to the other. "I'd like to speak to you in private," he said.

Lawrence felt Kat stiffen against him, and he tightened his embrace almost imperceptibly. "We've nothing to say," she said.

"I've left her," her boyfriend said, panic growing in his eyes, the desperation of a man who's broken up with the other woman only to find his first love doesn't want him back.

"I don't know what you want me to say, Brian. You made your choice perfectly clear two weeks ago."

Again, Brian looked up at Lawrence before talking to Kat. "I made a mistake, Kat. Please. Can't we talk in private?"

Lawrence saw the slight movement of her head, felt her entire body begin to shake, just the slightest trembling. "Brian? May I call you that?" Oh, Lawrence knew he could turn on the blue blood when he wanted to. "Katherine and I were . . . busy. I wonder if you could come back later."

"You have nothing to do with this," Brian said, and Lawrence saw with a certain sense of delight that the other man's fists were clenched.

Apparently, Katherine saw those fists, too, because to Lawrence's great disappointment, she stepped out of his arms. "Brian, come back at four. I'm not prepared to talk to you right now. You should have called."

"I didn't know the number," he said, and the look of desperation was back. "Please, Kat."

"Come back later, Brian," she said with a bit of steel Lawrence had never heard in her voice before.

"I am coming back," he said, then looked down at his bag. "Is it okay if I keep this here?"

"You're kidding, right? You thought you were going to stay here?"

"Well . . ."

"No. Later, Brian."

He nodded and walked down the porch steps, dragging his black overnight bag behind him.

Lawrence watched Katherine close the door, then press her head against it. "I'm sorry," he said. "I didn't know what else to do. It seemed like a good idea at the time."

She was shaking, her body wracked with it, the grief, the stress . . . the laughter. She was laughing.

"Oh, God, did you see his face? Did you? Larry,

you are a genius." She walked over to him and kissed him on the cheek. "A genius."

"Does this mean I get the house for the summer?" he asked.

"It means I'll let you stay a few more days. Just until we get rid of him."

Lawrence tilted his head to make certain he saw her expression clearly. "Are you sure you want to get rid of him?"

Her nostrils flared suddenly, and he thought she would cry. "Yes. I want to get rid of him." She looked up at him and for a second, he couldn't breathe from the pain he saw in her eyes. "But Brian is . . ." She let out a tired sigh. "I thought he was my forever. And when I saw him, I wanted to just hate him."

"You still love him?"

"I'm not sure. I don't want to. But you saw how I fell apart when I saw him. I want to believe him. I'm an idiot because the only thing stopping me from letting him in the house is you."

She suddenly got a fierce expression on her face. "You have to help me. Don't let me be alone with him. Don't let me cave in."

Lawrence suddenly wasn't so sure of his role. When Brian had come to the door, he'd acted without much thought when he kissed her. He just knew, for whatever reason, he could not let that man hurt Katherine. But she was tough; she could resist on her own. She didn't need him, and he wasn't sure he wanted to get involved, pretend to be her lover, hold her firm body against his. Lawrence wanted to laugh. If he had a devil on one side and God on the other, they'd both be saying to do it . . . but for far different reasons.

"I'll do it," he said, "but you have to tell me exactly what's going on between you two."

Katherine looked slightly ill but walked into the living room and sat down heavily on a love seat, her fingertips digging into the soft armrests. Lawrence took a chair opposite her and waited.

"You know I owned a housecleaning business. One of my biggest clients was a realtor who sold houses in this exclusive development in Keene. We'd clean the houses to get them ready to show, and she'd pass out our card. We got a lot of business like that, and she got immaculate houses to sell.

"There was this one house. It was spectacular. I loved it, and I made sure I was the one who got to clean it 'cause I was dying to see the inside. After I was done, the realtor came in to check everything, and we got to talking about how she thought she had a buyer for the house already. She was all excited. Some young couple with lots of money wanted this particular neighborhood and loved the house. She mentioned their names."

Kat closed her eyes against the memory because the pain of that moment still had the ability to devastate her. Brian was buying the house with another woman. At first, she hadn't believed it because Brian didn't have all that much money. He was a CPA, but she made more money than he did and that wasn't saying much.

"I said I knew a Brian Rindell from high school and wondered if it was the same person. It was."

"You're kidding."

"Nope. We were engaged, and he was out house hunting with another woman. And the worst thing was I'm the one who told him about the house. I loved it and talked about it like some far-off dream. Maybe someday we'll own a house like that. I actually said that to him."

Larry looked at her grimly. "That's just about the lowest thing I've ever heard of a man doing to a woman. And you say you're going to have a tough time resisting him?"

Kat let out a humorless laugh. "You have to know him. I'm sure he feels sick about what he did. Brian's not an evil person, just weak."

"What?" he said in pure disbelief.

"Okay. He's evil. And I'm cursed because even though I know he's a big time jerk and the worst kind of liar, when I saw him . . ." She let her voice trail off. "I didn't hate him. I wanted to. I know I should. But I didn't. That's what I need you for." She grinned, and he smiled back.

"I'll tell you what. I'll help you get rid of him in grand fashion if you help me."

Kat lowered her eyebrows. "Help you what?"

"Nothing nefarious if that's what you're frowning about. I'm having a bit of trouble with my writing, and well, I could use your assistance."

Unless he was doing research on how to screw up your life completely, Kat didn't think she'd be much help to him. "What's the trouble?"

Larry took a deep breath and looked more uncertain than she'd ever seen him. "My agent believes I need to write a book that is more appealing to . . ." He stopped as if searching for the right word. "Well, appealing to people like you."

"Me? You're going to write a romance?" She laughed aloud.

He gave her a quick smile. "What I mean is that I

have to write a book that appeals to the lower classes." He stopped and looked at her, gauging her reaction to his inadvertent and horrible insult. Kat knew he hadn't meant to sound like an ass, but that didn't mean he wasn't one.

"The lower classes," she repeated slowly.

"Well, that's not precisely the way I should have phrased it, but yes. Something that will appeal to the masses."

"I see. Something simple. Without all those big words and metaphors."

"Precisely," he said a bit uncertainly.

"For people like me."

"I've insulted you."

"Garsh, no. I'm just happy to have a smart, classy guy like you talking to one of the lower classes," she said in her best redneck accent.

Larry laughed. "You know I meant nothing by that." He smiled and looked so damned cute and sorry that Kat couldn't help but try to forgive him. This was a dangerous man. She should be heading out the door or kicking him out, but instead she was standing, smiling at him and thinking he was cute. Must be the accent, those dimples, those deep brown eyes that just sucked you in and made you want to forget he was a bit of a snob. Maybe it was that kiss.

"I need your help, and you need mine," he said.

Kat wrinkled her nose. "True. But what about the house? Who gets it?"

"I think for the time being, we agree to be room-mates."

"And here I thought we were so much more," she said, bringing back his theatrics in front of Brian.

"I thought I was brilliant."

"You were," Kat said laughing. "But I don't know if that kiss was really necessary."

"I had to make you look like you'd just been up to no good," he explained, and Kat wasn't sure she liked that gleam in his eye—especially coming from someone who'd so casually asked her if she'd wanted a summer fling.

Chapter 4

They walked silently, side by side, with the Atlantic Ocean to their right and Victorian water-view cottages to their left. Any brief sense of camaraderie that they'd had in the cottage was gone, and they were strangers thrown together with nothing in common but the awkward silence they were sharing. Kat put her attention on the houses they passed, mostly ornate Victorians with front porches, tower rooms, and gingerbread trim. The houses had been built at the turn of the century as summer cottages for New England Methodists who camped annually in the summer there. While the Methodists were long gone, many of the homes were still used only as summer homes or had been transformed into inns or bed and breakfasts like Roy had done.

Kat looked to see if Roy was on his porch and had a sudden pang of sadness for Carl, who'd wander over to Roy's at martini time, sometimes with Lila and sometimes without. "I bet Roy misses Carl," she said wistfully.

"I know he does. He's talked about him often," Larry said, looking over to his bed and breakfast. "I like Roy. He's the only American I've met who actually read one of my books."

"Ah, so he obviously makes the cut."

"Absolutely," he said without a hint of irony.

"Did he like your book?"

Larry looked out at the beach where several families were digging in the sand or splashing in the mild surf.

"He didn't?"

"He didn't actually dislike it. He just felt it was lacking something."

"What?" Kat asked.

"Soul. He said my book lacked soul. He must have read *The New York Times* review because that is precisely what that reviewer said when he tore it to shreds."

He'd said it lightly, but Kat had a feeling both the *Times* review and Roy's criticism didn't sit very well. "Not everyone can like everything. I'm sure someone liked it."

"I'm beginning to wonder." He stopped, braced both hands on the pitted, green-painted railing that separated the boardwalk from a steep drop to the beach, and looked out at the sea.

"Are you having a pity party?" Kat asked with a grin.

"A what?"

"Are you feeling sorry for yourself?"

He looked at her and gave her the oddest smile that, for some reason, made her breath catch in her throat.

"Actually, yes, I am. I've been lamenting my inability to write, but I'm beginning to fear that even if I could write, I'd end up writing . . ." he floundered.

"Something without a soul?" Kat offered.

"Yes," he said grimly. "Precisely."

"Maybe you need to suffer more. You've lived a privileged life, right?" He nodded. "So you need to suffer, to live."

"I've suffered enough, thank you."

Kat let out a snort. "Let's go find something fun and middle class to do. You're bringing me down."

Kat loved Oak Bluffs. Although Martha's Vineyard was a relatively small island, its small towns were decidedly different. Edgartown was posh, trendy, and touristy. Chilmark, with its green rolling hills and isolated beaches, was quiet and rural; Vineyard Haven, quaint; and Oak Bluffs, fun and a bit rough around the edges. Oak Bluffs, one of two towns on the island that served alcohol, teemed with activity in the summer months, thanks mostly to nonstop ferries that dumped boatload after boatload of day trippers onto its shores. It was one of the few places on the island where a family could eat for under thirty bucks. But its most well-known characteristic was the tiny gingerbread cottages that spread out in a labyrinth of narrow streets, placed side by side and painted fairy tale colors like pink and bright yellow.

The center of town was tacky and loud and wonderful, and its centerpiece was a century and a half old carousel called the Flying Horses that attracted hundreds every day. It wasn't one of those run-of-the-mill plastic carousels. Its carved wooden horses with real horsehair and glass eyes weren't all that fancy, and they were getting a bit worn, but riders actually tried to catch the brass ring as the horses whirled about the hot, wooden barnlike building.

Kat adored the carousel, and she made certain to ride it at least once every time she came to the island. Of course, Brian always refused and told her she looked ridiculous riding on it without a child, but Kat didn't care. She'd ridden the thing at least half a dozen times and never gotten that blasted brass ring.

She knew the place well enough to know that midday in July was the absolutely worst time to enter the carousel because it was always teeming with families and the temperature inside soared into the nineties. It was the worst place to be on a hot summer day if you were over the age of twelve. Kat brought Larry directly to the carousel.

It was a hot madhouse, the music seeming nightmarishly loud above the screaming of a little black-haired girl who apparently wanted to go on the ride again. Her parents looked sweaty and harassed, and they were probably wishing they were anywhere else on earth at that moment.

"This," Kat said with a flourish, "is normal people."

"Good God."

"And this is what we look like, what we do, what we are."

Larry looked at the screaming little girl, at her parents who were trying to push her stroller through the thick crowd, and turned around and walked back to the street. Kat jogged after him.

"How are you ever going to learn about us lower classes unless you mingle with us?" she asked innocently.

"I do not find you amusing."

Kat sighed. "I really would like you to ride that thing. We'll come back sometime at night. It's open until ten, and it's a lot cooler and a lot less crowded then."

"I don't understand the attraction. Those poor people looked miserable. What would make them do that?"

"It's the oldest carousel around. You'd be riding on a bit of history. And . . . it's fun," she said a bit defensively. "I know it seems stupid, but if you ride the carousel enough, you get really good at grabbing the rings. You can get two or three at a time, and your chances of getting the brass ring increase. It's a game."

"Perhaps later."

Kat shook her head. "You've got to try it. Then you'll get hooked. Your problem is that not only are you a snob, you're also a stick-in-the-mud."

Larry stopped walking, making the wave of people behind them part and go around. "Are you saying I'm boring?"

"Well, yes."

"Because I don't want to ride a child's amusement ride in sweltering heat?"

"Yes." And Kat thought, Brian was the same way. She could never get him on the carousel, no matter how much she'd cajoled. Of course, that had only made her want to ride again and again. Her little rebellion. And here was another guy, too stiff, too concerned about what others thought to look a little bit ridiculous and have a little fun.

"I assure you I am not boring."

"If you say so."

"Refusing to ride a carousel means nothing. It doesn't make me boring, and it doesn't make me a snob. It makes me practical. It was too bloody hot in there. Besides, the line was too long."

Kat tilted her head at him and studied his expression, trying hard not to notice how drop-dead gorgeous he was. Not that she was attracted to him. No right-minded woman with a broken heart would be attracted to any man. And she was a right-minded woman—who, okay, dammit, was attracted to him. At present, he was a hot, sweaty, gorgeous guy. Poor man was used to England, Kat thought, which had to be a heck of a lot colder than Martha's Vineyard. His near black hair was glistening with sweat around the edges, making it curl. Her hair drooped in the hot, steamy weather. He must have followed her eyes because he swiped at his hair.

"Is it always so hot here in the summer? I thought islands were supposed to be cool."

Kat forced herself to look away and began studying a group of teenage boys enthusiastically washing down a large recreational fishing boat with an ancient green hose.

"It gets cool at night. Are you saying you'll go on the carousel when it's cooler and the line is shorter?"

"Ah, the carousel. I don't see why not. I want to."

"Oh."

Lawrence looked down at her shining, open face and almost grimaced. He did not want to ride a carousel; he loathed the entire idea of it. But for some reason, Kat's disappointment got to him. She had him saying he wanted to—*wanted to*—ride a bloody carousel when he didn't.

"Let's walk," he said abruptly and stepped directly into the path of a little girl, making her ice cream cone fly out of her hands and onto the sidewalk. The scream that came out of her mouth was so piercing, Lawrence thought he had somehow broken one of her bones. He was horrified and immediately bent down to see what damage he'd done, moving his hands along her arms and legs to find any obvious injuries. That only made the girl scream louder until he thought his eardrums might burst.

"I'm so sorry," he said, looking up at the girl's parents and recognizing them as the same tortured pair he'd seen in the carousel.

The two rushed to reassure him. "It's the ice cream," the mother said. "She dropped it. It's all right; she's not hurt." The father tried to comfort the girl, which simply produced another earsplitting scream.

Lawrence looked around frantically—he wasn't sure for what—and he spotted an ice cream shop—Mad Martha's—with a line ten people deep.

"Excuse me," he said, pushing his way to the front. He spoke to the crowd of sweaty tourists wearing T-shirts and baseball hats. "That little girl screaming over there lost her ice cream because of my carelessness, and I was wondering if I could cut in front of you and buy her a replacement." *En masse*, twenty pairs of eyes turned to the little girl and her now mortified parents. When they gave a collective "awww," Lawrence knew he had them, and he smiled.

Kat watched in amazement as the crowd stepped back in unison and let Larry walk to the front. It's that smile, she thought. And the accent. Deadly combination.

Holding the ice cream like a hard-won trophy, Larry bent at the waist and presented it to the little girl, who was still wailing about her lost cone as her mother threatened never to buy her an ice cream cone for the rest of her life if she didn't stop screaming immediately.

"Miss," Larry said, "a replacement."

"No." And she swatted it down, out of his hand, and directly onto Larry's expensive-looking shoes.

"Kristy, apologize to the nice man," the mother said, horrified that her child was behaving so abominably.

"It's quite all right," Larry said, smiling politely and grimacing only slightly when the devil child screamed again.

"Sorry," Kat said to the parents, as if the entire episode was Larry's fault, and tugged on his arm.

"Good God," he said when they were finally away from the family. "That is why I will never have a child. Did you hear her? I think I'll be hearing those screams for the rest of my life." He looked surprisingly upset about the entire incident.

"She was probably just tired."

"Yes, she was tired. She was hot. Children are always something."

Instead of handing the tissue to him, Kat bent down and cleaned the shoes off herself without a second thought.

"She probably sensed you hate children. Animals and children are like that, you know."

"Animals and children love me, typically. I'm just not that good around them. I'm missing the correct gene, I believe."

"You mean the human gene?" she teased. He smiled, and Kat felt inordinately glad that she'd gotten a smile out of him. He'd become way too serious on her. "Kids can also be sweet and love you unconditionally."

"So can a dog," Larry said darkly.

"That's horrible," Kat said, truly outraged. But she laughed anyway.

Larry seemed mildly surprised that she'd laughed. "But true."

"You've obviously never been around children."

He looked off to the water as if suddenly interested in the fleet of fishing boats tied up along the wharf. "I've been around enough of them to know I need to avoid them. Oh, don't look at me as if I'm a monster."

"Thank goodness your mother and father didn't think that way."

"They did. That's why we were sent away to school when we were seven and why when we were home, we had a governess. My parents were exceedingly intelligent."

Kat stopped and looked up at him. "This explains everything," she said.

"Explains what?"

"You've never been in love, have you?"

"Of course I have," he said quickly.

"And you didn't feel loved by your parents," Kat went on as if he hadn't responded. "A child who's never felt love . . ."

"My parents loved me," he said, clearly losing his patience with her.

"A man who's never been in love . . ."

"You really are beginning to grate, you know."

"And books without a soul," she said triumphantly, having a wonderful time baiting him. She didn't mean a single word that was coming out of her mouth.

"You're insane."

"But right," she said and then started laughing when she took in his horrified expression. "My goodness, I didn't mean it. I was just teasing you. I do that."

"No. No, you're right," he said.

"No, I'm not. I'm sure your parents sent you to school because they wanted the best for you because they loved you."

He shook his head, denying her assurances. "No. They sent us to school to get us out of their hair."

"I was only teasing you."

"And I haven't been in love. Not really. I was just a boy then. I thought at the time I was in love, but look at me. I'm thirty-four years old and unmarried, and I have no real desire to get married. I have no one. I'm a shell. Vacant. Soulless, like my books."

"For God's sake, Larry, I was just kidding," Kat said, exasperated.

And then he grinned, and she knew. He'd been playing her, reeling her in like a trophy fish.

She quirked one eyebrow. "Are you finished?"

"I believe so."

"You are oh so witty."

"I do try."

She smiled up at him, and he smiled back, and in that split second, the attraction meter flew off the scale, which made her realize she'd better be very careful with Larry Kendall. Because not only did he have that accent and killer looks, but he could also make her laugh.

"I still think you should keep an open mind about kids," she said.

Larry shrugged as if he didn't care or really hadn't given it much thought.

"I suppose not everyone is cut out to be a parent," she conceded. "You were nice to that little girl though. You didn't have to buy her another cone and charm yourself to the front of the line," she pointed out.

"I just wanted her to stop the racket."

Kat gave up badgering him. Brian hadn't had any huge desire to have kids either. She needed to meet someone who wanted children as much as she did. She wasn't thirty yet, no clocks ticking, but Kat knew kids were going to be part of her future.

They were walking past a T-shirt shop, and Kat stopped. "Perfect," she said and walked into the store. Five minutes later, she was back holding a large tank top with a cartoony great white shark emblazoned on it. Out of its mouth was poking a furry black tail and the words "Sharks Eat Black Dogs."

"Very anti-establishment," Larry said dryly. "It's perfect."

"I knew you'd think so," Kat said with a grin, right before she clutched his arm in horror. "What time is it?"

He looked at his wrist watch and grimaced. "You're late." When Kat began to dash off, he held her arm. "Let him wait."

Kat swallowed. "Right."

"Are you certain you don't want to take him back?"

"Yes." She chewed on her lower lip. "I just wish he didn't want to talk to me in private."

And then Larry did something Kat would never forget. He took her face in his large hands and gently made her look into his eyes. "You are the toughest girl I've ever met. If you can't resist him, then you weren't meant to."

She nodded, mesmerized by his intense gaze. "I wish I were as confident as you. I'm not as tough as I look."

He laughed, let her go, and the moment was over. "I didn't say you looked tough. You look as tough as a puppy."

"A pit bull puppy?" she asked with mock hope.

"That's the ticket. Now let's send this chap packing, shall we?"

Chapter 5

Lawrence hovered on the staircase just in case Katherine needed him. He heard only the low murmur of her voice and a single "Please, Kat" from the boyfriend. Frankly, he didn't know what could be taking so much time. "Get out, I never want to see you again" would take about five seconds to say. They'd been in there for nearly a half hour. He realized with a small start that he was actually worried about her. He hadn't been worried about anyone but himself in such a long time—it felt slightly foreign, and it reminded him uncomfortably of a time when he'd routinely put himself last. He was just about to sneak down to see if he could hear something of the conversation when he heard footsteps.

He watched from the stairs as the two of them walked to the door, and he silently scooted up a couple more steps to keep out of sight.

"You're wasting you time, Bri," he heard her say.

"Not if there's a chance I'll get you back."

"You won't. I told you. I'm sorry, but there's no going back after what you did. I'd never trust you again. Do you really want to live that way? I know I don't."

He tried to pull her to him, and Lawrence had the undeniable urge to throw himself down the stairs and physically heave the man out the door.

"Stop it. It's over, Brian." She said those words with far more kindness than she should have.

"I can tell in your eyes that you don't mean it."

"I mean it. If I have to, I'll get a restraining order."

"Bravo," Lawrence said softly, smiling at her spunk. He knew she was tough.

"I haven't done anything to warrant a restraining order, and you know it."

True enough, Larry thought with regret.

"Just leave me alone."

"Please, Kat. I love you. I made a mistake. A huge, horrible mistake." The guy actually started to cry, and for the smallest moment, Kat's face crumpled, but she gathered herself together remarkably quickly, given the fact Brian was nearly blubbering in front of her.

"A one-night stand is a horrible mistake," she said, her voice strong, betraying none of the emotion she must be feeling. "Getting engaged and buying a house with another woman is pathological. Leave."

"I'll be back." Lawrence had to give the guy some credit—he could do the wounded dog look with the best.

"You'll be wasting your time. And mine. Goodbye."

After he left, Katherine immediately looked up the stairs and smiled. "I couldn't have done it without you, Larry."

"Lawrence," he corrected. "And I'm not certain eavesdropping qualifies me as hero of the year."

"I think you know that if I didn't know you were

sitting up there watching us, I would have folded. I wouldn't have thought you had it in you to be so nice."

Lawrence walked down the stairs, one eyebrow raised. "Based on what?" He actually was a bit insulted. He was a nice guy, wasn't he?

Katherine walked toward the living room, and he followed, sitting across from her. "Remember I Googled you? You didn't seem like a guy who goes around rescuing damsels in distress. Unless they're blond. Nearly every picture of you has you standing next to a tall, skinny blonde."

"This is true. And beautiful—don't forget that they are all beautiful." She made a face, and he laughed. "What is wrong with a man liking to be around beautiful women?"

She drew her legs up onto the couch, wrapping her arms around them. "If all men like beautiful women, what happens to the rest of us?"

"Who do you mean?"

"Like me. And other women like me. Ordinary woman without big boobs and long legs and blond hair."

"You're quite pretty," he said. "In fact, you have moments when you border on beautiful. Let me guess—you think a man should fall in love with a woman's soul first, is that it?"

"Yes," she said, even though she was just as shallow as the next person. Still, she persisted. "Just look at all the beautiful women who fall in love with older men. Ugly men. Look at Donald Trump. He's not good-looking, but look at the women he gets."

He started laughing; he couldn't help it. "Oh, good God, you're kidding, right? Do you think those women were with me because they thought I was a wonderful person? Let me tell you something—when the money dries up, an amazing thing happens: the beautiful women disappear. Present company excepted, of course."

"You are very cynical," she pronounced.

"I wouldn't say Brian is ugly, would you?"

Kat smiled, enjoying herself far more than during her emotionally draining conversation with Brian. "What does that have to do with anything? We were talking about you and how shallow you are."

"Is your ex-boyfriend ugly?" he repeated.

"Well, no. He's good-looking. A jerk, but good-looking."

"Ah-ha," he said, pointing a finger at her.

"Ah-ha, what?"

"You were able to overlook the fact he is a jerk because he was good-looking. You are just as shallow as I am."

She looked at him as if he were crazy, even though she knew he was partially right. "I didn't know he was a jerk until very recently."

Larry stood up. "I'm going to try to get some writing done. Maybe some of your woeful tale will inspire me."

"One can only hope. Good luck, Larry."

He was walking away and paused. "Lawrence," he corrected, and she just grinned.

When he'd gone, Kat let out a long breath and looked up at her aunt in all her glory and remembered she'd meant to call her days ago. She grabbed up the phone and dialed California where her aunt lived.

"Lila, it's Kat."

"Hi, sweetie. Did you make it to the cottage okay? Is everything all right?"

It was weird having a conversation with her aunt sprawled in front of her in her altogether, so Kat turned away from the painting. "Everything's fine. But it turns out I have a roommate. You know Lawrence Kendall?"

"Oh, no."

"Oh, yes. Apparently Carl said he could have the cottage for the summer. Did he forget to tell you?"

"He talked about it, but I didn't know whether he'd finalized anything with him. I completely forgot, to be honest. He was so sick, and we knew we weren't going to make it to the Vineyard this year. I'm so sorry."

Kat twirled the phone cord with her finger. "Everything's worked out so far, I guess. Neither of us wants to give up the place, so we're in negotiations."

"If I know you, you're winning," she said.

"Do you know him? He seems like an okay guy, but . . ."

"I never met him, but Carl thought the world of him. He did strike me as a very complicated man."

Kat furrowed her brow. Larry seemed like a nice guy, a bit shallow, but certainly not complicated. Then again, she didn't really know him. "Complicated is not a word I'd use to describe him," Kat said.

Lila laughed her soft, lilting laugh. "Have you read any of his books?"

"Have you?" Kat asked with disbelief.

"His last three. He's quite good, but not really what I prefer to read."

"Your complicated man suggested we have a

summer fling. I think he was half-serious, but I'm not sure."

Lila laughed again, apparently not worried about her niece being propositioned. "What did you say?"

"No, of course. I hardly know the guy. And I just broke up with Brian, remember? And speaking of that rat, he showed up here."

"No."

"Yes. But I sent him packing. At least I tried. I think he plans to hang around here until I change my mind. But I won't, and I do have Larry to thank for that. Brian thinks Larry is more than my housemate, and I let him go on thinking that."

"Good for you. And Lawrence is gorgeous, so I'll bet that didn't go over very well with Brian."

"Lila," Kat said, slightly shocked, "I thought you liked older men."

"I do, but I can appreciate a younger one, too. Don't worry about Lawrence, Kat. He's one of the good guys. At least, Carl thought so. Having said that, a man's opinion of another man is not always something to consider."

"That's true."

"I'll bet he's lonely," Lila said, her voice going all soft and breathy. "Men like that are profoundly lonely."

Kat snorted. "Lila, you're more of a romantic than I am, and I thought I was hopeless. I'll let you go; I just wanted to make sure this guy was safe and to thank you again for the cottage, even if it didn't turn out the way I'd planned."

"Actually, I'm glad you called because I was going to call you. Something very upsetting is happening. Carl's children are contesting the will, even though he was very generous to them. They want the cottage," Lila said, her voice breaking. "I wanted you to be aware that they might send someone, a lawyer or something, to take a look around. I can't lose that cottage." Kat gripped the phone, knowing her aunt was crying on the other end.

"Is there anything I can do?"

She sniffed. "Just let them in. I've hired a lawyer, too. We were so happy there."

"I know." Kat closed her eyes, picturing Lila snuggled up next to Carl on the porch swing. Brian had thought it was creepy for a woman so young to show so much affection for an older man, but Kat thought it was beautiful. Carl loved Lila to distraction, and she adored him. "If I can do anything, just let me know."

"I will."

Kat hung up the phone, feeling sad for her aunt. The house was worth a small fortune, but Kat knew that wasn't why Lila wanted it. Perhaps his children had fond memories of the old place, too. After all, it was likely that they'd spent summers at the house when they were growing up. As much as Kat loved her aunt, maybe it wasn't fair that she get the cottage. Then again, if Carl left it to her, he probably knew what he was doing.

Kat picked up her book and tried to read, then put it down, too tired to make sense of the words. She still couldn't believe Brian had shown up to win her back. It was insane. Still, as she trudged to her room and peeled off her clothes, she couldn't stop thinking about what she might have done if Larry hadn't been listening in on them. When Brian had started to cry, she'd almost lost it.

Maybe she *should* have a summer fling to get over Brian. How crazy it would be to do something like that. No strings.

She laughed aloud. "Not in this lifetime."

After trying to write for two frustrating hours, Lawrence decided what he needed was a beer and a blonde, so he walked down to Oak Bluffs looking for both. Four hours later, Lawrence left the Blue Moon Cafe feeling a bit unsteady. The blonde he was with wasn't much better. She giggled a lot, which he found annoying, but a man had to do what a man had to do. And he hadn't done what he wanted to do with a woman in too long.

"You're so cute," she said and mashed her lips against his.

"Likewise."

"I just love your accent. And you're so serious," she said, putting on a serious face. "Say something else. Talk to me." She flung her arms wide and spun around a bit, almost stepping off the curb and into traffic. Lawrence hauled her back, and she gave off a squeal, followed by the inevitable giggle. "Where're we going?"

"I thought we could go to my cottage. It's just down the street." For the first time all evening, she hesitated, and Lawrence had a sinking feeling he wasn't going to get what his body so desperately needed.

"Well," she said, drawing out the word interminably, "I suppose I could. Sure." And she threw herself against him with only the abandon a woman half-drunk could. He laughed, enjoying her exuber-

ance and refusing to think about Katherine and her
ex-boyfriend and how she felt leaning against him.
He didn't want to think about Katherine, so he
pulled the blonde close and kissed her.

"Wow. You can really kiss," she said, gazing up at
him, her pretty blue eyes gone hazy.

"Lots of practice."

She smiled, revealing brilliant white teeth. "You're
so cute," she repeated, walking alongside him.

Lawrence was trying not to find her annoying, so
he let his eyes drift to her bouncing breasts and got
over his annoyance quickly. Ah, nothing like a beautiful, blond, willing woman.

"Here we are," he said as they reached the cottage.
Thankfully, nearly all the lights were out, which
meant Katherine was asleep. He didn't know why,
but he felt slightly guilty bringing a woman home.

"Wow. You own this place?" the blonde said. She
was "the blonde" because even though he was quite
certain she'd given him her name, he'd forgotten it
entirely.

"I'm just here for the summer."

"Oh." And in that syllable, he heard her disappointment, the mental calculation in her head that
told her this guy wasn't as rich as she'd thought.
Then she brightened. "I'm here for a week," she
gushed and ran up the porch stairs.

"Do try to be a bit quiet. I have a roommate," he
said, fighting his conscience for bringing this
woman home. He didn't know why—it was purely
ridiculous—but he had the strangest feeling he was
being disloyal to Katherine. Pretending to be her
lover was fogging his brain, he decided. Katherine
wouldn't care if he brought a woman home any

more than he'd care if she brought a man home. Even as he considered that reality, his mind rejected that image.

The blonde comically clamped a hand over her mouth to make herself quiet, and he couldn't help but think how darling she was. He fumbled briefly with the key and let them both inside.

"Do you have any beer?" she asked, heading toward the kitchen.

"I don't think . . ."

"Oh, my God, what crap," she said, holding up a half-full bottle of Katherine's Arbor Mist.

"It's my roommate's."

"And you can't have it," said a voice from behind them. Lawrence let out a sigh and turned to see Katherine standing there, her hair sticking up in spikes, her face flushed from sleep. She wore a tank top and sweat shorts, and for the life of him, he could not seem to tear his eyes off her, even with the gorgeous blonde standing next to him.

"This is Katherine," he said to the blonde.

"Corey," the blonde said, and Lawrence said a little silent prayer of thanks that he'd learned her name.

"I'm Kat. And I'm not his roommate. He's only here temporarily."

Lawrence rubbed his hands together. "Now that all the introductions are complete, good night, Katherine." He wanted to get rid of her, out of sight, out of mind, because at the moment, with her standing there barefoot and sleep-tousled, her small breasts nicely outlined by the thin tank top, it was difficult to concentrate on the blonde.

Katherine's eyes went from him to Corey, and they

stayed on Corey so long he began to feel a bit uncomfortable.

"Do you mind if I ask you a question, Corey?" Katherine asked calmly.

The girl shrugged. "Go ahead."

"How old are you?"

That question gave Lawrence a start, and he decided to give Corey a closer look as well. Oh, good God, he thought with dread. Please be twenty-four, please. Even twenty-three would be all right . . .

"Eighteen."

"Oh, Christ."

Katherine nodded and gave the oddest smile. "Eighteen. Wow." Then she turned to Lawrence. "Eighteen, Larry. Not that it's any of my business since I hardly know you, even though we were, briefly, lovers, and given your reputation and your thrilling proposition earlier, I suppose I shouldn't be surprised. But you've got to be kidding."

He held out both hands as if warding off an attack. "I didn't know. How could I know? We were in a bar; she was drinking; I assumed she was at least the legal age to drink."

"I took one look at her, and I knew she was probably still in high school."

"I graduated this year," Corey said defensively. "And it's not statutory rape if I'm an adult."

Lawrence let out a strangled sound. "I think you better go, Corey."

"Oh, come on. Just because she's all old." Corey crossed her arms in front of her. "How old are you?" she asked him cautiously, studying his face in the light for the first time.

"I'm"—he swallowed—"thirty four."

"Oh."

"Yeah. 'Oh,'" Katherine said. "Just go home and count yourself lucky that you didn't become another notch in Lawrence Kendall's bedpost."

"I guess I should go. My parents are already going to kill me for being so late." Lawrence let out another little sound of horror. Corey went up to him and pulled his face down for a kiss, one that Lawrence just couldn't bring himself to respond to. She was a kid, and Katherine was standing right there, looking as if she wanted to kill him. "Good night," Corey said and walked out the door with a little wave.

"I didn't know," he said, turning to Katherine, who still stood there looking at him as if he were some sort of child molester.

Then she started laughing.

He felt himself bristling. "What is so blasted funny?"

"You go into a bar, pick up a pretty blonde," she said, emphasizing *blonde*. "And you bring her home without even bothering to find out how old she is? God, you're about as complicated as a fence post."

"You don't even know me."

"I read all about you, remember? England's most eligible bachelor. You asked me if I wanted to have a summer fling, remember? And then you come home with a teenager on your arm. Does any of this sound a bit depraved to you?" He gave her a crooked grin, and Kat couldn't help but get off her high horse.

"I suppose when you put it that way, it does all sound rather sordid."

"Yes, it does." She remembered what her aunt said

about Larry, that he was a lonely man. She called bullshit on that one. He was a horny man who had enough charm to get most women into bed. Well, she was not most women. She was not going to be one of a string of women who slept with him. No, sirree. No way. Even if he did look incredible in his khakis and untucked, partially unbuttoned, wrinkled white dress shirt. He should look like a slob; any other man would have. But not Larry.

"I am a bit put out with you though," he said, settling down on the sofa. The way he sat down all loose-limbed made Kat realize he was a bit drunk.

"How so?"

"If you hadn't come waltzing into the room, I never would have found out how old she was, and I could be having a wonderful time right now."

Kat wrinkled her nose in disgust, and he laughed.

"I'm joking," he said. "I'm a bit weak in the knees, but I'm not fully blotto."

"I don't think you are joking."

"I am," he insisted.

Kat chose to believe him and flopped down on the couch next to him. "I just don't get guys, and I guess I never will. It really doesn't matter who you sleep with, does it, as long as she's beautiful."

"And blond," he put in, making her laugh. "Not all men are like me. Some of my best friends have settled down, and they seem happy enough."

"Happy enough for what?"

That question seemed to throw him for a minute. "Happy enough not to live like me, I suppose."

"Brian got bored. He must have. Otherwise, he wouldn't have cheated on me. Isn't that why you haven't gotten married? Boredom?"

"There are dozens of reasons a man doesn't wish to marry. As for me, fear of boredom is not one of them. But please don't compare me with Brian. He's an idiot."

Kat pressed her lips together and took a deep breath. It was a waste of time and energy to dwell on something she couldn't change.

"So are you saying I'm better or worse than your ex-fiancé?" Larry asked.

"Worse, from a woman's perspective. I bet every woman who's dated you thought she might be the one who makes you fall in love," she said. "You are the worst sort of man. A challenge with just enough charm to make women not hate you."

"You know me so well," he said, and she couldn't be certain whether he was being sarcastic or not. "And not every one was trying to marry me," he said slowly, as if he were tallying them all up in his head.

Kat let out a snort. "Someday, it'll happen to you. You'll fall in love, and then you'll find out what it feels like to be me and all the other women who were dumb enough to fall in love."

He raised his eyebrows. "Are you saying you're in love with me?"

"You *are* hopeless," she said blandly. "I wouldn't fall in love with you if you were the last man on earth." She meant every word.

"All the more reason to sleep with me," he said with mock sincerity.

"You need therapy."

He laughed, and Kat just shook her head, got up off the couch, and headed for bed.

"Good night, Romeo."

"Good night, Juliet."

Despite herself, Kat smiled all the way to bed, wondering what it was about Larry that allowed him to get away with what he did. He was so damn likable, so accepting of his flaws, so charming.

And so very, very hot. Was she influenced by a beautiful face? Probably not. Kat usually found good-looking men either obnoxious, boring, or intimidating. Larry was none of those things. She snuggled under the covers because with the air conditioner blowing softly on her, it was a bit chilly in her room, and she willed herself not to think of the man sharing the cottage with her. Then she decided it was much better to dwell on Larry than Brian. Much, much better.

Chapter 6

Kat, used to getting up at six each morning, had been up for four hours before Lawrence made his way downstairs looking showered and none the worse for his late-night adventure. She'd been to the tiny Stop & Shop in the heart of Oak Bluffs, finished her shopping, put the groceries away, and grabbed her book to head to the front porch when he stopped her.

"I feel I should apologize for last night," he said so formally Kat almost laughed. It was only his sincere face that stopped her. "I don't usually drink so much, and I swear to you I have never knowingly taken a girl under twenty home ." He hesitated, and Kat was about to let him off the hook when he said, "And I want you to know I was never serious about the whole summer fling thing."

Kat struck a pose of dejection. "And here I was ready to accept." He gave her a withering look. "I suppose I was just shocked because I'd known you for all of a single day before you mentioned it."

"The only explanation I have, then, is that I was overwhelmed by your dazzling beauty."

Kat shook her head. "I know there are women out there who fall for that stuff, but I still find it hard to believe."

"You are making it very difficult to get out a simple apology," he said, sounding slightly put out.

"Apology accepted. Now, if you'll excuse me, I'm going to read out on the porch." Kat left him standing there looking confused and off balance. It was almost fun making him think she was completely oblivious to his charms. Poor man was so mystified. She curled up on the porch swing and was just about to open her book when the screen door squeaked open.

"What about our research?"

"I don't think that's going to work out. If you really want to know what it's like to be middle class, then get a job at a McDonald's."

"It just might come to that," he said under his breath.

Kat gave up trying to read for the moment and gave Larry her full attention. "What is your book about, anyway?"

"It's about nothing. I've written nothing," he said with surprising exasperation. "I need inspiration. I need . . . something."

"How about a book about a murder in a small New England seaside resort?"

He shook his head. "I don't write mysteries."

"It wouldn't have to be a mystery. It could be a story about how a murder divides a community. The local sheriff suspects the girlfriend murdered her cheating fiancé, and then the sheriff falls for the girl even though he doesn't trust her, and then she falls for him and . . ."

He held up a hand to stop her. "I don't write romances either," he said.

"Maybe you should. The supermarket's loaded with 'em. They must sell a bunch. Then again, how can you write about falling in love when you've never fallen in love? You're right. No romance."

He looked for a moment as if he might want to murder her himself. "I don't need ideas; I need inspiration. You've got to help me. Tell me about yourself."

Kat was dubious about the whole idea, and she really was dying to sit on the porch by herself and read, but she figured she'd indulge him for a little while. And he had helped her with Brian far more than she'd helped him understand the middle class. "I'm twenty-eight years old, and as you know, my fiancé just dumped me because he fell in love." She rolled her eyes.

"Was she blond?"

Kat looked to the side and pretended to speak to an invisible friend. "And then she killed the writer, and the jury acquitted her because they decided he deserved to die."

Larry laughed. "Go on, I'm sorry."

"Anyway, at about that same time, I killed that dog, got sued, lost my business, and will probably lose my apartment, and here I am telling my life story to a spoiled playboy who's moaning and groaning that he's got writer's block. Boohoo."

He looked a bit taken aback. "I sense a bit of undeserved hostility."

Kat let out a sigh. "Sorry. It's just that my life is going to shit, so it's a little bit difficult right now for me to feel sorry for Britain's most eligible bachelor."

"You shouldn't believe everything you read,

Katherine," he said, and something in his voice made her look at him.

"You're right. Sorry. I'm sure my life captured in black and white wouldn't be a very accurate picture either. Anyway, I never went to college officially, but I did take some business courses. I was actually doing pretty good before this summer."

"What about family? Any brothers or sisters?"

"Thankfully, I'm the only one. Mom worked mostly as a waitress my whole life. She never got married, a fact that I used to thank God for every night when I was a kid. Anything else?"

"That's all for now," he said, acting like a teacher hearing a book report.

Kat couldn't stand the thought of his feeling sorry for her, so she went back inside. She shouldn't care what he thought, but Kat realized she did. One of the reasons she'd worked so hard at her business was because as much as she loved her mother, she didn't want to end up like her. She wanted to end up living in that dream house and driving a Volvo. She wanted to forget that she was the kid who shopped at Wal-Mart for clothes and thought fancy dining was Ponderosa Steakhouse.

Kat loved her mother, was proud of the fact she'd raised her alone, cherished their close relationship. She wouldn't trade a minute of her life with her mother—the day they'd colored her hair black when she was thirteen, the time her mother took her to get her ears pierced and had nearly fainted. The facts seemed so sordid without any of the beautiful color that made up their lives.

She went to the screen door and yelled, "I love my mother. I have a wonderful life."

She could hear his footsteps running down the stairs, and she turned to see him smiling broadly at her. "I know," he said almost fervently. "It's wonderful. It's . . ." and he smiled, "inspirational. You go read; I've got to jot down some things. Tonight, let's do something. Let's go for a walk."

Kat smiled at his sudden enthusiasm, then narrowed her eyes. "No strings attached."

"None," he said, grinning. "But if we do run into Brian, I just might have to kiss you again."

Why did she suddenly hope they ran into Brian?

"I've got just the place. Have you been to Aquinnah yet?"

"I haven't even been out of Oak Bluffs."

"If you rent a car for the day, I'll take you to the most beautiful place on the whole island. But we have to make it there by sunset. Deal?"

"Deal."

Most tourists traveling the long, winding roads to what the locals still call Gay Head stop at the lighthouse, buy a cheesy souvenir, look through the metered binoculars above the cliffs, eat a picnic lunch, then go back to their hotel or cottage. But Aquinnah, renamed to honor the island's native Americans, held a secret—it is one of the most beautiful places on earth at sunset.

Brian was a lousy fiancé, but he had a talent for finding the road less traveled. Down the street from the lighthouse was a small dirt parking lot, and off that, a long sandy path led down to a pristine beach that stretched for miles. Parts of it were so secluded that it was an unofficial nudist beach that attracted couples and a number of gay lovers, a point that had absolutely nothing to do with the area's former name. You could tell how long someone had been on the island by what they called the cliffs.

Lawrence stood at the top of the path looking down toward the beach and smiled. To his left was a beach house nestled in a little valley, surrounded by beach roses and scruff pines. The house, with its gray, weathered clapboard, startlingly white trim, and a porch that looked out over the Atlantic, looked hauntingly familiar.

"It's the house in the painting in the dining room, isn't it?" he asked Katherine. "My God, it's spectacular."

"Every time I see that house, it tugs at my heart for some reason. I think it has that same effect on a lot of people."

The sun was getting low in the sky, but it was still warm as the two made their way down the sandy path. A few people passed them along the way, but they mostly had the path to themselves. When they got to the beach, Lawrence stopped again. The beach was littered with large rocks made smooth and rounded by the sea. People had piled them up or used them to create designs in the soft sand, little monuments that gave the beach an almost mystic look, as if a cult of beach worshippers met at night and performed rituals. Driftwood, shells, and seaweed made some of the creations seem almost satanic, and despite the warm wind, he shivered.

"Rather creepy, isn't it?"

Katherine laughed. "I thought so at first, but I think it's cool the way people have created these things. Brian and I did it once, and I always wondered how long it stood there before it fell apart. Come on, this isn't the best part."

Walking in the soft sand was difficult, so Lawrence followed Katherine's lead and took off his boat shoes to walk along the edge of the surf where the sand was far firmer. The water felt impossibly warm, and he walked so that he touched the edge of the surf. They walked toward the setting sun, the sea to their left and a high cliff to their right. The cliff was made of reddish orange clay that was brilliant in the setting sun. Deep trenches had been carved into the cliffs from rainstorms, revealing several different shades ranging from stark white to deep red. "This is fantastic," he said, and Katherine smiled, her teeth white in the twilight.

Up ahead, the surf got more violent as it struck large boulders at what looked like a tip of land. The further they walked, the fewer people there were on the beach, and it seemed strange to Lawrence that something so beautiful could be so deserted.

"Wait until we go around this bend," she said.

They climbed over large boulders to get around the bend, and Lawrence stopped. Curving as far as the eye could see was a nearly empty beach. The only inhabitants were a fisherman standing in the surf and what appeared to be a family. Katherine, smiling broadly, pointed to the top of the cliff, and there was the lighthouse, its beam cutting through the misty air.

"Thank you," he said and looked at her and tried not to think about how pretty she was standing there in the last glow of the sun, her skin a soft peach, her dark hair blowing about her head.

"I thought this might inspire you," she said cheerfully. Any maudlin thoughts that she'd had earlier in the day were gone, and Lawrence was beginning to believe she was the most buoyant, most cheerful person he'd ever met. He'd known plenty of men and women who were nauseatingly morose after a breakup, something he found difficult to understand, having never suffered any ill effects from ending a relationship. "You have no sense of empathy," said one woman after she'd broken up with a fellow she'd been seeing all of two months. She'd gone on and on about how she'd thought he was "the one," and when he told her she should simply go out and find another man, she looked at him as if he'd gone quite insane.

Katherine, on the other hand, had just ended a long-term relationship that she'd thought would be her last, and here she was chipper and smiling. She was either amazingly resilient, or she hid her pain well. She walked slightly ahead of him, and his eyes drifted to her bum—a very nice one, actually. If she were any other woman, he just might try to kiss her. Maybe he'd try anyway. Later.

"I wish I could paint," she said, sighing. "I mean, have you ever seen anything more idyllic? It comes complete with a happy family and a guy fishing."

They walked toward the family, enjoying the feel of the cool sand beneath their feet. The water lapping ashore felt bathwater warm, and Lawrence gave a fleeting thought to jumping in when the woman on the beach gave a little cheer.

"Daddy's got a fish," she yelled, and the three kids who were scattered along the beach came running. She grabbed a camera and began taking pictures of her husband as he fought with what, from the bend of his pole, appeared to be a large fish. Caught up in the moment, Lawrence moved closer to the family so he could watch. In the surf, a fish splashed to the surface. A big fish.

"Did you see that?" he asked, forgetting for a moment his practiced reserve.

"My daddy caught a big fish," said a little girl as she jumped up and down. She was a freckle-faced little thing, her hair a strawlike mess, and looking at her hurt his heart. "It's the threed fish so far."

"Third," one of the bigger kids corrected.

Before long, the man climbed off the boulder he'd been standing on and walked toward his family carrying by the gill an impossibly big fish. His family rushed to the edge of the water, and they all admired the fish while the man posed for a few pictures. It was a big, fat thing with a white belly and horizontal stripes along its beefy body. Then he laid it on the beach, and his wife handed him a measuring tape.

"How big?" Katherine asked, poking her head around one of the kids.

"Thirty-eight inches," the man said, grinning, his face alight with the joy of the moment. Apparently, that was a lot because the man's wife clapped.

And then the man did an amazing thing. He kissed the damned fish and gently put it back into the water, holding it in the surf until the fish gave a sudden jerk and swam away. The kids went back to the hole they were digging; the woman went back to the blanket, tucked the camera in a large tote bag and watched her husband walk out into the surf.

"That was remarkable," Lawrence said softly and began walking down the beach away from the family.

He felt, for a moment, insanely jealous of that man, for his joy, for his family, for the pure pleasure he'd gotten from catching a silly fish. Insane, indeed.

Kat hugged herself, filled with the pleasure of the moment, the beauty of the beach, the happy little family who could find such joy in catching a fish. Larry walked a bit ahead of her, his head turned slightly to the sea, his thick, dark hair blowing in the warm breeze. In that moment, he looked like a blustering sea captain in love with the sea.

"Getting inspired?" she teased because she really didn't know how else to talk to him.

"I've never seen anything like that. This is exactly what I needed," he said. "You can't know what it's been like to have my brain be dead, to have nothing going on inside."

He shook his head. "Nothing solid yet, but it's there," he said, tapping the side of his head. "I can feel it moving about."

"E-ew."

He chuckled. "It's not as bad as all that. It's wonderful, actually."

They walked on until the family was a distant speck, then settled down to watch the sun slide into the Atlantic. Kat pulled a bottle of Arbor Mist out of her backpack and unscrewed the top.

"No cork?"

"Nope. Handy, isn't it? Want some?" Kat took a gulp right out of the bottle and handed it over to him. He gave the bottle a dubious look before taking it.

"Beggars can't be choosers, I suppose."

"That's right. You might even develop a taste for it."

His grimace told Kat he probably wouldn't.

"I've never done this," he said after a while.

"Drunk out of a bottle?"

He gave her a quick grin. "No. I mean walk down a deserted beach for the pure pleasure of it. That family." He shook his head as if he couldn't quite explain what was happening in his head.

"I suppose you're used to the jet-set crowd. Night clubs and fancy restaurants. No kids. All that."

"It's true. I am. They looked so happy."

Kat laughed. "Believe it or not, some people are happy."

"Of course." He shook his head as if she misunderstood him. "Not to break this idyllic mood, but I feel I should give you fair warning—I have friends coming over next week. I invited them because I was going mad here with boredom, not to mention I wasn't writing at all."

"Oh? That's okay. Are they staying at the cottage?"

"Yes. They're the old crowd," he said vaguely.

"Is that good or bad?"

He let out a small chuckle. "Bad. I was bored and needed a bit of excitement. But now . . ."

"Now?

"Now I think inviting them was a mistake."

Kat shrugged. "I get along with most people," she said.

"These are not most people," he said, taking a swig of wine and wincing a bit, a strangely endearing reaction. "I don't even get along with them anymore."

"You can hang out with me then," she said, and in that moment, he looked over at her, and she felt her entire body get hot. Instantly. Like the snap of a finger. She'd been attracted to him—he was a gorgeous man, and a woman would have to be half-dead not to be attracted to him. But the attraction hadn't reached anything hotly sexual until that moment.

She looked away, hoping he hadn't seen the immediate reaction she'd had to him . . . and sort of hoping he had. Despite what she'd said, she kept hearing over and over in her head, "summer fling." What harm, really, would it do? It had an end point; he was gorgeous; she was needy and wildly attracted to him. *What was the downside again?* she asked herself. Maybe she'd just kiss him madly and see if there was any chemistry between them. That other kiss had been way too quick to tell, she lied to herself. Just because she thought he was hot didn't mean he was truly interested in her.

She steeled herself and looked over to him only to find him still looking at her. "What?"

"It's only that you look beautiful in the sunlight." He said it without embarrassment, as if he were stating a fact. "You're one of those women who grow on you."

She frowned. "Was that supposed to be a compliment?"

"What I mean is that when I first saw you, I thought you were a bit attractive. But there are moments, like now, that you are quite breathtaking."

Kat bit her bottom lip and gave him a skeptical look, wondering if he had seen her lust-filled expression and realized he should take full advantage of her state.

"You don't believe me."

"No, I do. But I also believe you're trying to get me to sleep with you."

"Oh, that," he said, waving a hand at her. "I've

stopped trying. And I wasn't really serious anyway. You know that."

Kat was more than slightly dubious. "You're saying that if I came on to you, you wouldn't be interested?"

"Good God, no. I'm saying that I've given up the pursuit. If you came on to me, I'd be more than receptive."

"Well, don't hold your breath," Kat said, even though she had been contemplating having that fling about thirty seconds ago.

"For instance," he said, ignoring her, "if you were to lean over and kiss me, I'd let you."

"How nice."

"Why not give it a try?" he said, acting boyishly hopeful. He was so darned handsome at that moment, Kat was more than tempted. "Just lean a bit and . . ."

And she did, and right before their mouths touched, his eyes widened in surprise, and she almost laughed. But the laughter died as soon as their lips met because the strangest and most wonderful thing happened, something that had never happened before. Kat melted. Her body got all boneless, and she simply had to reach out and grab his neck to keep from sagging into the sand. Her lips had just been lips before, but now it seemed as if every nerve ending in her body was centered there and was directly connected to between her legs. His lips were firm and soft and gentle and rough, and God, he knew how to kiss.

She pulled back, trying not to look dazed, trying to look as if she were still playing a game and he was playing along. Except he looked as dazed as she was trying not to look.

"You have an amazing mouth," he said, his dark eyes dipping to her lips. "Let's have another go."

Her head screamed no, because it wasn't normal to have such a strong physical reaction to a no-tongue kiss. She shouldn't be ready to tackle him and strip him naked and ride him like some porno star. But that's what she wanted to do, which was very, very scary. And not at all like her. He leaned forward, and she leaned back, her lips pressed together as if they'd been superglued.

"I can't kiss you if you keep backing away," he said with laughter in his voice.

"That's the point," she said and scuttled back like a crab.

He pulled back and looked slightly annoyed. "What's wrong?"

What was wrong? Nothing was wrong, and that was the problem. She'd known this guy for all of a week, and here she was on a beach kissing him, and for some reason, it felt okay. More than okay. That's when Kat's body made the decision for her. "Nothing, absolutely nothing, is wrong," she said and grabbed his collar with two hands and pulled him toward her and met his mouth with hers, open and wet and so damned hot, and let out a sound no man had ever heard her utter. She could only hope that he felt half of what she did because otherwise, she was making a complete idiot of herself. She didn't care; he felt so good, he tasted so good. They kissed and kissed until Kat felt like screaming for him to touch her breasts, between her legs, any of the places that were on fire.

Then finally, finally, she felt his hand on her breast, heard his low moan, let out a moan of her own; then he stopped cold. He drew away from her, out of breath and laughing slightly. When he saw her confused look, he jerked his head a bit, and that's when Kat noticed a couple, buck naked, walking toward them. The two men were holding hands, the gifts God gave them dangling for anyone to see, so Kat immediately averted her eyes. As the two walked past, they each said hello, so Kat and Larry said hello back. Kat tried to be sophisticated about the whole thing, but seeing a gay couple walk by naked was not part of her everyday life experience.

"Did you see that chap's wanker?" Larry said.

"No, I did not," Kat said, turning beet red.

"It wasn't natural. It was hitting his kneecaps."

Kat laughed. "It was not."

"Ah-ha. So you did look."

"I did not," she said. "Not much. But enough to know it wasn't *that* big."

"You're blushing," he said, tilting his head to get a better look in the waning light.

"Of course I'm blushing. Two men holding hands just walked by me buck naked."

He shook his head, smiling. "You've never been to Greece, I take it."

"I've never been out of New England," she said truthfully.

"You're kidding."

"Nope."

He looked at her as if she were a strange being, but Kat refused to let him intimidate her. "You've never been to California? Or Florida?" he asked incredulously.

"Are those in New England? I told you. I haven't traveled. I spent every day of my life working and building my business so I could travel someday. We were supposed to go to Bermuda on our honeymoon, but obviously, that got cancelled."

"I'll take you," he pronounced grandly. "I'll show you the world. Spain, Italy, Greece."

"Montana?" she teased.

"Even Montana. Good God, Katherine, you cannot spend the rest of your life in one place."

"Why not?" She wrapped her arms around her legs, not liking this conversation.

"Because there is so much to see. Imagine if I never left England. I wouldn't be here with you on this beach watching the sun set. I would have missed out on this."

Kat stared silently at the sea, watching as the sky darkened, as the water lost its shimmer and color and turned black. She thought about her mother, who'd never been anywhere either; about herself; about the life she'd been so perfectly happy living. Until now. "Some people are perfectly happy staying in one place," she said, echoing her thoughts. She was happy. Well, other than the fact she'd lost her business and her fiancé, she was happy.

Oh, God, she was miserable, and she hadn't even known it.

Kat glared at Larry. "People like you move around so much because you don't have a home, no roots to hold you down. You travel because whether you know it or not, you're searching for happiness."

"Here we go again," he said on a sigh.

"It's true. If you had a family, a wife and kids, or even a relationship, you wouldn't be gallivanting around the world."

"Sure I would. They'd just be with me."

That stopped her cold because she suddenly had

the painful image of a family standing beneath the Eiffel Tower and they were so happy. And the worst thing was she was that mom and Larry—good grief—Larry was the dad. "You'd take them with you?"

"The reason I was so struck by that family is because they seemed so free, so alive. But I'll happily live vicariously through other families."

"You don't strike me as that happy a person. Are you saying you're happy?"

"Yes," he said without hesitation.

"I'm happy," she said, but with the slightest bit of defensiveness, which made her seem unsure.

"I didn't say you weren't happy," Larry said, and from his tone, Kat could tell he was getting annoyed.

Kat fell silent again and stared out at the ocean. The only thing visible was the red and green running lights on a boat passing by in the distance and the white caps of the waves as they came ashore. Down the beach, the family was gone, and there were no naked couples in sight.

"I think if we kiss again, we'll both feel better."

Kat laughed and stood. "I think we did enough kissing for one night."

"I suppose you're right."

Kat gave him a suspicious look that he'd given up so easily, but he was walking down the beach away from her, seemingly unconcerned that they were done for the night. Was he being nice or was he completely uninterested? Kat wasn't sure what she wanted him to be thinking, but she couldn't stop the twinge of disappointment that he hadn't argued with her even a little about that kiss.

Chapter 7

The sound of the door chime startled Kat and then made her feel slightly ill. It must be Brian, she thought, come back to beg her. She wished Larry were in the room with her. It wasn't that she couldn't handle Brian on her own, but having Larry there listening in made being strong easier somehow. But when she got to the door, she saw a woman she didn't recognize, and she thought for an instant it must be the lawyer Lila had warned her about.

Kat realized almost immediately that this woman was no lawyer. What she noticed first was the mass of curling hair that seemed to sprout from her head in a lovely auburn cascade that fell to her waist. The second thing she noticed was her red, swollen eyes, and Kat knew without a doubt who was standing on her aunt's doorstep.

She pretended not to know anyway. "Can I help you?"

The eyes, blue and beautiful despite being red-rimmed, immediately filled with tears. "I'm sorry. I'm so sorry."

"You're looking for Brian, aren't you?" Kat said,

her tone defeated and not at all hostile. Funny—if she had pictured this scene in her head beforehand, she would have seen herself with her hands around the other woman's throat. Instead, she stepped aside. "Come on in."

"I'm so sorry. I didn't know what else to do. He never puts his cell phone on. I don't even know why he bought it." That stung, Kat thought, because she didn't know how many times she'd complained to Brian about just that thing.

"I'm Kat."

"I know," she said and made an attempt at an apologetic smile.

"Okay, you got one on me. You knew about me, but I didn't know about you."

"This is horrible," the woman said, and she dashed away another tear. "I'm Emelia."

Lovely name for a lovely girl. "I don't know where Brian is."

Emelia looked momentarily stunned. "But I thought he'd be here. He said he was coming to get you back."

"And you thought I'd take him back? Are you crazy?" Kat asked with surprising good humor.

Emelia nodded her head. "I made a terrible mistake."

"We have that in common," Kat said dryly.

"You don't understand. I broke up with Brian. I threw him out, and now . . . now . . . now . . ." She choked, and Kat thought for an instant she was going to have to give her the Heimlich to get the rest of the sentence out.

"Wait. *You* broke up with *him?* And then he came here to win me back, and you're here to stop him. Is that right?"

The poor girl was breathing now, but she still couldn't talk.

"You can have him. Lock, stock, and barrel."

Her sobs suddenly became louder. "What if he doesn't want me?" she wailed.

Kat looked at the woman in front of her in disbelief and realized at that moment she didn't love Brian anymore because all she could think of was how insane this woman was to want him back. She didn't look mad, but she must be crazy as a loon.

Emelia took a tissue out of her handbag and blew her nose loudly, managing to smile an apology. "I thought he was only marrying me for my money," she said softly.

"And I thought he was marrying me because he loved me," Kat said, not bothering to hide the bitterness.

"I know this is terrible for you. But Brian really did feel awful."

Kat tilted her head and studied this other woman, wondering how someone so young and so completely stupid could have amassed enough money to buy her dream house. She must be a trust fund baby. "Can I ask you a question?"

She looked a little wary but nodded.

"How long have you known about me?"

Emelia ducked her head and pressed the tissue to her nose. "Since always. He told me from the beginning he was involved. And that he loved you and didn't want to hurt you. Then he fell in love with me, and he was really tortured, you know? He was torn in two."

"How touching," Kat said quietly, stunned by what she was hearing.

"Do you know where he is?"

Kat shrugged. "I don't have a clue."

"It's really important that I find him," she said, as if Kat were lying.

"Listen, Emelia, I don't know where he is. If I did, I'd call a taxi and pay for the fare myself. You can have him."

"Really?" she asked, as if Kat was giving her a gift. She was adorably dimwitted, Kat had to admit. She could almost see why Brian was attracted to her. Emelia clearly was pretty, and she had all that gorgeous hair, and she probably made Brian feel like he was a god.

"Really. But are you sure you want him back? I mean, while he was cheating on me, he was also cheating on you."

Emelia seemed stunned, as if she hadn't given that much thought. "There's *another* woman?"

Kat blinked twice. "No," she said slowly. "Me. I was the other woman. To you." She narrowed her eyes. "Get it?"

Emelia let out a funny little laugh, embarrassed that she'd been so dense. "Oh, yeah. I really haven't thought about that."

"Maybe you should," Kat said, suddenly feeling foolish to be giving advice to the woman Brian was cheating on her with.

"I only know I love him. And . . ." Emelia hesitated, "I'm pregnant."

Now *that* hurt. Kat felt as if someone had sucker punched her in the gut. If she was truthful—and she usually was—the thing she was most looking forward to after the wedding was having babies. This cotton candy-haired girl was having her baby and living in her dream house. Kat suddenly felt ill.

"I think you should go," Kat said, her voice hollow. "If I see Brian, I'll tell him you were here."

Emelia stood. "Please don't tell him about the baby."

Kat looked at her and had to use all her willpower not to shriek. "I won't," she managed.

"This is where I'm staying," Emelia said, dropping a business card on the end table quickly as if finally sensing that Kat was barely holding it together. "Thanks."

Kat watched her walk out the door and stood in the middle of the room staring at nothing, trying only to breathe because suddenly that was getting really hard to do. And then her eyes started burning, and her throat convulsed. She brought her hands to her throat as if she could hold in the sobs that were screaming to be let out. Some strange noise escaped her mouth at about the same time she thought she heard someone coming down the stairs. Kat launched herself out of the living room and toward the first floor bathroom. She turned on the faucet, ran the shower, flushed the toilet, and then sat on the closed seat and cried as she hadn't since she was little.

She couldn't stifle the sobs; she couldn't control the massive heaves shaking her body. She couldn't stop. She sat there, fists clenched unknowingly on her lap, as tears streamed down her face, down her neck and soaked into her tank top. She cried for a full ten minutes before a soft knock sounded on the door.

"Are you all right in there?"

Kat squeezed her eyes shut at the sound of Larry's polite inquiry. "Fine," she said, grimacing at how stuffed-up that one word came out. Clearly, she was not fine.

He didn't say anything for a moment, and Kat could picture him standing on the other side of the door undecided, one hand hovering by the doorknob. "Are you crying?"

Kat could have lied, but it was so obvious that she had been crying, was still crying that she figured it made no sense to lie. "Yes."

"May I come in then?"

She stared at the door. "No."

Lawrence opened the door slowly and peeked his head into the bathroom. "What's happened, Katherine?" Through her misery, he could tell that she was annoyed with him for opening the door.

"Nothing."

"Yes. I can tell that you are the type of woman to cry about nothing." He stood there feeling helpless and wondered if he should just let her be. But he could not stand to see her look so sad, not when a smile made her look so incredibly beautiful. "Tell me what happened."

"You wouldn't understand." She let out a sigh, blew her nose rather noisily, then looked up at him, the picture of dejection.

"Brian's girlfriend showed up."

"Ah, Jesus, Katherine."

She waved a sodden tissue at him. "No, no, that's not it. I was okay. I was really okay. She's pretty and young, and I thought, 'You can have him. In fact, good riddance.'"

"Good for you," he said.

"And then . . ." she swallowed and squeezed her eyes shut. "She's pregnant," she choked out. Then she opened her eyes, and he'd never seen eyes so tortured, except on himself. "With my baby," she shouted and sobbed and then laughed as if she'd heard how ridiculous what she'd just said was.

He pulled her to him, and she wrapped her arms around him, laughing and crying in equal parts.

"It just hit me," she said, sounding stuffed up and adorable. "He's living my life. My dream. He never wanted to get married and have kids and have that house. That house was my house, and now he's living in it."

Lawrence pushed away from Katherine just far enough to offer her another tissue. "He won't be happy," he said, trying to say something that would make her stop crying.

"Of course he will. He's got everything. The pretty wife with long hair, the big house. The baby," she said, and her face crumpled.

"It'll probably be a nasty baby. And the wife will get fat. And he'll go bald."

Katherine looked up at him and gave him a smile through her tears. "He's already thinning," she said, a small hopeful note in her voice.

One more nose blow, and she seemed to get herself together. "I think I was overdue for that. I haven't really cried since we broke up."

"You made up for lost time, I take it?" he said, nodding toward the small trash can that was nearly overflowing with used tissues. She smiled, truly smiled this time, and something inside him gave the strangest sharp tug. "All better?"

"Better," she conceded. "Whew. I feel so much

better now. All that bottled up grief that I didn't even know was there. That's what I do. Nothing bothers me—at least, nothing seems to—and then something will set me off, and I'm a basket case. I'd actually convinced myself that the breakup wasn't bothering me." She seemed fascinated by this particular flaw. "Sorry you had to witness that."

"Not at all."

The way she was looking at him made him feel slightly uncomfortable, as if he'd done something wonderful. "You know, you're a nice guy."

He frowned. "No, I'm not. I'm cold and heartless."

She shook her head. "You couldn't stand me crying, could you?"

"Of course not. It was rather annoying, all that blubbering and nose blowing."

"You are nice," she said, poking gently at his chest. "Admit it."

"I'll do nothing of the sort," he said, but he couldn't help himself and smiled.

"Fine. I know the truth."

From the living room, the doorbell rang, and he could tell by the look of horror on her face she was afraid it was Brian.

"If it's him, give him the business card on the living room coffee table. It's where his girlfriend is staying. I can't see him right now," she said, waving a hand toward her swollen, red eyes.

Lawrence nodded grimly, giving her shoulder a squeeze before heading to the living room to retrieve the card, his body taut with unleashed rage. The anger he felt toward her ex-boyfriend was unreasonable—he knew that—but he also knew he'd have to tap into everything his mother had taught him about being a gentleman to prevent himself from thrashing the living daylights out of Brian if he was, indeed, standing outside the door.

He grabbed the card and opened the door.

"Where is she?" Brian asked, his stance so belligerent it was all Lawrence could do not to smash his fist into his face.

"To whom are you referring?" Lawrence asked, his voice hard but infinitely polite.

"Kat," the other man said with clear derision. Tough guy.

"She told me to give you this," Lawrence said, holding out the card. "It's from your other girlfriend."

Brian looked momentarily confused. "Em's here?"

"If you ever step foot on this porch again, I will hurt you," Lawrence said, all politeness gone.

"Hey," Brian said, backing off a bit. "I don't have any beef with you."

"I'm afraid you do. Leave. Now."

Brian stepped off the porch so quickly, he stumbled a bit, but he gripped the card like it was a winning lottery ticket, and Lawrence wished he'd given in to his baser instincts and coldcocked him.

Lawrence heard a noise behind him and turned to see Katherine standing there with the saddest smile he'd ever seen.

"He's gone."

Lawrence nodded.

"You should have punched him," she said.

"I wanted to, believe me." He studied her for a moment. "Are you all right then?"

She let out a big heaving breath. "No, but I'll get

over it. Tell you what. Why don't I take a shower, and you and I can do something middle class."

He couldn't help but be charmed by such a suggestion. "What do you suggest?"

"How about riding the carousel?"

When they arrived at the carousel, it was suppertime, and, Katherine informed him, the perfect time to ride as most families were off eating. The line was relatively short, with a few families and more teenagers waiting their turn. Lawrence stood in line while Katherine went to get the tickets, and he wondered when the last time was that he'd ridden a carousel. He must have been a young child, so young he had only the barest memory of it. Katherine beamed at him, holding the two tickets, and he couldn't help but smile. She was unlike any other woman he'd ever known, completely unpretentious, beguiling, and cheerful. She didn't pretend to be anything other than what she was, and that was something he was unfamiliar with. The women he'd spent time with were charming, rich, sophisticated, intelligent. Boring. They all wore the right designers, went to the right spas, drove the right cars, and lived in fear that they'd somehow lose their place in society. He was quite certain that Katherine wouldn't know the right anything if someone handed it to her. She was wearing green cargo shorts and a yellow tank top and hiking boots. She should have looked dowdy, but for some reason, she looked sexy. He couldn't put his finger on why because Katherine was not the type of woman who normally attracted him. Her dark brown hair was straight; her eyes, brown, her body, trim and athletic. She wasn't beautiful unless she smiled, and then she could take a man's breath away. At least his, he realized uncomfortably.

"What?" she asked self-consciously, and he realized suddenly he'd been staring at her.

"Oh, nothing. I was just thinking you've bounced back well today." He thought he saw a flash of pain in her eyes, and he could have kicked himself for bringing up the day's traumatic events.

"All I needed was a good cry," she said, a bit too chipper to be sincere, and he had the sudden urge to hold her against him, an urge he stalwartly ignored.

The music ended, and the carousel came to a slow stop.

"Okay," she said, looking intensely at the carousel. "You want to get an outside horse. Try to grab as many rings as you can as you go by. See? They come out there," she said, pointing to an arm that jutted out toward the ride. "That increases the chance of getting the brass ring. You put your rings on top of the horse. See the little post?"

He leaned down to her and said softly in her ear, "You're taking this rather seriously, aren't you?"

"This is serious business," she said, obviously trying not to smile. "And please don't embarrass me by dropping any of the rings. And if you get the brass ring, I'm going to have to murder you in front of all these children. I've ridden this thing ten times, and I've never gotten it."

"What a fierce little thing you are."

"I'm very competitive. It's an illness." The line moved forward. "Here we go."

Lawrence, for the rest of his life, would remember sitting on that ridiculous horse and staring at Katherine, at the pure joy on her face as she tried to grab the brass ring. He sat three horses back from her, watching her, unable to take his eyes off her. He was so enthralled with her he forgot to grab for the rings a couple of times. A bell rang, and someone announced that the brass ring was entering the arena. He heard a screech from behind him as a teenage girl got the lucky ring, and then he heard Katherine laughing, laughing, watched her hair ruffle in the breeze, her strong arm grabbing the post. And he smiled, that sharp tug he'd felt earlier turning into something stronger and fuller and . . . And then he frowned as his gut clenched hard as if he might be sick.

You are not in love. Idiot. You cannot fall in love with a girl so quickly. You cannot.

He couldn't breathe suddenly, and the heat of the place immediately became oppressive. Lawrence didn't wait for the carousel to come to a complete stop; he bolted off it, stumbling slightly, lunging for the door, for light, for air.

"Hey, are you okay? Get dizzy?"

She was laughing at him, unaware that he was a drowning man. He was suddenly glad his friends were coming. They would bring him back to reality, back to a place where men did not fall in love with women in a week. He needed a blonde with large breasts, not some dark-haired American who would get him thinking about things he didn't want to think about. Like families playing on the beach. Like riding carousels.

"Larry?"

"I told you, several times actually, my name is Lawrence," he bit out.

She backed away slightly, her smile less certain. "Now, Larry, anyone who rides a carousel is much too young and carefree to be called Lawrence."

God help him, but he laughed, all irritation blown away. "You seemed to enjoy yourself on the ride," he said.

"I still didn't get the brass ring," she grumbled good-naturedly. Then she smiled. "The consolation prize is a kiss."

He stopped cold. "I think we should remain friends," he said, unable to meet her gaze.

"Oh."

"I have friends arriving soon, and I don't want to complicate things."

Dawning realization hit her. "Women friends."

"Perhaps," he said evasively, feeling rotten but knowing for his own good he was doing the right thing. He did not need to be walking around like some love-struck idiot. He needed to nip this in the bud before it bloomed into something he couldn't control. He needed to write. He needed to live his life. He did not need some pretty young American getting under his skin and making him do things he would never do in a normal state of mind. And, he reminded himself, she wanted children.

"Just friends," Katherine said as if testing the concept. "That's fine."

"I know I joked about us having an affair—"

"And you did kiss me," she pointed out.

He cleared his throat, the memory of that kiss, the way her small breast felt in his hand seared into his mind. "Yes, a moment of weakness caused by cheap California wine."

"You mean you don't like me?" Katherine asked and struck a pose of abject misery, flinging her head back and resting the back of her hand on her forehead.

"I think you're quite nice," he said darkly.

"Don't sweat it, Larry. Maybe I'll hook up with one of your male friends. There are going to be men, right?"

He swallowed hard against the image of Katherine with Thomas. "At least one. And he is not your type."

"Too sophisticated? Too rich?"

"Too crude."

She waved a dismissive hand at him. "I come from New Hampshire; that's the way they make men in the Northeast. You're trying to protect me? That's sweet but completely unnecessary."

Lawrence ground his teeth together. "Do whatever you wish then."

Kat looked at him, knew she was torturing him, and smiled. For whatever reason, Larry didn't want her dating his friends. She didn't care one way or another, but it sure was fun baiting him. "Is he cute?"

He stared at her a full second. "Women adore him."

"Do they adore him as much as they adore you?"

"More so."

"Wow."

Larry gave her sideways glance. "Thomas uses women the way most people use napkins."

"Then you two have a lot in common," she said and tried really hard not to laugh. Then she saw the look on his face and took pity on him. "I'm only kidding. I told you this morning you're a nice guy. You're not using me, and you could. I'm very vulnerable right now," she said, not being able to resist teasing him a bit more.

He stopped walking and looked down at her, the oddest expression on his face. "What do you mean?" he asked, his words measured.

Kat could feel her cheeks redden. "You know, the whole summer fling thing. I was thinking it might not be a *horrible* idea. Not a good one," she said quickly, "but not horrible. Not unthinkable."

For a few seconds, Kat was sure he was going to kiss her, the look on his face was so . . . intense. "Let's just let things be," he said finally.

"Good idea," she said, but she was disappointed. Something had happened between them today. Maybe it was the way he held her, maybe it was her realization that she was truly over Brian, but the thought of sleeping with Larry had suddenly become not so bad. And for some reason, for him it had suddenly become not so good. Perhaps she was a bit too enthusiastic on the beach. Maybe he didn't like the way she kissed. Maybe the chemistry she'd thought she'd felt had been completely one-sided. That must be it, she thought, flooding with embarrassment.

"I believe it would be a mistake," he said, driving his point in painfully.

"I get it, Larry; you don't have to spell it out," she said, trying to sound completely unaffected by the rejection.

He looked as if he might say more, then stopped.

"I'm not blond," she said, a teasing note in her voice.

"No." He shook his head slowly.

"And let's face it, I'm not as endowed as most of your dates."

His eyes drifted down her body, making her feel hot and slightly weak-kneed. "You have a nice body." He said it casually enough, but his eyes got that hot, intense look.

She frowned, wondering why she was getting such mixed messages from him and also wondering if it was just her imagination. Maybe he wasn't giving her hot, intense, I-want-you-now looks. Maybe he looked like that all the time. She hardly knew him, after all. "Thanks. You're not too bad yourself. Let's go home. You want to help with the laundry?"

"I think I'll stay in town for now. I'll see you tomorrow."

Another rejection that she was not going to let bother her. Of course he'd rather stay in town than go back to the cottage with her and do laundry. "If you bring home another girl, please keep the noise down, okay?"

"Sure," he said distractedly.

Kat walked home confused about Larry and about herself. One minute, he was looking at her as if he wanted to strip her naked, and the next, as if he wanted to be anywhere but standing next to her. It didn't matter. In four weeks, she'd be home in New Hampshire, and he'd be across the ocean doing whatever it was that he did when he was home. And for some ridiculous reason, she felt that awful burning in her throat. This time, she shook it off.

"Hey, Roy," Kat said, waving as she passed.

"Where's Lawrence tonight?"

"I left him in town. I think he's going skirt chasing," she said, smiling widely to let him know that it didn't matter to her in the least.

"One of his talents, I understand."

"Yup." Kat gave him a wave and went into her cottage, wondering what Larry was up to. He was probably sidled up to a bar, drinking something nasty and eyeing the joint for a big-breasted blonde. And she didn't care one whit.

Lawrence leaned against the bar telling himself he didn't really mind the smell of sea and diesel from the marina across the boardwalk. He was indeed eyeing a big-busted blonde and trying—rather desperately—to feel anything. He sipped his beer and looked at the gorgeous creature as she laughed at something her bright red-headed friend said and then glanced his way in a manner that he found practiced and slightly distasteful. He gave himself a mental shake because there wasn't a reason in the world why he should find it distasteful that a beautiful woman was blatantly flirting with him. He should find it exciting or at least satisfying that she'd noticed him. Since when did he find a woman's overtures distasteful? What the hell was he doing? he thought, finishing off his beer and putting it back on the bar with determination. He walked toward the woman; saw her quick look of pleasure before she pointedly looked away; noticed the redhead lean toward her, nod, then move slowly away. A clear path.

"Hello," he said.

"You're British," she said and gave him a measured smile. "I studied in London for a year. English lit. I'm sorry I was staring at you, but you look familiar. Perhaps I saw you in London. I was back there last spring visiting friends."

He didn't recognize her at all and told her so.

She shook her head slowly. "No. I'm very good with faces. I know I've seen you somewhere, and it's going to drive me insane until I figure it out." She laid a hand on his forearm and laughed. She was gorgeous, seemingly intelligent, everything he always loved in a woman. And the next thing out of her mouth should have clinched the deal.

"What's your name?" she asked as if she truly did know him.

"Lawrence Kendall."

"You're kidding," she said, her eyes flashing attractively. "You're an author. I've read you. I had to critique your book for a project."

"And?" he asked, beginning to get intrigued by this woman. She was classically beautiful, with a soft, educated voice; gorgeous blue eyes; and an air of general affluence. And she'd read him.

She looked down, apparently embarrassed. "I'm afraid I was brutal."

"Is that so?"

"Your book wasn't nearly as bad as I said it was, though. I was just trying to impress my professor with my biting insight."

He laughed, thinking that perhaps he'd been a bit hasty in declaring himself to be falling for Katherine. Perhaps it was the close proximity and the novelty of her that was getting under his skin. He couldn't be falling in love with Katherine if he was finding that he was interested in this woman. "I hope your article wasn't published."

"No. It wasn't written well enough for that. You do write brilliantly. I wrote down passages that struck me. It's just . . ."

"It's just that my work lacks something."

She gave him an apologetic look and another pat on his forearm. "It wasn't my cup of tea," she said gently, and he knew she was lying to spare his feelings.

Lawrence could feel himself sliding back into the man he'd been for the past seven years; into that guy who slept with beautiful blondes, who wouldn't in a million years fancy himself falling in love with anyone. He felt much more himself now, and he waved at the barkeep to order another beer.

"I have another of your books at home, and I promise I'll read it and enjoy it as soon as I get back."

"Where's home?"

"Boston. I'm Jocelyn, by the way." She held out her well-manicured hand, smooth and unwrinkled. Well-pampered.

He looked at her, at her fresh, unlined skin; her blue eyes; straight teeth; her general perfection. "How old are you, Jocelyn? Don't be offended," he said after seeing her alarmed expression. "I almost got myself into trouble the other night, and I'm just trying to be overly cautious."

"I'm twenty-five. Does that scare you?" she asked in such a practiced, seductive voice he almost laughed.

He smiled, enjoying himself, finding himself on territory he was familiar with. This woman, this conversation, *this* was what he was. He wasn't a man who fell in love with brokenhearted girls with dreams of families and began thinking—even in the most abstract of ways—about what it would be like to spend a lifetime with one woman. "You," he said, "do not frighten me in the least."

She smiled and gave her blond hair a practiced toss. "How long are you on the island?"

He translated: Are you going to be here long enough to justify sleeping with you? Ah, he loved women.

"I don't have a set departure date. I'm here to write."

She smiled again. "I'm here for two weeks. We have a cottage in Edgartown, but sometimes, I like to come to Oak Bluffs. It's more fun. Now I'm glad I did."

"We?"

"It's my parents' cottage, but I'm here with three other girlfriends. We do this every summer. I almost didn't come this summer."

And he said what he was supposed to because they were following a script, after all, one that would end up very nicely with both of them in one of their beds. This was exactly what he needed. "I'm glad you changed your mind." For some reason, Jocelyn frowned, and for a second, he thought he'd said the wrong line, misread the scene entirely. Then he felt a hand on his arm, his entire body grew hot, and he almost groaned aloud.

"Katherine."

"Hey. Sorry to interrupt." Katherine gave Jocelyn a sunny smile. "But your agent called and left a message for you to call. He said you could call him up until eight, so there's still time to catch him if it's important. I just thought you should know."

"I'm sure it's not important," Lawrence said, trying to stop himself from feeling so happy to see

her. Happy and angry, if that were at all possible.
Angry because he was happy. Angry because he was
back in the groove, back in his own territory, and
here she was looking up at him and smiling and not
caring that he was with another woman when he'd
want to rip the head off any chap who was coming
on to Katherine. "I wish he'd call my cell. The man
has a strange aversion to cell phones. And I'm sure
he's only calling to harass me about my book."

"Tell him you're being inspired," Katherine said,
a teasing note to her voice.

"You don't have to go, do you, Lawrence?" Ah, Jocelyn inserting herself back into the conversation.
He'd almost forgotten her.

"No. I'll just give him a quick ring so he can torture me for five minutes, then I'll be right back."

Jocelyn's eyes went from him to Katherine, silently
questioning who the heck she was.

"I'm his housekeeper," Katherine said.

"Oh."

Lawrence gave Katherine a look, which she ignored, before walking away from the noise of the
bar and calling his agent. Katherine followed him,
smiling like a child with a secret.

"Why did you say you were my housekeeper?" he
asked when they were away from the bar.

"I don't know. She looked a little concerned about
me, so I thought I'd help her relax."

"Very thoughtful," he said without a speck of sincerity.

"I didn't want to ruin your chances with the
blonde. They *are* all blonde, aren't they?"

"Actually, yes."

"What if I dye my hair blond?" she asked, her eyes sparkling with humor.

"Then I'd have to ravish you on the spot."

Katherine laughed. "I'll think about it," she said, walking away. "Good night."

He let her walk perhaps five steps before calling her back. "Don't go," he said, not quite believing what he was saying. He had a sure thing with Jocelyn, and here he was telling Katherine to stay. When had he stopped knowing what he was about to say before it came out of his mouth?

"Three's a crowd," Kat said, trying valiantly not to let him know how much it bothered her that he'd been cozied up to the bar with a beautiful woman. She felt slightly ashamed that she'd used the flimsy excuse of his agent calling to go looking for him, but she'd been dying to know what he was up to.

"We'll ditch the blonde. Come on."

She didn't like this. She didn't like the way her heart felt at this moment, like it was beating too fast, like it actually might burst out of her. Her heart was not fully recovered from that afternoon, and she knew she could get herself into deep trouble with Larry. "Make your phone call, and I'll think about it."

She watched him dial and wondered what she was letting herself in for. She'd be dead not to be flattered that he'd rather be with her than with a woman who was so obviously beautiful. Jocelyn was the kind of woman men like Larry ended up with. She was the kind of woman who had been on his arm in nearly every picture she'd seen of him online.

And he still wants to be with you.

For now.

"He wasn't in his office, but I left a message for him to call my cell. He won't. What do you want to do?"

Kat laughed. "I know you're not going to just leave that woman without saying goodbye."

"I suppose. You wait here; I'll be right back."

He was only gone for a minute before he came bounding back. "Let's get an ice cream," he said.

"There's an art gallery opening tonight. I saw an article in the *Vineyard Gazette*. That's the real reason I came back to town," she said, flushing slightly at the half-truth. She really had intended to go to the gallery if she hadn't found him. "I figured if I saw you on the way I'd give you your message. We can go to that and then get an ice cream."

"Art show. That's much too cultured," he teased.

"Well, you can watch a middle class person's reaction to art. Won't that be fun?"

He grabbed her hand, and they walked like that, Kat feeling silly and happy and wondering a bit if somehow he'd managed to get himself a little drunk in the short time she'd left him on his own. She looked up at him, but he didn't seem drunk, just happy. Weirdly happy.

"You're in a good mood," she said and held up his hand in hers as evidence.

He stopped walking and looked down at her, and the look on his face made her feel as if her heart had stopped.

"I'm going to kiss you."

"I thought we were through with all that."

"I am," he said right before he bent his head and gave her a kiss. "Don't tell me I have to stop doing that."

Kat turned away and dropped her hand from his,

suddenly scared to death, suddenly knowing that she couldn't have a summer fling with this man. Kisses and hand-holding and lovemaking would only lead to one thing—a broken heart. She liked Larry. A lot. A little more than a week, and she felt as if she'd known him three months. She'd never liked someone so quickly before, never reacted to a man so physically. It was wonderful and scary and definitely not something she wanted to happen. She couldn't trust herself right now, not after Brian had begged her to come back and Emelia had told her about the baby. She was ripe for another broken heart. That's all she needed—two broken hearts this summer.

"I'm sorry," he said, sounding truly distressed. "I know this is not the best timing."

"Larry."

"Don't tell me not to kiss you again."

"Larry . . ."

"Don't tell me—"

"Don't kiss me again."

He sagged against a nearby storefront. "You are cruel," he said.

She walked to him and leaned up against the wall next to him as tourists walked by, oblivious. Turning her head, she took in his beautiful profile and wondered if she was insane. Maybe she could guard her heart. Maybe she couldn't.

"Here's the thing," she said. "I just broke up with a guy, and you are very, very tempting. I've got to think about this, Larry. You could hurt me."

He turned his head, and the look on his face made her want to launch herself into his arms. Larry had probably unintentionally left a trail of brokenhearted women across the globe, but he didn't want to break hers.

"Katherine," he said softly, and she suddenly liked the way he said her given name. "Don't tell me not to kiss you."

She was about to say it again, and he put his finger over her mouth to shush her. "Don't," he said, moving closer until his lips were against his own finger. "Don't." He moved his finger away slowly, and his mouth pressed against hers, and he was kissing her again. It was a small, gentle kiss, one that wouldn't offend even the worst prude walking by, but Kat felt as if her entire world were tilting around her.

"That wasn't nice," she whispered.

He smiled. "I've never pretended to be nice."

"I mean it, Larry." She pushed away from the wall, feeling the tiniest bit angry. She was feeling raw and wounded, and she wanted him more than she thought she should.

She felt him touch her arm, and she stopped as if he'd yanked her back. "I'm sorry." Then he grinned. "I'm not really sorry."

"I know," she said. "Let's just go to the art show." She pretended to be mad for about five seconds, then subtly held out her hand and smiled the tiniest bit when he almost instantly took it.

Chapter 8

"They're here," he said, frowning out the window at the small group of British tourists standing outside the cottage with looks of bewilderment and disbelief on their pale faces. New England charm, apparently, was escaping them at the moment, and Lawrence had to admit this "cottage" was a far sight shabbier than his last residence in Mayfair.

"Open the door, Larry. Invite them in," Katherine said. He looked at her, at her smile, her fresh-faced innocence, and he wished for the hundredth time that he hadn't invited this group. They were the worst of the lot of rich, lazy friends he'd socialized with when he'd been younger. Lately, they'd found good ol' Lawrence a bit of a bore with all his writing and lack of funds. But they'd been particularly bored when he called them three weeks ago and invited them to the islands that the Kennedys and Clintons went to. Clearly, they were not impressed with the Vineyard so far.

"Better yet, since I'm the housekeeper, I'll answer the door. Do you think I should have rented a maid uniform?" Katherine asked, teasing him as always.

"Yes. One of those little French numbers with the skirt up to here," he said, pressing a hand high on his thigh. "But you can get that when my friends leave."

Katherine opened the door, that big smile beaming, letting in the lions to feast.

"We almost died," Clarice said to Lawrence, dropping her bag as soon as she cleared the doorway. "You said the island had an airport. That," she said, pointing in an arbitrary direction, "was not an airport. And that was not a plane. It was a toy." Clarice was a complainer. It was what she did and who she was, and she was just witty enough about it to make it mostly charming instead of vastly annoying. He'd thought about dating her at one time, but they became friends before he could make up his mind and had remained so for years. He was content with the relationship, and he'd discovered through a mutual friend that she was not. Her pale blond hair was unnaturally straight, and she'd gained a few pounds in some very obvious places. Clarice had always been too thin, but now, she seemed to have thrown all caution to the wind.

"It was a bit rough," Thomas Bartlett said, his voice booming, and Lawrence could tell by his flushed cheeks that he was drunk. In fact, they all looked a bit glassy-eyed.

"How charming," Emma Ryder said, putting her bag down far more gracefully than Clarice and handing her sweater to Katherine, who accepted it with a look to Lawrence that was filled with silent laughter. Emma never seemed to fit in among his more disreputable friends because she always appeared to be so subdued and detached. Emma hid her wild side well from the outside world. Only their little circle knew she was slightly off, a bit batty even.

"Katherine," he warned. Even though she ignored him, he could tell by the small twitch of her lips that she was trying not to smile.

"Shall I show them to their rooms?" Katherine asked, and the two women looked utterly relieved to have someone take charge of them and their belongings.

"Katherine is my housemate," Lawrence stated, just to clear the air. "Her aunt owns this house, and there was a bit of a mix-up, so we've been sharing."

"Really?" Clarice said and gave Katherine a long once-over as if he'd said instead, "She's my sex slave."

Lawrence breathed in harshly through his nose and could feel his nostrils flaring as he tried to keep his temper in check. Because if he really thought about it, Clarice hadn't done anything she hadn't done a dozen times with other women. This time, though, it made him see red.

He turned to his friends and indicated the living room featuring Lila's boa-ed portrait. "Please make yourselves comfortable. I'll be right back. Help yourself to the bar." And then he took Katherine's arm and led her to the kitchen. "You are not to let them think you are anything other than what you are," he said in a low voice that he thought brooked no argument.

Katherine nearly collapsed against the door in silent laughter.

He stalked over to her, planting one arm above her head. "What is so funny?"

"Them. And you. I feel like I've walked into one

of those British dramas. I'm sorry. It's the accents or something."

Lawrence tried not to grin, but damn if her smile wasn't completely infectious. "They are unique," he said. "I warned you about them."

"Yes, you did, but seeing them in person is much more fun. Can't I pretend to be the maid? The naughty maid?" she managed to say before nearly collapsing in laughter.

"You will not pretend to be my maid." He leaned over her, hoping to look slightly menacing.

"But it would be such fun," she said, wiping at one eye. It was much nicer to see her wiping away a tear of laughter instead of sorrow, he thought.

"If you do, I'll drag you into my arms every time you pass and kiss you."

"Is that supposed to be a deterrent? Because I gotta tell you, that doesn't sound half bad," she said, clearly teasing him again. For some reason he couldn't explain, this time he didn't like it.

"Don't tempt me," he said darkly, pushing away from the door.

Kat was immediately contrite. "I'm sorry. I was just having fun." She dipped her head. "Okay?"

"No, Katherine. It's not okay. You have to decide what you want." And he walked out the door, leaving Kat behind feeling foolish and slightly angry.

He was right. Sort of. She couldn't have it both ways, even though she wished she could. It had been three days since they'd kissed on the sidewalk, and since then, Kat had tried to avoid Larry. It wasn't all that difficult; he'd spent an abnormal amount of time up in his lair trying to write. She knew he wasn't having much success because he'd walked around the house like an angry grizzly bear giving her no more than a couple of grunts that she took as greetings.

This morning, though, he'd gotten up early, shaved, and even put on clothes that weren't completely wrinkled. He'd acted more like himself, or at least more like what Kat knew. She had to remind herself that even though she felt like she knew Larry, she really didn't know him at all. It hadn't even been two weeks since she'd walked through that door. It was so strange, the attachment she had to a man she hardly knew, who hardly knew her. It would be so easy just to go to him, have wonderful sex—she knew it would be wonderful—and throw all caution to the wind. But she also knew her heart was already far more engaged than it should be. One night with Larry, and she knew she'd be a goner. She'd hoped she could joke with him, witty banter, a bit of flirtation that wouldn't lead anywhere. She was just fooling herself.

Kat went out to the living room and offered to bring the bags up just because she wanted to be a good hostess.

"I'll help," Larry said and hurried toward the bags. When they reached the top of the stairs, he turned to her. "What am I going to do with them for two days?" he asked, his voice slightly panicked.

"What did you use to do?" Kat asked.

"Drink. Heavily and frequently. We'd go to clubs; the women did a few lines in the loo; we'd dance and drink and have orgies in hotel penthouses."

Kat studied him and couldn't tell if he was telling the truth or not. She hoped not. "Well," Kat said slowly, "you could do that. But I don't think any of the hotels here have penthouses."

Larry let out a groan. "I don't want to do that. Well, not entirely. It was what I did not too many years ago."

"Maybe they've changed, too," Kat said doubt-fully.

Larry pressed the heels of his hands against his eyes. "I don't know what I was thinking."

"Oh, come on. I'm sure they're harmless. And the guy is cute in a British sort of way. A little like Hugh Grant, only blonder. Let's take them dancing in Edgartown. There're a few clubs downtown."

"You're not going anywhere," he said. "And what do you mean, in a British sort of way?"

"You know, blond, pale, scrawny. *You* do not look British."

"Oh?"

"You're dark-haired, brown-eyed, have a five o'-clock shadow at noon. And you're big, football player big."

He crossed his big, beefy arms in front of his big, beefy chest, and Kat knew he was flattered by her description. "Which do you prefer? Pale and scrawny or dark-haired and . . ."

"Beefy."

"Yes, beefy."

Kat grinned. "Like all American women, I prefer pale and scrawny. So that guy is perfect for me."

"I don't think Thomas and you would be a good idea," Larry said cautiously. "In fact, I don't think your being with any of them is a good idea.

"Why not?"

"I'll handle this. They're really not your crowd."

"I can keep up with the best of them," Kat said, lying through her teeth. A "wild" night for her had been two beers at the American Legion and a dart tournament.

"I'm sorry if I don't believe that. Truly, Katherine, these people make those Hilton sisters seem like nuns. They're from another world. Hell, I don't fit in with them anymore."

"I'm not a complete idiot, if that's what you're saying."

He looked at her as if she was, indeed, an idiot. "I don't want you near them. They are not like you."

"I see," she said, her entire body going rigid.

"No, you don't. Katherine," he said, his voice going soft, "you are . . ."

"Lawrence, you haven't any gin anywhere."

He looked in the direction of the female voice calling up to him, murder in his gaze. "We'll have to go to the half-license to get some more," he yelled down. Larry turned back to her and put his hands gently on her upper arms. They felt warm and strong and too right. "I don't dislike you," he said, then stopped abruptly, looking briefly as if he were in pain. "What I mean to say is that I like you. Quite a lot. And I don't want that bunch down there corrupting you."

Kat narrowed her eyes and wondered if he were being sincere or simply changing his tactic to avoid hurting her feelings. "I'm not twelve, Larry. I may never have done drugs myself, but I've seen people snort coke. I've *heard* of orgies," she said, smiling weakly.

"Thomas makes a game of women."

"Like I said, I'm not twelve. Maybe I make a game

of men. I reduced Brian to tears, remember?" She said it to make him smile, but he still looked dead serious. He was being overbearing and ridiculous, but Kat knew he was only looking out for her. Misplaced chivalry for sure. "You win. I'll let you go off with your friends. But I want you home by one."

"There's my girl," he said with a relieved smile.

"But I might change my mind," Kat called after him as he brought suitcases into one of the bedrooms. "And I'm not *your* anything."

He poked his head back out through the doorway. "Not even my housekeeper?"

Kat just shook her head and grabbed another suitcase.

"You haven't screwed her yet?" Thomas asked, clearly shocked.

Lawrence did not like this conversation, but he smiled anyway. "Not yet."

"I'll screw her," said Clarice, making the lot of them laugh.

"Clare's decided she's into women now. Not that she's ever been with one," Thomas said.

"I have," Emma said.

"We know you have. You'll sleep with anything that stands on two legs," Thomas said.

"And you won't?" Clarice said, one graceful brow arching significantly.

"I didn't say that now, did I?"

The four of them sat in an Edgartown bar exchanging witty sexual comments and drinking heavily for hours, with Lawrence unsuccessfully trying to relax and enjoy himself. His friends were decadent, but they had always been a lot of fun to be around. Maybe this was exactly what he needed to feel grounded, to remember what it was like when he was young and the drive to write superseded everything else. These people had made him forget the worst time of his life; they'd pulled him through by introducing him to a world where no one had any cares or problems, where people didn't talk about death or pain. He'd party with his troupe for days, then write nonstop until he had a rough draft done. He wrote his first two books that way, half hungover, sleep-deprived. Everything would be just fine as long as he kept Katherine out of his thoughts and their plans.

"Your housemate is gorgeous," Thomas said, and Lawrence had to fight hard not to clench the fist that held his Guinness. "Very brash and American-looking. Tight little bum. You notice that?"

"Of course he did," said Emma. "It's what Lawrence does, notice tight bums. Isn't that right?"

Lawrence lifted up his glass in a mock toast, as if agreeing with her.

"I'd really like to have a try, if you don't mind," Thomas said grandly. "I've never been with a Yank."

Lawrence swallowed hard. "She's engaged," he lied, because he knew the worst he could do was tell Thomas to stay away from her.

"Engaged," Thomas said distastefully.

"Then she's not *married*, Tom," Clarice said, trailing a fingernail slowly across her glass. "Leave it up to her."

They all laughed, except Lawrence, who had to force a smile.

"Since when have you let something like an engagement ring stop you, Lawrence?" Clarice asked, draping her arm around his neck. She leaned close to his ear. "You usually don't let anything stop you."

Clarice was right; Lawrence couldn't argue with her. And he couldn't tell these louts that Katherine was different. A man didn't simply screw someone like Katherine; at least he couldn't. Not now. "I'm not attracted to her is all," he lied.

"Have you been neutered then?" Thomas said, laughing. "I don't believe you. You hit on her, and she rejected you. That's it, isn't it?"

"Precisely," Lawrence said in a tone that clearly indicated he hadn't hit on anyone. God, he wished he'd never invited these people.

"Lawrence," said a female voice, and Lawrence looked up and nearly groaned. It was the blonde from the bar, Jocelyn, the one who'd read his book and hated it. He had a sudden and nearly uncontrollable urge to get up, leave the bar, and find Katherine.

All three friends turned and looked at Jocelyn with interest. She was beautiful—he had to give her that. "I'm so glad I've run into you," she said, looking around the table with interest, clearly seeking an invitation to sit down.

"Jocelyn, these are my friends from England. Clarice, Thomas, and Emma."

Thomas raised a knowing eyebrow as if now understanding his not screwing Katherine, which Lawrence found unreasonably irritating.

"Why don't you join us?" Thomas said, and Jocelyn gave him her brilliant white smile, pulled up a chair next to Lawrence, and waved to her two friends across the room.

"Jocelyn lived in England for a time," Lawrence said to make conversation, hoping that was all he would have to contribute. He wanted to go back to the cottage.

"I'm a real Anglophile," Jocelyn said.

"I'm a beautiful womenphile," Thomas said, and Jocelyn gave him a musical laugh.

"I'll be right back, if you'll excuse me," Lawrence said and got up. He was gratified when Thomas moved over to his seat and began chatting with Jocelyn. Maybe if he stayed away long enough, the two of them would hit it off, and he'd be rid of both of them for the remainder of their stay.

Lawrence walked outside into the charm of downtown Edgartown with its colonial buildings and electric lanterns. The sidewalks were crowded with tourists, all dressed a bit more stylishly this time of day. The air was fresh, tinged with salt and tantalizing scents of seafood from nearby restaurants. Couples sat on a restaurant's balcony across the street, their faces lit by candles, and he smiled at the sight of them. Damn. What the hell was wrong with him? Sex. That was it. He needed sex, and he'd just walked out—again—on a beautiful woman who would surely fill that need. Why would a sane man do such a thing?

Because you are not sane, a voice answered in his head. What sane man believes he is falling in love with a woman he's just met? What sane man would rather be sitting on a balcony fully clothed than naked and in bed with another beautiful woman? Of course, he'd take being naked with Katherine in a bed over sitting on a balcony a hundred times over. Yes, Katherine naked, looking up at him, kissing him, touching him. God, he could almost taste her, feel her beneath his hands, hear her moan against his mouth.

Lawrence turned toward the waterfront because it was slightly cooler there. He might just jump into the water and stay under until he got himself together. He glanced at his watch—midnight. Katherine was probably already asleep, and if he left now, his friends would have to take a taxi because he'd have the rental car. He might as well go back to the bar and pretend to have fun. Maybe Jocelyn was exactly what he needed to return to sanity.

Kat woke up briefly at two AM to the sound of a woman giggling and the low tones of a man as they made their way up the stairs. Shortly after came the embarrassing sounds above her head of a bed creaking rhythmically and the screams of a woman in ecstasy. It couldn't be Larry. He wouldn't be that insensitive, would he? Chances were it was Thomas and Clarice or Emma. Not Larry. And even if it was Larry, he was an adult, and he could do whatever he pleased, she told herself as the woman let out a particularly loud screech. Maybe she was being murdered, not ravished. It was difficult to tell, really.

Kat stared at the ceiling annoyed and embarrassed and, she had to admit, hurt. It wasn't as if she and Larry were dating or even engaged in a meaningless summer fling. She tried to tell herself it would be okay if it was Larry getting some, and she tried to ignore the murderous jealousy that she knew was completely unfounded. But she couldn't. After the rapturous ending of the love scene above her head—one long, exceedingly drawn out scream and a short male grunt—it took a long time for Kat to fall asleep.

She woke to the unfamiliar sounds of pans clanking together in the kitchen. She threw on a thigh-length thin terry robe over her shorts and T-shirt and headed to the kitchen to help whoever was trying to make breakfast.

"Good morning, Clarice," Kat said, forcing good cheer. But when the blond woman turned, Kat couldn't stop the look of shock, the plummeting heart, the raging jealousy.

"Oh, hello. You're the housemate." It was the woman from the bar, the one Larry had left to be with her. And here she was, the screamer, well-satisfied and smiling and looking at Kat as if she'd won some sort of contest.

"Kat," she supplied, feeling foolish and stupid.

"I'm Jocelyn. Sorry to invade your kitchen, but I'm starving, and everyone is still sleeping. We were up a bit late last night. I hope we didn't disturb you."

The orgasmic screaming was a bit disruptive, but I managed to fall asleep.

"No. I didn't even hear anyone come in."

Jocelyn smiled, and Kat felt a sharp pinch in her gut. The woman was drop-dead gorgeous and exactly the type of woman Larry went for.

It doesn't bother me, nope, no sireee. You had your chance, baby, and you passed. So don't you dare get all riled up because Larry is doing with someone else what he asked you to do.

Kat had a vivid, quite nice image of herself hurling across the kitchen floor and tearing out Jocelyn's hair clump by painful clump.

Jocelyn turned to the pantry, and Kat knew she'd find nothing breakfasty in there.

"We don't have much for breakfast really. Just some eggs," Kat said, trying to be big and understanding and not care that the woman Larry'd just slept with was standing in the kitchen with her cheeks glowing and her hair bed-messy and her lips slightly swollen from some of Larry's wonderful kisses. God, his lips had just been on hers not a few days ago, and he'd been putting them on this woman.

Jocelyn turned, her arms filled with several items. "Pancakes," she said, dumping everything on the counter. "You go relax, and by the time I'm done, everyone should be awake." She was much, much too happy and nice to hate. Damn, damn, damn.

"Hey, gorgeous," said a male British voice.

"Good morning," Jocelyn said, all dewy and happy.

Kat turned, and there stood Thomas. It was Thomas Jocelyn had slept with. Not Larry. Oh, thank God, not Larry. Kat was frighteningly giddy with relief.

Thomas wrapped his arms around Jocelyn and nuzzled her neck as if he'd known her years instead of a single night. "I'm going to have to thank Larry for disappearing last night," he said, kissing Jocelyn and making Kat feel as if she were a voyeur.

"He was there," Jocelyn said, laughing lightly. "We just didn't notice."

Kat laughed, too, because suddenly she was inordinately happy.

"I'm taking her home with me," Thomas said,

grinning like an idiot, as if he'd found a puppy and decided to keep it.

"Why don't we see if we can stand each other after today?" Jocelyn said, rolling her eyes, and Kat had to give her another point for being intelligent. Thomas was the sort of man who was easy to fall in love with. He was charming and open, and he probably was that way with every woman he met.

"If you two are going to be groping each other all day, please warn us all so we can go somewhere else." Larry entered the kitchen, his face half-covered with dark beard, his hair sticking up in all angles, his feet bare, and his eyes bloodshot. And Kat's heart melted on sight.

"Good morning, Lawrence. As a matter of fact, I plan to spend the entire day with Jocelyn away from all negative influences so I can entice her to move to England with me."

Jocelyn shook her head. "How long *had* it been since you had sex?" she asked.

Thomas laughed, and Larry frowned.

"It's just you, darling," Thomas said, giving her another hug. Thomas hugged with his entire body, wrapping himself around Jocelyn like a tourniquet, but she didn't seem to mind.

"He's like this with all women, I'll bet," Jocelyn said with a laugh at Thomas's exuberance.

Larry stared at the two of them. "Actually, I've never known Thomas to spend the night with a woman. He's never been in love, never even dated someone more than a week. And as far as I know, he's never, ever invited anyone to come back to anywhere with him." He might have been a doctor telling a patient the grim news of a terrible disease.

"Oh." Jocelyn's smile disappeared as she contemplated what Larry had told her. And then, slowly, her face lit up until a man would have to be a fool not to see how happy she was. "I'm not convinced," she said. "But you have five days before I have to leave."

"You can't fall in love in five days," Larry said, his voice tinged with disgust.

Everyone in the room gave him a dark look.

"Who the hell mentioned the word love?" Thomas asked, then kissed Jocelyn's neck, making her giggle. "I never said love. Did you say love, darling?"

"No."

"Not yet anyway," Thomas said.

"Well, you're talking about bringing her home and looking at her all cow-eyed. It's ridiculous," Larry said.

Thomas's good humor faded, and he stepped away from Jocelyn. "What the hell is your problem?"

Larry let out a harsh breath and seemed to force himself to relax. "Nothing. Nothing is wrong with me."

"He's jealous," Kat said, hoping to make him laugh. It didn't work.

"What in God's name do I have to be jealous about?"

He was being such a jerk; Kat just shook her head.

"No, tell us, Katherine," he demanded.

"I was joking, but you *were* interested in Jocelyn first, weren't you?"

He looked at her as if she'd grown a potato on her head. Then he turned to Jocelyn.

"Jocelyn, please don't take this personally, but I am profoundly glad that you and Thomas are together."

"No problem," Jocelyn said, and Kat could tell that she was getting uncomfortable as well. "Thomas, why don't we go out for breakfast. There's a little place right down the street by the ferry landing."

She didn't have to ask twice; they practically threw on their clothes and were out the door in five minutes, leaving Kat standing in the kitchen making coffee with Larry hovering behind her like some brutish hulk.

"What is your problem this morning?" she said finally.

"I didn't sleep well," he said.

"Well, who could with the sex Olympics being carried on?"

"I've never seen Thomas act that way." Every word out of his mouth this morning had been tinged with anger.

"So be happy for him. Would it really be the end of the world if he fell in love with Jocelyn?"

"Yes," Larry said, throwing his hands out to his sides. "The man is a womanizer. He makes me look like a monk. If Thomas falls in love . . ." He stopped and looked at her as if it was her fault his friend was falling in love.

"What?"

Larry shook his head and left the kitchen.

Lawrence showered and threw on the cleanest clothes he could find with the idea that he'd walk along the shore and clear his mind. And maybe something would enter it except thoughts of Katherine. He needed a story and quickly. He needed to be writing, not entertaining friends, not following an American girl around this Godfor-saken island hoping that something would fly into his brain.

Roy was out on his porch sweeping when he walked out of the house. Now there was a lonely guy. Or a lucky one. Lawrence hadn't made up his mind about that yet.

"Good morning," the older man called, and Lawrence walked on over.

"How about some company tonight?"

"Sure. You're always welcome." He passed the broom over the gray-painted wood, pausing to look up. "Now, what do we have here?"

A man wearing a suit and carrying a briefcase was walking from the ferry, looking about as out of place as a guy in a beauty salon. As the two men on the porch watched, the suit crossed the street, con-sulted a piece of paper, and began walking up the steps to Lawrence's cottage.

"May I help you?" he called over right before he heard the screech of a car from down the street.

"Good God Almighty," Roy muttered, his atten-tion drawn away from the guy in the suit to a blond blur crossing the street lugging huge animal print suitcases while managing to hold on to a small bug-eyed dog that yapped at the cars, the people watch-ing, a leaf blowing by. As quickly as Lawrence could absorb what he was seeing, Roy was off the porch and jogging down the street to grab the suitcases from the grateful-looking woman. He figured it must be a customer Roy was expecting.

In every way, the woman now tiptoeing quickly down the street in shoes as impractical as the dog-like animal she was dragging behind her was over the top. She had white-blond hair, breasts that would make a stripper happy, lips as red and luscious as any Marilyn Monroe look-alike, and curves that would make an old man tip back his bottle of Viagra.

Lila had come to the Vineyard.

Chapter 9

The man in the suit looked over to Lawrence, hesitated, and smiled. "I'm here to take a look at this property. It's part of a legal proceeding in probate."

"Oh, no, you don't," said Lila, who moved amazingly quickly in the pair of flimsy three-inch heels she was wearing. She now carried the doglike thing in her arms. Roy stopped at his porch and released the rolling suitcases, a bemused look on his face.

"This ought to be interesting," he said to Lawrence, who'd stepped down from Roy's porch.

"I own this property, and unless you have a court order allowing you access, I forbid you to take one more step," she said in a wispy little girl voice that Lawrence guessed was supposed to sound fierce but that failed miserably. She sounded like a breathier version of Melanie Griffith.

"Ma'am, my name is Ryan Davidson. I'm from the law offices of Schefflin and Morgan out of Boston. We were retained by the family of . . ."

"I know who retained you," Lila said and held the animal in her arms closer as if the bad lawyer man would steal it. The animal barked, so Lawrence figured the thing she was carrying was a dog, though he'd never seen anything quite like it. It looked like a cross between a Chihuahua and a rat.

The lawyer looked over at the two men watching from next door, a look of beseeching on his face. Then he opened his briefcase and brought out a document, holding it out for Lila to examine.

Lila looked crestfallen as she handed the order limply back to the attorney, all bluster and fierceness sucked out of her by a legal-sized piece of paper.

"Ma'am, I just need to look at the property, take some pictures. I'm here two days, and tomorrow, I'll be here with a bank and fine furniture appraiser. It's all routine. No one is going to take the house from you today."

"They're going to sell it?"

"I have no idea. I'm just here to take a look at the property."

"No. I'm sorry. Not today."

"I have a court order," the attorney said.

"Goodbye, Mr. Davidson."

The lawyer gave the two men another look. "If I have to come back with the police department, I will," he said, sounding tired and like it was the last thing on earth he wanted to do.

"We'll see you later then," she said cheerfully and waggled her fingers at him.

The lawyer looked slightly sick as he passed by the men, and Roy chuckled. "Looks like she got the best of him," he said, clearly delighted by what he'd just witnessed. He picked up the suitcases and began rolling them over to Lila, who stood like a sentinel on her front porch. A sentinel with a rat-dog in her arms.

"Roy," she breathed. "Can you believe this? They're trying to take the house away from me."

"Carl's kids?"

"Yes. He left me the house specifically. He knew I'd take care of it." She looked down the street, her cornflower blue eyes squinted and angry. "You know what they call me? Anna Nicole."

Lawrence almost laughed aloud because she did resemble the buxom blonde in more ways than one.

"I suppose it's understandable given the circumstances," she said, surprising Lawrence with her honesty.

"Lila? What are you doing here?" The door flew open, and Katherine rushed into her aunt's arms, though it seemed strange to think of Lila as Katherine's aunt because they were so close in age. The two women didn't look like they could have come from the same gene pool. Katherine was petite, dark, and dressed about as conservatively as a woman can while Lila was bright and anything but conservative.

"I got wind that the kids' lawyer was on the way, so I tried to head him off at the pass," she said lightly. "They'll be back though. With reinforcements."

"The lawyers were here?"

"Lawyer. And he'll be back with the police later because I refused to give him access to the property," Lila said, letting out a small giggle.

"She was ferocious," Roy said, smiling up at Lila.

Kat gave her aunt another hug. It was so nice to see her acting more like herself. The last time Kat had seen Lila was at Carl's funeral, then her aunt had looked pale and deflated, as if this time she really couldn't go on. But Lila was not a woman who could be kept down, which was one of the things that attracted older men to her. She was so full of life it bubbled out of her.

"Was Lila as ferocious as this little guy?" Kat asked, giving Lila's little dog a scratch behind its ear. "Were you a tough guy, Killer, were you?"

"Killer?" Larry asked, staring at the dog with undisguised distaste.

"Carl named him," Lila said, giving the little dog a nose nuzzle. "He was such a fierce little puppy. Weren't you?" The dog gave a strange whine that sounded anything but fierce. "You must be Lawrence. I've heard so much about you," she said, holding out her hand to Larry. He took it and kissed the top of her hand, his eyes dancing when he saw Kat's look of disbelief.

"He didn't kiss my hand when he met me," Kat said.

Lila turned and gave her niece the good-natured once-over she always got from Lila. "Well, just look how you dress, sweetie." Lila dressed ultra feminine, and she had never been self-conscious about her endowments. If anything, she wore clothing that made her seem sexier than she actually was, and she was constantly lamenting that Kat didn't follow suit. Her dress was white with large, bright yellow polka dots placed rather enhancingly around the fabric. It went down low and came up high, and a man would have to be dead not to notice her. "If you dress like a housecleaner, that's what people will think you are."

"I *am* a housekeeper," Kat said with exasperation.

To which Lila responded with a maddening, "See?"

"Then she's the prettiest housekeeper I've ever seen," Roy said kindly.

"Thank you, Roy," Kat said pointedly. "Would you

mind bringing Lila's bags in . . ." She stopped dead. There was no bedroom available.

"What's wrong?" Lila asked.

"Go ahead and bring Lila's things in. Roy, do you happen to have a free room available for the next few days?"

"Why?" Lila demanded.

"We have a full house thanks to Larry and his houseguests," Kat said.

"They can all leave," Larry said quickly.

"No, I'll leave," Kat insisted. "Do you have a free room, Roy?"

"If you leave, who will keep the place clean?" Larry said without a hint of humor.

"I'll only be next door. And it wouldn't kill you to do a little bit of work around here. Roy, is there a room?" Kat asked for the third time.

"The single is available. But it's small," Roy said.

"I'll stay with Roy," Lila said and immediately turned to walk out the door.

"Lila, get back in here. This is your house," Kat said and looked at the two men for help.

"Yes. My house, and I say you all stay in it. I arrived unannounced. I told you that you could stay here for the summer. Carl told Lawrence he could stay. You two managed quite well, and I'm the unexpected guest," Lila said, sounding sensible.

"But it's your house," Kat insisted.

"So I get to choose. And I choose the bed and breakfast. Roy makes a mean mushroom omelet and the best martini on the East Coast. Is that all right with you, Roy?"

Roy hesitated for a split second before nodding. "Fine with me," he said.

"Lila," Kat persisted.

"Sweetie, I don't want to stay here right now," she said, and her eyes misted slightly. "It's too hard yet. I'll be happier next door."

Suddenly, Kat felt awful and insensitive. "Sure."

"Now, Roy, if you could grab my bags one more time," she said, and she walked out of the cottage like a queen expecting to be followed. When Roy didn't follow, she turned.

"The dog," he said, jerking his head toward Killer. "I don't usually allow animals."

"But he's so small," Lila said, acting slightly bewildered, and Kat narrowed her eyes to watch a master at work. "He'll be quiet as a mouse."

"I think he's part rat anyway, so you're not so far off," Larry said under his breath, and Kat did all she could not to laugh.

"Besides," Lila said, looking all dewy, "he's all I have."

Roy gave a look as if he knew he was being manipulated, but he began dragging the bags out anyway. "Looks like a yapper," he said, apparently just to show he was not a complete sap.

Lila smiled at him, a blazing flash of white teeth against her full ruby lips, and Roy looked for a second as if he might actually have been paralyzed by the smile. Then he scowled and followed Lila, her polka-dot behind swinging to and fro.

"See you tonight, Roy?"

Roy grunted an answer, and Larry chuckled.

Damn, damn, damn, double and triple damn. Roy did not want Lila in his house, and he didn't even want to think of all the reasons why. But the most important reason was that he could just see Carl up in heaven laughing his ass off as Lila sashayed across the porch and through his front door.

He and Carl went way back. He couldn't remember a time he didn't know Carl because when he was just a kid growing up in lonely Martha's Vineyard, Carl had been the coolest adult around. Carl and his first wife started spending summers in the house next door when Roy was just a baby, so Roy grew up with their kids and spent half his summers in their house. Roy and the McKnights were inseparable, roaming about their little piece of the island, turning brown in the sun, tracking fine white sand over everything. Summers seemed endless, and the McKnights were a part of some of the happiest times in Roy's memory.

He'd never forget the summer the family never showed up, those long, tedious, horrible days of staring over at their boarded up house wondering what had happened. And then the next year, Carl and the kids showed up without Mrs. McKnight, and everyone wondered what had happened to the lady. Roy had been just twelve years old, not quite old enough for his parents to talk about divorce, but he got it out of Betty McKnight during a game of truth or dare.

And the three McKnight kids grew up, turned into teenagers, into kids who didn't want to spend their summers on an isolated island where there was nothing to do and nowhere to go. Carl had a realtor rent it out a week at a time so that a steady stream of strangers were in and out of the place. He didn't see Carl for years—and never saw the kids again—until he married Lila. By then, Roy had been married and widowed, had grown up and grown old, and here was his boyhood memory, white-haired and ancient, with a knockout blonde on his arm. It just didn't seem real.

It took only a few days for Roy to see that Lila truly loved Carl and that Carl was crazy about her. Sure, it was hard to believe at first, but he watched and listened as they sat on his porch night after night, and nothing Lila did or said made him think she was anything than what she pretended to be: a young woman deeply in love with her husband. They spent four summers together, shared eight months total with him before Carl decided to rock his world.

Roy still remembered that summer night nearly a year before. Carl must have suspected or perhaps even known he was dying because after two martinis, he turned to Roy and made him think things he had no business thinking about with another man's wife.

"I'm not going to live forever," Carl had said, gazing at the ocean through his glass.

"None of us are," Roy said pragmatically.

"Cut the bullshit," Carl said. "I'm 80 years old, and I'll be dead long before most people walking on this earth."

"You sick, Carl?" Roy asked, straightening up in his chair.

"Nothing specific. Nothing other than old age." And then he'd said it, one word that would stir up all kinds of things that he didn't want stirred up. "Lila."

Roy's gut had clenched because he could guess what was going to come out of Carl's mouth next. "Nice woman," Roy had said, trying to be as neutral as possible, though God knew it was difficult for any red-blooded man to be neutral about Lila.

"She's going to be alone. Lila doesn't like to be alone."

Roy almost said something insensitive like, "She ought to be used to it by now, losing two other husbands already." But he didn't. He simply nodded and waited for the axe to fall, waited for Carl to put into words the things he wouldn't allow his mind to think.

"I want you to look after her."

Roy shifted in his chair. "She's only here two months a year," Roy said, trying desperately to be pragmatic. "Hard for me to look after her if she's in California." He knew, he *knew* what Carl was asking, but he'd be damned if he let his mind go there before it was spelled out to him.

"I think you know what I'm asking, Roy. You're a good man. A young man. Lila needs someone like you. She needs someone steady, someone who needs her, and you've got to be the neediest son of a bitch I've ever met."

Roy would have argued the point, but he suspected he'd lose that argument. After all, he was running a bed and breakfast out of his home out of sheer loneliness.

"I can't think of Lila that way, Carl. You're my friend. We've known each other for years. Hell, I grew up with your kids; I watched your marriage end. Lila's more like a s—"

"Bullshit. No one not related to Lila could ever think of her as a sister, and if you do, well, then you've got other problems I don't care to discuss right now."

Roy chuckled. "Okay. You've got me there."

"Just think on it. I don't want to have to worry about her. She's already been through so much. I want her to have a place to go to, a place where she feels safe."

Roy had agreed, knowing then that if Carl did die any time soon, Lila would be far away, would probably never step foot on the island again. In fact, when he'd heard of Carl's death, he'd half-expected to see a "for sale" sign pounded into the lawn within weeks.

Instead, she was not only on the island, but also in his house. Wearing that dress that showed off every curve on her luscious body. All those places that Roy hadn't allowed himself to go when Carl was alive, when Lila was still Carl's wife, he realized he could now go. He could let his mind, if not his eyes, wander all over the place knowing he had Carl's blessing. Except he didn't want to because in his mind, Lila was still Carl's husband, no matter that he was probably smiling down at him right now. Right about now, Roy was darn mad at Carl for sticking those thoughts in his brain, as if Lila would in a million years consider someone like him. Living on the island for a summer was one thing, but living there permanently was another thing entirely. It certainly wasn't for everyone. He'd seen plenty of people who thought retiring to the island was a wonderful idea only to move out after one long, bleak winter. Lila loved to shop; she loved museums and lectures and eating out at fancy restaurants. Her husbands had taken her to Paris and Rome. Roy supposed he could do that, too—he certainly had enough money—but he really didn't give a fig about going to those places.

Damn Carl for putting that bug in his brain because now she was on the Vineyard where he didn't think she'd ever be again. And she was in his house.

"I'm afraid the only room available for the next two nights is the small one at the top of the house," Roy said, struggling with the large suitcases. Dragging them around by the wheels was one thing; lugging them up three flights of stairs was something else entirely.

"I love that room," Lila called down. "I don't know how you keep this house so nice, Roy. You have a rare and wonderful gift for making people feel welcome."

Roy tried not to grumble because he really didn't want Lila to feel welcome. He didn't want her here at all. He didn't want to feel his heart pick up a beat or let his mind put him places he would never be. Like in her bed, his head nestled against her breasts, his hands trailing down her wonderfully round bum.

She opened the door to the bedroom and flew across the room to look at the view. Then she turned, her face bright and filled with such happiness his heart squeezed painfully.

"Oh, Roy," she said, her eyes filling with tears. "It's so good to be home."

Chapter 10

Kat slowly hung up the phone, trying to gauge how she felt about being dumped by Brian for the second time in a matter of weeks. She'd done enough crying already, so it wasn't a good cry that she needed. While she was trying to understand how she felt, she realized she didn't feel anything—not sad or happy or angry. Nothing. The thing was, she didn't know if that was good or bad or if she was going to start sobbing at some highly embarrassing moment because she was inadvertently bottling up her grief.

Do I feel sad? Kat let out a small sigh. Yes, she did. But she realized she didn't feel sad about Brian; she mourned a lost dream, and dreams were something she was getting used to losing, sadly.

Kat picked up her romance novel, knowing with certainty the hero and heroine would end up together and everything would be resolved nicely. Unlike her life, she let herself think. She had read approximately two pages when she heard her name being called by a British man with little patience.

"Katherine, I can't find my Burberry pants."

Kat sighed and went to the laundry room where Larry stood amid piles of clean, folded clothes that she hadn't had a chance to bring upstairs yet. "Which ones are the Blueberry?"

"Burberry. The ones with the plaid along the waistband. You know, Burberry."

Kat gave him a scowl. "I wouldn't know Burberry if it landed on my head."

"Plaid," he repeated as if repeating the word to her would cause an epiphany.

Oh. Plaid. Burberry. Of course.

"They cost nearly two hundred pounds, which I can ill afford now."

"Two hundred dollars for a pair of pants?" Kat said, shocked.

"Two hundred *pounds*," he stressed. "That's nearly four hundred dollars. Do you know where they are?"

Kat stared at him, wondering what sane human would pay four hundred dollars for a pair of pants. "In a museum somewhere being guarded?"

"Very funny. Ah, here they are," he said, lifting up what appeared to be a rather ordinary pair of khakis.

"See?" he said, folding over the waistband. "Burberry plaid."

"That's just plain nuts. I can buy you a pair of Dockers that look exactly the same at T.J. Maxx and pay twenty bucks for them."

He gave her a superior smile. "Dockers are not Burberry."

"Well, la-dee-da," Kat said, rolling her eyes at him. "Just for your information, the masses that you are trying to appeal to typically don't spend more than fifty bucks for a pair of pants and even then, they have to think about it real hard."

"Ah. The masses." His good humor vanished almost instantly.

"I take it you haven't been inspired by me yet?"

"If you're asking how the writing is going, it is not going. At all."

Kat couldn't feel all that sorry for him. Now that his friends were visiting, she hadn't even heard him mention writing once.

"Where are you going in your Burberrys?" she asked, giving the pants a curious look.

"I'm taking the girls to town. I'm afraid they are exceedingly bored as well as exceedingly horrified by Thomas's behavior. They made a desperate appeal to me to bring some excitement into their lives. As such, I've hired a boat to sail us about the island for a couple of days. We set sail tomorrow morning with whoever wants to join us from our adventures this evening." He began walking away, then paused midstep. "You're free to come along."

To Kat, the invitation was so uninspired she hardly felt the need to respond. "I'll just stay here and enjoy the peace and quiet while you're all gone."

"Lovely."

Kat shook her head. Any American male saying the word "lovely" would sound ridiculous. But when Larry said "lovely" it sounded right, masculine even. Sexy.

"Brian called," she said. "Guess he learned to use a phone book."

He stopped abruptly, his eyes searching her face for any signs of grief.

"It's okay. He was calling to tell me he was dumping me. Again."

"Good riddance. Right?"

Kat smiled because he truly looked concerned, and she liked having someone worry about her. "Right."

He walked over to her, and for a second, she thought he was going to draw her into his arms. God knew she wanted him to. "You're really fine?"

Kat nodded, willing him to reach out, willing herself to step into his arms. But he backed away slightly, and the moment was gone.

"I am heading over to Roy's before I go out for the evening. Care to join us?"

That sounded much more sincere than his invitation to go on the boat. It really was cute the way he was protecting her from his nefarious friends. "Sure, as long as you don't make fun of my wine."

"I'd never dream of such a thing," he said. "And thanks for washing these." He held up the pants and smiled as he headed toward his room to, she assumed, change into his precious Burberry pants.

She supposed she'd been right not to sleep with him, Kat thought after he'd gone. He seemed more infatuated with his damn pants than he had with her. She told herself she was glad he'd seemed to have lost interest in her sexually, glad he was sailing around the island "with whoever wants to join us." All he'd wanted was a distraction from his writing troubles, and at first, Kat had filled that role.

The thing that bothered her most was that she was still attracted to him, still liked him, still would find it difficult to push him away if he ever decided to kiss her again.

When Kat had been in her early twenties, she would have jumped at the chance to sail around the island partying and rubbing elbows with international jet-setters. She hated to admit it, but she just had no interest in that sort of entertainment anymore. She'd suffered enough hangovers to know she never wanted to be hanging again. She'd grown up while apparently Larry and his friends had not.

Because they hadn't needed to. Because none of them worked, none of them needed to work. Attending some charity event on the arm of some debutante was not work.

Feeling vindicated and superior to all that was Larry, that night, Kat brought out her bottle of Arbor Mist and a tall glass filled with ice and headed over to Roy's at the appointed hour. The two men were already out there, martinis in hand, along with Lila, who was wearing a brilliantly white, draped outfit that she made look chic. The only thing that ruined her look was Killer, bug-eyed and wary, sitting on her lap.

"Kat, hurry up; they're talking sports and not even the same ones at the same time."

Roy chuckled. "I was talking baseball and the Red Sox, and he was talking cricket, which no one plays and no one cares about."

"Aren't they practically the same sport anyway?" Kat asked, just to bug both men at the same time.

"Hardly," Larry said, giving her the affronted look she knew he would. "Cricket is a game of finesse and style whereas baseball is a game of brutes on steroids."

"That's all over now," Kat said, then leaned toward Larry. "Let me give you a little lesson about New

England. You can't say anything bad against baseball or the Red Sox."

"Or football and the Patriots," Roy said. "And that's real football, not soccer. I have never understood Europe's fascination with a sport as dull as soccer."

Larry smiled. "I'm not much of a fan myself, but I never own up to that back home."

They sat in silence for a while, enjoying a late afternoon breeze off the ocean, and watched the ferry leave the landing after giving off a single loud blast.

"Larry's going to be sailing around the island tomorrow," Kat announced.

Roy leaned forward in his chair. "Oh?"

"My friends and I are renting a small sloop," he said.

"Apparently he's picking out his crew tonight in the bars." Kat avoided Larry's gaze, which suddenly turned toward her.

"We do plan to invite a few more people along for the ride."

"Preferably blond and leggy," Kat muttered. Okay, she knew what she was doing now and she knew why, but she just couldn't help herself. This sudden abandonment of her when he'd acted just days before as if she was beautiful or at least someone worth pursuing was beginning to grate on her nerves. She was jealous, and she knew it and, for the life of her, couldn't stop herself.

"Precisely. Don't forget large-breasted and beautiful."

"I haven't received an invitation yet," Lila said, laughter in her tone. "Are my legs too short?" She straightened out her legs and wiggled them a bit.

"Oh, Lila, you're much too old for this little

cruise," Kat said, turning to Larry. "What is the age limit? Twenty-two? Twenty-three?"

Ah, now he looked annoyed, and Kat felt exceedingly happy that she'd gotten to him.

"I did invite you, if you recall," he said as if Roy and Lila weren't on the porch.

"You were only being polite, and you know it."

He took a sip of his martini and didn't bother denying what she'd said.

"It's supposed to be nice out tomorrow," Lila said with false cheerfulness, an obvious attempt to change the subject. "You know, Roy, when was the last time you took a couple of days off? You should go with Lawrence, and I'll mind the store here."

Roy immediately shook his head. "The last thing Lawrence needs on the boat is me," he said, but Kat was surprised to sense that he actually seemed to like the idea of going along.

"You must come," Larry said, suddenly animated and friendly. "You know these waters and would be an invaluable help to us."

"Well, I don't know."

"Go, Roy. How hard can it be to make a few beds and prepare breakfast? You already know I'm a terrific cook. Go."

"I won't be cramping your style?" he asked Larry with endearing caution.

"God, no. Chances are you'll be the only chap on board I'll be able to have a decent conversation with."

Roy leaned back in his rocker and steepled his fingers beneath his chin, his eyes studying each person on the porch in turn. "I'll tell you what. I'll go along if Kat here does."

Kat blinked slowly, feeling like an animal watching a trap close in slow motion. She did not want to be stuck on a boat filled with college girls batting their eyes at Larry, but how could she possibly deny Roy his day out on a sailboat?

"That's not a fair condition, Roy. I don't want to go. Really."

Roy shrugged. "Deal's a deal."

"There is no deal," Kat pointed out.

"Kat," Lila said with exasperation.

"Okay. I'll go," Kat said through gritted teeth. She happened to look over at Larry at that precise moment and saw his expression. He looked more than unhappy that she was now part of his plans.

"I was blackmailed," she said, then gave Roy a glare, but he simply smiled at her in that maddening male way. Kat took a long sip of her watered-down wine and wished for the first time she could stomach something stronger.

"Isn't that one of your friends?" Roy asked, pointing out a couple walking along the boardwalk. They were clinging together as they walked and somehow managed not to bump into anyone even though they were staring deeply into one another's eyes.

"Thomas," Larry said, looking at his friend with distaste.

Kat looked at the couple and couldn't stop the feeling of envy that swept over her. She'd never had anyone hold her like that. And the way Thomas was looking at the girl—it was as if she were the most beautiful creature on earth. "He's in love," she said softly.

"So it would seem," Larry said, sounding irritated.

"That's sweet," Lila said.

"It's a bit idiotic if you ask me," Larry said.

"We didn't," Kat pointed out.

"They met yesterday, for God's sake."

Larry had a point, Kat knew. But she knew a person could at least begin to fall in love with someone in a day. It wasn't impossible, and it wasn't idiotic. "Just because you've never been in love and never felt that way doesn't mean there's anything wrong with it."

"I fell in love with Carl in a week. That's pretty quick," Lila said, and Kat gave her a quick smile of thanks.

"You've never been in love?" Roy asked. "Don't believe that for a second."

"He hasn't. Ask him," Kat said, ignoring the daggers that were flying from Larry's eyes.

"I have actually," he said, and Kat gasped at the lie. "But then I came to my senses."

"Then it wasn't love," Kat said.

"Obviously not," Larry said.

"Because when you love someone, you just don't fall out of love."

"Then you still love Brian." Larry had a superior look on his face that Kat was just dying to slap off.

"No. But I am still getting over that, and thanks so much for bringing that up."

Lila gave Larry a fierce look. "He betrayed her. That was the man she was planning to spend the rest of her life with, and he cheated on her."

"Okay, Lila," Kat said before her aunt said too much.

"She had everything planned. The wedding, the reception, the honeymoon. You don't just get over something like that." Lila turned to Kat. "Honey, I don't know how you're ever going to trust another man again."

"I don't think all men are like Brian. Roy here's nice," she said, purposefully leaving Larry out.

"She came here to lick her wounds," Lila said, as protective of Kat as her own mother.

"Lila."

"Her heart was broken."

"Okay, Lila."

"She doesn't need to be reminded of that heartache."

Larry had the oddest expression on his face, almost as if he'd never been scolded in his entire life. "I know, and I apologize," he said.

"I don't know how the conversation turned to me," Kat said, "but we were talking about Thomas and how lucky he was to have fallen in love."

"He's not in love," Larry said. "He's infatuated. He'll come to his senses before the week is over." He glanced at his empty martini glass. "Do you have another of these, Roy, because this one doesn't seem to be doing the trick."

Later that night, after Lawrence and Kat went their separate ways, Lila sat with Roy in his private sitting room, Lila reading a novel and Roy reading the *Boston Globe*. He was one of those people who read a newspaper cover to cover and didn't like to be interrupted. The only time of day he could do that was in the evenings when his guests were out. He liked Lila despite not wanting to. It went without saying that he was attracted to her, more attracted than to any other woman since his wife died. She might look like a bit of fluff, but she was an intelligent, warmhearted woman who was nicer than she needed to be. She didn't have a hard edge to her, and for a man, that was damned attractive.

"What do you think of Lawrence and Kat?" she said, breaking a long, comfortable silence.

"I think he's half in love with her."

"Really. I was under the impression they didn't get along very well."

"Have you ever seen a couple bicker like those two who weren't in love?"

Lila shook her head and laughed lightly. He liked the way she laughed, a soft, bright sound. "I don't know. He really didn't seem to want her on that boat, and she didn't seem to want to go. Is that why you made that bargain—to put the two of them together? You're not playing matchmaker, are you?"

"Sure. You should see the two of them together. Sparks fly every time they're within six feet of one another. Even if they don't end up together, it's the best entertainment I've had in years."

Lila put her book aside and gave Roy her full attention. "What about you, Roy? Any girlfriend?"

Roy could feel his face flush, and he shook his head. "Not a large pool of women looking to live on an island twelve months a year."

"Carl used to worry about you being so alone here all the time. Can I tell you something he said?"

Roy swallowed hard, wondering if Carl had been fool enough to say something to Lila about the two of them being together. "Sure," he said, nearly choking on the word.

"When he knew he was dying, he told me he didn't

want me to end up like you, alone. You bothered him, you know. And I think I know why."

"Why?"

"He just couldn't figure out how a man so alone could be so happy."

Roy forced a smile he didn't come close to feeling. Happy? He wouldn't have used that word to describe himself in a million years. "Guess I'm just used to being alone."

Lila sighed, a soft breath that made Roy want to close his eyes just to capture that sound forever. "I think I'm going to have to get used to being alone, too. I've been married or dating my entire adult life. I need to find out who I am by myself."

Roy couldn't help the aching disappointment he felt in his gut. It wasn't until that moment that he realized how much he'd hoped that Lila would somehow become part of his life. "Well, I sure know who I am," Roy said, forcing a laugh.

"Who?"

He thought about lying for a moment, then said the truth. "Lila, I'm the loneliest man on this island."

Chapter 11

If there was one thing Lawrence was finding out, it was that he wasn't twenty-five anymore and he didn't want to be. That was not the case for Clarice and Emma who he didn't think would ever grow up. Then again, they had both just turned thirty; their fun hadn't reached that sad, desperate level he'd seen in other women—and men, for that matter.

"You've become a bore," Clarice said with a pout. "You didn't invite a single person on this boat with us, and now it's going to be a boring tour of a boring island with boring people." When she said boring people, she was looking at Kat who was at that very moment getting a lesson in sail folding from Roy. Kat, for all her reluctance to go sailing, seemed to be embracing everything about the boat with an enthusiasm that was charming.

"Why don't you just stay on land then?" Lawrence said, wishing for the hundredth time he'd never called his friends to invite them to the island.

"You know what? That's the best suggestion you've had all week," Clarice said. "Let's go, Emma. We can find our own fun."

Lawrence watched in disbelief as the two women grabbed their overnight bags and climbed off the boat onto the dock. "Come on, girls; don't be like that," he pleaded halfheartedly. And when they continued walking away with a little wave, he yelled after them, "I don't know why I'm always the one assigned to find the fun people."

Emma stopped, turned, and took enough steps closer so she wouldn't have to shout. "You've always been the one to attract the liveliest crowd. We always leave it up to you. And Thomas. But he's gone batty, and you've gone boring." From her tone, Lawrence couldn't tell which she found more disturbing.

"Come on, Emma; we'll still have fun," Lawrence said.

Emma seemed to hesitate, then Clarice came back and grabbed her friend. "No hard feelings, Lawrence, but I think we'll have more fun on shore. You didn't even buy any tequila," she accused.

Behind him, he could sense Roy and Katherine watching the scene unfold. Absolutely nothing was going according to his well-planned script. The last place on earth he wanted to be at this moment was confined to a forty-foot yacht with Katherine. Roy was not nearly enough of a buffer between them. He was of a mind to cancel the entire trip.

"We lost part of the crew?" Roy asked far more cheerfully than seemed necessary.

"I'm afraid they wouldn't have been much help anyway," Lawrence said. "As it is, it doesn't make much sense for just the three of us to go."

"Let's just take her out for the day, and if it goes well, we'll keep her until the morning. Katherine here's a fast learner, and I could sail this boat myself if I had to." Roy clearly wanted a day away from the bed and breakfast, and Lawrence wasn't going to be the one to tell him his mini vacation was cancelled, so he agreed to a short trip. Short being the operative word.

He hadn't looked at Katherine all morning, had been too afraid that he'd make an idiot of himself and stare at her like some drug-hazed fool. He knew what she was wearing because of the quick glance he'd made when she'd first arrived. She had on cargo shorts that were too big for her so they hung low on her hips and a bikini top that was probably modest but to Lawrence was painfully revealing. That's all he knew and all he was going to know unless he found some way to stop his stupid body from reacting to her.

It was insane, this thing going on inside him. He couldn't shake her, couldn't ignore her enough, couldn't be without her enough to make himself stop thinking about her constantly. Wanting her. Lusting for her. It was not like him at all, and he didn't know what to blame anymore. He'd really thought his friends would be a big enough distraction to bring him back to sanity. They would come, remind him of what he was, and all would be well. But they'd only reinforced the aching reality that he was falling in love with her, if not already there. He was not going to make a complete ass of himself the way Thomas was, mostly because Katherine seemed so completely indifferent to him. He knew that she was not suffering because he was on the boat, other than that she might be slightly annoyed by him. She was not in physical pain every time she looked at him. She wasn't ready to commit herself to an asylum for the completely mad.

"Sorry about your friends," she said, and his entire body tightened. He managed a shrug—God his charm was in full force today, he thought cynically. Next thing he knew, he'd start grunting at her. It had been so much easier to be charming when he hadn't cared about her.

"Roy said we could go fishing off the boat. He brought some poles, and we could cook it in the kitchen. I mean the galley," she said, all chipper and oblivious to his suffering.

"Sounds lovely."

"Larry?"

"Yes," he said, sounding impatient because he was desperate to get her away from him. Any moment now, he was going to give in and look at her and see her standing there in her baggy shorts and too tight bikini, and then he was going to make a complete fool of himself by declaring himself in love.

"Listen, I know you didn't want me to come along, and I'm sorry if I ruined this trip for you."

He swallowed and looked up at her and knew in that moment he shouldn't have. His insides sort of turned to mush, and he thought for a moment something was medically wrong. She was so close to him, closer than she'd been in days, and she was looking at him with those beautiful brown eyes, her short hair blowing about her head like some sort of romantic music video.

"I'm glad you're here," he said, and his voice sounded strange to his ears, as if he were talking into a glass. She didn't believe him—he could tell by her eyes, full of skepticism. He could only imagine her expression if he told her he was half in love with her.

She turned to Roy. "Are you ready to cast off?"

Lawrence moved to the bow of the boat and undid the line from the cleat, then moved to the stern and did the same there. Roy turned on the engine and backed the boat out of its slip. Before long, they were ready to hoist sail with Katherine clutching the wheel like a seasoned sailor even though she'd said this was her first time on a large boat.

"Just keep her going into the wind," Roy called.

"How do I do that?" she yelled back.

"Keep her straight," Lawrence said, hopping down to the cockpit beside her. "See that buoy?" He pointed to a red buoy a distance away bobbing from a powerboat's wake. "Just head for that. It's just easier to raise the sails when you're not fighting the wind."

"Toward the buoy," she muttered and moved the wheel a fraction of an inch, enjoying the fact that the boat moved in the direction she meant it to.

Kat held to that wheel as if it might swirl out of control if she let it go. That's what always happened in the movies, and she wasn't about to let it happen to her. Though she hadn't planned to steer the boat, she found she liked being in charge. Captain Kat. She grinned and moved the wheel slightly just to see what would happen.

"Windward," Roy called out, and Kat quickly brought the boat back to wind.

Roy and Larry hoisted the sails, and they snapped in the wind and seemed to heave the boat on its side. She gave a little scream—at least she thought it was little—but Larry came bounding off the top of the boat to find out which limb had been ripped from its socket.

"What's wrong?" he asked, looking around wildly for whatever had caused the apparently blood-curdling scream she'd just emitted.

"The boat nearly tipped over," she gasped.

Larry looked at the boat, which was tilted at perhaps a four-degree angle. "Darling," he said in a voice that made her blood slow, "next time you scream like that, you better have a shark hanging off the end of your foot. Are we clear on that?"

She gave him a mock salute. "Yes, sir." That salute cost her a bit of control of the wheel, and she quickly grabbed at it just as Roy was jumping down to stand next to them.

"I'll take over," he said grimly.

"A mutiny, hm-m-m?" Kat said, reluctantly giving up the wheel.

"I think we'll all be a bit safer if Roy has the helm," Larry said, and Kat gave him a face.

From his spot, Roy reached over and yanked on a couple of ropes, and the sails stopped their ruffling sound and the boat leaned over a bit further, but this time Kat was ready and even found herself enjoying the way the boat sliced through the waters. Then they hit a wake; Kat lost her balance and found herself steadied by something warm and iron-strong round her upper arm.

"This one's not going to find her sea legs any time soon," Larry said to Roy, who chuckled.

Kat wanted to argue, but the truth was she hadn't found her sea legs yet. She'd been watching sailboats from shore for as long as she could remember, and she'd thought it would be so wonderfully serene and quiet. It wasn't. The sails snapped, the bow hit the waves with violent *whumps,* and the damn thing sailed crooked. It was fabulous.

Then something really awful happened. Larry took off his shirt. And he was beautiful. More beautiful than she remembered. Sure, she thought, flaunt your perfect abs, your beautiful biceps, your wonderfully hairy chest, that line of dark hair that extends from your perfectly shaped navel down to your sexy bathing suit. Why not just wear a sign that said, "You could have had this, you dolt."

Kat didn't want to stare. Not true. She did want to stare to her heart's content, but she did not want Larry or Roy to see her stare. So she looked back at the island and pretended that was something she wanted to stare at instead of Larry.

At the bow of the boat was a relatively flat area that Kat looked at longingly. It seemed like a fairly safe place to be, and in all the times she'd watched sailboats pass by, there always seemed to be someone lounging on the front of the boat looking extremely relaxed and happy. Larry stood next to her, close enough that she could actually feel the heat of his naked arm, which rested casually on the boom thingy. She needed desperately to move away from him. With a deep breath, she hoisted herself up and walked, albeit a bit unsteadily, to the bow of the boat.

"Where're you heading?" Roy called. "'Cause we're going to be tacking real soon, and unless you've got a good grip on something, that jib's going to throw you overboard."

Kat turned to Larry. "English, please."

"Roy is going to turn the boat soon, and you'll probably get whacked by that big sail up there. When we turn, we move the sails from one side of the boat to the other."

"I knew that," Kat said even though she really hadn't thought much about it.

"You can settle down on the bow and relax once we round that point," Roy said, pointing to a spit of land up ahead.

Kat scootched back and settled down on a bench-like seat, trying not to let either man know how desperately she wanted to get away from Larry.

"You look a little sick," Larry said, easing down into the seat next to her.

She didn't look at him but at the island slowly passing by, at people on the beach, at a seagull, at anything but the man sitting next to her.

"I'm fine," she said and wished that were true.

Forcing herself to feel brave, she let her gaze drift slowly over Larry. He was just an ordinary guy. Well, not ordinary. He was excessively good-looking, and he did happen to have quite a nice body. He was witty and charming and sexy, and he made wonderful fodder for some pretty hot fantasies. And that was the problem. Larry wouldn't be able to live up to the fantasies that Kat had built in her head. No man could.

"Coming about," Roy yelled.

Suddenly, the boat whirled, the sails snapped, the boom crashed; Roy and Larry grabbed ropes and pulled, and Kat felt more alive than she had in weeks. Then they were sailing again, fairly serenely, heading away from the island.

"We're heading around that point," Larry said, nodding back to the island.

"Oh." Her eyes drifted to his mouth, that wonderful mouth that had actually kissed better than her fantasies, and she wondered suddenly if everything would be better. She wondered if he'd look her in the eyes when he was over her, if he'd kiss her while he was slipping inside, if he'd move his hands over her body and groan and . . .

"Katherine."

Her eyes darted up, and her cheeks flushed, caught red-handed in the middle of a very nice fantasy. "Yes?"

"Would you like a mimosa? Lila packed some for us."

"Yes, please." Something cool and with alcohol. Perfect.

Sailing was . . . lovely, Kat thought as she stretched warm and content on the top of the boat, a soft towel beneath her, the sun hot and bright above her. She had a nice little mimosa buzz, just enough to take the edge off her fear of Larry and make her fully appreciate how very nice it was to be on a boat sailing around Martha's Vineyard. The good life. The life of the rich and famous.

"Feeling better?"

Kat kept her eyes closed and smiled when she heard his voice, deep and as warm as the sun. "M-m-m-m-m," she managed.

"We thought you fell asleep up here," he said, chuckling.

"I think I did." Kat turned to her side and found

Larry's face four inches from hers. She could see the gold specks in his brown eyes, the hairs of his beard poking through his sun-flushed skin. He looked young and completely harmless at the moment. "You're pretty," she said, and he laughed. "You are," she insisted.

"No one's ever called me pretty."

"You have perfect features," she said, realizing that little mimosa buzz might be a *big* mimosa buzz.

"And you, darling, have consumed too much champagne too early in the morning."

"Alcohol is a truth serum," she said with a little shrug.

"I haven't had a drop to drink so you can take this any way you want. You are . . ." He stopped, let his eyes drift closed for maybe two seconds. When he opened them, she could tell something had changed—or shut down.

"I am what?" she insisted, even though she knew that whatever he had been going to say he wouldn't say now.

He moved back a bit. "I was just going to say you have nice eyes."

She gave him a skeptical look. "They're almost exactly the same color as yours. So what you're really doing is complimenting yourself."

"Precisely."

Kat frowned. "What were you going to say?"

He gave her a look that almost seemed as if he were proud of her for seeing through him. "Some things," he said, tapping her on the tip of her nose, "are better left unsaid."

She turned over onto her stomach. "You're no fun," she said sleepily.

"So I've heard," he said dryly.

"Maybe we should have invited Thomas and Jocelyn. They were fun."

"They were nauseating."

Kat laughed and turned her head toward him. "You're clearly jealous of the love Thomas has found, having never been in that state yourself."

He pulled his knees up, wrapped his arms around his legs, and grabbed the wrist of his other hand. Kat couldn't help but scan his legs, long and hairy and very masculine. She loved men, she decided, every muscly, hairy, scratchy bit of them. "Actually, being in love isn't all it's cracked up to be," he said finally.

"Ah-ha. You were in love and had your heart broken. I knew no one in their thirties could have escaped completely."

"Not quite." He studied her for a moment. "I loved a woman—briefly—who didn't love me. It was unfortunate."

"That's so sad. No wonder you're so bitter."

"I'm getting over it. And I'm not bitter."

Kat propped her head on her hand. "You mean you're still in love with this woman? Is she blind? Or stupid?"

He gave her the oddest look. "Neither. Just . . . not in love. Can't really explain it. Most women do like me."

"I like you," she said, trying to make him feel better. "But I suppose that doesn't help."

"Not at all, actually."

A thought occurred to her just then. "You have told her that you love her, right?"

"Good God, no."

She looked at him as if he was a complete idiot.

"Maybe she's in love with you, and you don't know it. Maybe she doesn't think you love her. Ever think of that?"

Lawrence stared at her for a long time, wishing he'd never said a word to her because it only confirmed that she didn't love him. "I'm quite confident my feelings are not reciprocated."

"You never know, Larry. Maybe she's just waiting for you to say something. It isn't Clarice or Emma?"

"No."

"That's good. I'm sure they're nice and all, but I really don't see you with one of them. What's this woman like, anyway?"

He looked away because he'd be damned if he gave himself away at this point. He wanted to tell her that he'd never met another woman like her, no one so open or nice or funny. No one who could see through him so well, and no one he could fall in love with so easily. "She's exceedingly annoying," he said finally.

And she shouted, "It's me," dissolving into a fit of giggles. Thank God, Larry thought, because if she had looked at him at that moment, if she had seen his eyes, the way his fists had clenched, she would have known the truth in a split second.

"You are very perceptive," he said, forcing out a laugh.

He felt himself being stripped, layer by layer, down to the man he used to be. *You are going too far out of character,* he thought, feeling slightly panicked. He'd thought he'd been living a lie all those years ago, but now he realized he really was living one now.

Chapter 12

Kat would always remember what a beautiful day it had been. They sailed for a few hours, then dropped anchor and had a lunch of tarragon chicken sandwiches on focaccia that Lila had prepared. Once Kat got some food into her, she lost that warm, wonderful feeling the two mimosas had given her. It was such a pretty day she didn't need champagne to give her the warm fuzzies. Larry was giving her enough warm fuzzies, thank you very much.

The wind calmed down, and the sloop moved gently on the small waves beneath a brilliant blue sky decorated with just enough cottony clouds to make the scene more interesting.

"You know, kids, I think we should head on back this afternoon. I'm feeling really worn out," Roy said, putting down half his sandwich. "Think I might be coming down with something." He stood, wiped the sweat from his forehead with a napkin, and dropped like a lead weight onto the deck.

Kat remembered screaming, wishing she'd brought her cell phone, looking helplessly to the shore that seemed so far away. And then she remembered stepping back and watching as Larry, with clinical precision, worked on Roy. There was no panic, no hesitation, nothing but practiced hands moving over Roy, checking his pulse, his heart, his breathing.

"My cell phone is in the galley. Get it, call 911, and hand it to me," he said without looking away from Roy, who lay there as if he were dead.

"Oh, my God."

"Go, Katherine," Larry said, his voice still controlled but laced with steel.

Kat ran down to the galley, frantically searching for Larry's cell phone. She found it, her hands shaking badly as she tried to figure out how to dial because it was a different model from her own. Finally, she pressed a little green phone, dialed 911, and ran up to the deck where Larry was hovering over a now conscious Roy.

"The phone," he said, holding out his hand, again without taking his eyes off Roy, and for an instant, Kat felt as if she were on one of those medical shows where the doctor was issuing orders to an incompetent nurse.

"Yes. I have a fifty-five-year-old man in cardiac arrest on a boat approximately one mile northwest of Vineyard Haven. He's conscious. Pulse is weak, heartbeat regular at 90." He looked up at Kat. "Go in the galley and look in the medical kit and see if you can find any aspirin."

Instead, Kat ran to her purse where she knew she had a little tin of Bayer.

Kat handed the aspirin to Larry, who helped Roy take it, making him chew the bitter medicine.

"Tastes like crap," Roy said, and Kat nearly cried to hear his voice sounding so normal.

Larry pushed off the phone and handed it to Kat. "They're sending out the harbor police," he told Roy. "They should be here within twenty minutes. How are you feeling?"

"Like a ton of bricks is sitting on my chest. What the hell happened?"

"You had a heart attack. Pretty good one, too. Any history of heart problems? High blood pressure, angina?"

"Naw. My father died of a heart attack when he was fifty though."

Larry looked at the older man grimly. "You're not going to die. Not today anyway. Just try not to have another one before the medics get here."

Roy slipped in and out of consciousness a few times before the medics arrived, and each time he did, Larry quickly listened to his heart, pressing his ear against Roy's chest, and taking his pulse. Kat watched, stunned by his calm, professional demeanor. Not only did Larry seem to know precisely what he was doing, but he also did everything without hesitation. As if he was trained to do so.

After fifteen excruciating minutes, the harbor police arrived, efficiently tied up to the boat, and transported Roy to the power boat. Larry spoke in quiet, urgent tones to the rescue crew before untying the boat. And before they shoved off, a woman said clearly, "Thank you, doctor."

And Larry waved them off before crumpling in the seat near the boat's wheel and putting his head down between his knees. Kat rushed over to him.

"Are you okay?" He was shaking, his entire body

covered with sweat, and he gripped his head with his hands, kneading his hair convulsively. "Larry, what's wrong? Roy's going to be fine. You saved his life."

She heard him breathing—long, harsh breaths, slowly gaining control.

"Christ," he said, his voice rough and low. "I'm all right now." He looked up at Kat, and she was shocked by the hollow look in his eyes.

"No, you're not."

He let out a short laugh. "I'm getting there."

Kat stroked his back, not knowing what to do or say because she wasn't quite sure what was wrong with him. "You were wonderful, Larry. If I'd have been alone, Roy would have died. You saved his life."

He let out a long sigh. "I suppose I did," he said, strangely impassive.

"Larry. That woman called you doctor."

"A mistake."

"You didn't correct her," she pointed out. "Why would she call you doctor?"

"I must have sounded like a doctor."

"Larry," she said, knowing he was keeping something from her.

He looked like a man facing certain torture. "Let's get the boat underway, open another bottle of champagne, and I'll tell you the sordid story of my life."

They were heading to Vineyard Haven where the island's only hospital was located. Lawrence didn't bother hoisting the sails; instead, he powered along the shore, his heart beating so painfully in his chest he wondered if he might be having a heart attack as well. He had to give Katherine credit for patience

because she waited a good long time before finally
turning to him, her face expectant and horrifyingly
admiring.

"I suppose you want me to talk."

She nodded, and he let out a deep breath.

"I didn't lie to you earlier. I was a doctor, but I'm
not any longer. Not for seven years anyway. I was
twenty-seven and working in the emergency room in
University College Hospital. It was busy that night, but
not as bad as I'd seen it. A bus accident had injured
several people, and for some reason, the ambulances
brought them all to us. A little girl was brought in with
trouble breathing, and I checked her quickly. She
had a punctured lung, and we were losing her. She
was so little—I can still remember intubating her,
trying to get that pediatric tube down her throat. Her
mother was there, begging us to save her. We did
everything humanly possible. She died. Just like that.
We couldn't bring her back; we couldn't save her. She
was so little. The mother started screaming at us, begging us to bring her back."

Lawrence kept a tight grip on the wheel, his eyes
staring at the horizon so he wouldn't have to look at
Katherine, grateful that she'd remained silent. The
guilt of it, no matter how misplaced, had nearly de-
stroyed him. He'd tried to move past that moment,
but he couldn't. She'd been his first young patient
to die, and he found himself paralyzed by the sim-
plest things at the hospital; the most arcane problems were beyond his ability. Other doctors seemed
to get over similar instances, but he couldn't. The
nurses began talking about him, began questioning
his decisions, probably because he questioned himself constantly. What if he made a mistake? He

couldn't get over it, the fact that he'd been unable to save that little girl's life. He couldn't stop seeing those blue eyes looking at him, pleading with him to help; he couldn't stop seeing her little body, lifeless in her mother's arms.

"I don't dislike children," he said, finally looking at Katherine. He could tell by her face that she didn't expect him to say something like that. "I'm frightened to death of them, you see. They all become her."

"That's a terrible story. I'm so sorry that happened to you."

He looked at her and could see tears in her eyes and fell in love so hard he thought he just might cry right along with her. "It was a long time ago."

"I don't understand why nothing I read mentioned that you were a doctor."

"I wanted that part of my life put behind me. I never talked about it. I wanted to reinvent myself," he said. "I'm not a doctor anymore, and I have no desire to go back to that life."

"I saw how you saved Roy. I saw how hard that was for you, but you did it anyway. You were incredible. I can't believe you're that man I watched save another man's life. You're not the shallow jerk you try to make yourself out to be."

"That's where you're wrong, darling," he said, his voice going low. "I'm exactly that."

Kat and Larry didn't talk again except to communicate to get the boat into its slip. She just couldn't wrap her mind around the fact that Larry—playboy, hard-drinking, womanizing Larry—had been a doctor. He wasn't the selfish, self-centered, self-involved guy she'd thought he was. He was the opposite—at least he had been. A shrink would have a field day with him, she thought as she watched him secure the boat to the dock.

He was stone-faced and distant, and Kat knew why. She'd discovered his deep, dark secret . . . and it was a doozy. Brian's deep, dark secret, other than the fact that he was a class A jerk and she hadn't known it, was a drunk driving charge ten years ago. After Brian had told her, he'd been incredibly self-conscious about drinking in front of her, and he'd even accused her of counting his drinks. She hadn't been, had trusted that he'd learned his lesson, but he'd regretted telling her. There was no worse position to be in than a woman who knows a man's greatest fear and greatest failing.

"I'm going to take a taxi to the hospital," Larry said, finally looking at her. "You take the car and let Lila know what's happened."

"Okay."

He stood there looking blindly toward the water, his white shirt open at the throat, the tails sticking out of his shorts, his dark hair rumpled and wind-blown, and Kat had to force herself to look away. She wished she could hold him, take away just a tiny bit of his pain. But she wasn't his girlfriend; she wasn't his anything.

Larry didn't return to the cottage until after midnight. Kat was on the couch reading by the only lamp lit in the room, her feet tucked under her, a pillow on her lap. She was exhausted, but she refused to give in to it because she wanted to talk to Larry about Roy before she went to bed. When he came in, he gave her a weary smile and sat down next to her without a word. Then he lay down and rested his head on the pillow as if it was something he'd done a hundred times. Kat wasn't quite sure what to do with her hands, so she laid one tentatively across his chest and the other near the top of his head, barely touching his thick hair.

He took her arm and held it to him, closing his eyes briefly, and Kat had the oddest feeling that he must think she was someone else because this was far more intimate than their most heated kisses.

"Larry? You okay?"

"Not really. This has been one hell of a summer."

"No kidding. How's Roy?"

He squeezed her arm. "Roy's going to have to be transferred to Boston tomorrow. They want to make certain he's stable enough before they put him on a helicopter. He had another small attack after they got him to his room."

"Oh, no." Somehow, the hand near his head had started burrowing into his waves, and his eyes drifted close again.

"He'll be fine. Boston's got some terrific heart surgeons. He's got some major blockage apparently."

Something happened to Kat's heart as she looked down at him. It got a weird heaviness that felt slightly painful, and Kat frowned because she knew what her heart was doing, and she didn't like it. Or maybe she did, just a little. *Don't you dare fall in love with him. Don't. You. Dare.*

"You're tired," she managed to say.

He let out a long, low sound that vibrated the arm he held tightly across his chest.

A movement outside caught Kat's eye, and she realized Lila was on the way over. "Lila's coming," she said, getting tense. She didn't want Lila to see them cozied up on the couch together. Lila would definitely come to the wrong conclusion.

Instead of sitting up, Larry simply turned his head. "I'm too bloody tired to move, if that's what you're getting at," he said.

Lila saw them through the screen door, so she didn't bother knocking. "How is he?" she said, rushing over to the closest chair and sitting down. It was obvious from her red-rimmed eyes that Lila had been crying. "I just can't believe it. I can't." Her eyes welled up, and she dashed the tears away almost angrily.

Larry finally sat up, but he laid a hand on Kat's thigh where it sat warm and heavy. "They're going to transport him to Boston tomorrow, and he'll probably have open-heart surgery within days. Maybe as soon as Tuesday. He told me to tell you not to worry about the business. All the guests are listed in his register, and you can call and cancel."

"No," Lila said, looking horrified. "We can't do that." She bit her lip and looked to Kat. "Honey, you have to do me a big favor. You don't have to be home for any reason, do you?"

"Sadly, no," Kat said dryly. "I know where you're going. Of course I can help out at the bed and breakfast."

"I don't want you to help out; I want you to take over. There is no way on this earth I am going to let that man suffer through open-heart surgery alone. Stanley had that operation before he died, and I thank God every day that I was there by his side when things went wrong."

"Roy's a young man, Lila," Larry said firmly. "He's not going to die."

"And he's not going to be alone suffering either. It's a horrible and painful surgery, and he'll need someone there," Lila said, her voice like steel.

"Of course I'll take over the B&B," Kat said. It wasn't as if she had a job to go back to. Or a life.

"I'm sure you'll be a big help to Roy, Lila," Larry said. "But doesn't he have any relatives who could help out?"

Lila shook her head, and her eyes welled up again. "Roy's all alone. His parents died years ago, and he was an only child. You know about his wife."

"He doesn't have any children?" Kat asked.

"He's completely alone."

"Wow. That must suck," Kat said. She'd never really thought about how alone she'd be if her mother died. She was an only child, too. Her grandparents were still alive, but how long would that last? Someday, she was going to be like Roy, fifty-five years old, dying alone in a hospital without a single person in the world to care. "I never realized how alone he was." *How alone I am.*

Lila sniffed. "I didn't either. And there was something he said the other night that just tears me up inside. I thought he was content to live his life, to have his guests. Carl and I talked about it, about how happy he seemed living his life the way he wanted to. I thought he liked being alone."

"I did, too," Kat said, and Larry shifted uncomfortably, obviously not wanting to share his thoughts. "What did he say?"

"He said that he was the loneliest man on the island. Can you believe that? I just about cried right then and there and didn't know what to say. And now he could be dying alone in a hospital."

"He's not dying," Larry said forcefully. "He suffered a moderate heart attack. He's going to be transferred to one of the finest heart surgeons on the East Coast who is going to fix his heart, and he'll probably outlive us all."

"Alone," Kat said, shaking her head sadly.

"I wonder why he never remarried," Lila wondered out loud.

"Maybe she was it for him. His one love. Sometimes, you only fall in love once, and that's it."

"No. It's too easy to fall in love," Lila said, her voice wistful.

"Not for most people. I'm twenty-eight, and the only one I've ever loved was Brian, and now I'm not so sure that I even loved *him*. I think I just convinced myself I did. I never fell head over heels. I never lost my appetite or got all stupid over him like people say happens. We were never, ever like Thomas and Jocelyn." She shook her head, rejecting her own argument. "I'm pretty sure I loved him. I was going to marry him, for God's sake."

Larry chuckled, and when she looked at him, she saw that crooked grin that was so damned appealing.

"What's so funny?"

"Nothing," he said, putting on a straight face.

"No, no. Tell me Mister Relationship Expert."

Larry looked at Lila as if she was a partner. "When you fall in love, nearly every thought is of that person. You want to touch them constantly. You find yourself thinking of doing things that you wouldn't in a million years think of doing just to make that person happy. You love to make them smile, and you die a little when they cry. And when they love you back, you're in heaven."

"Oh, Lawrence," Lila said, tears again making an appearance to Kat's annoyance. "You're in love."

Larry gave Lila a startled look, then shook his head. "God no, I . . . no." He looked sheepish. "I think I read that in a book. Obviously, not one of mine."

Kat looked at him intensely, suspecting he was lying. Just that afternoon he'd told her he'd been in love. "You are a liar," Kat said with theatrics. "You told me you had fallen in love."

"I've decided that wasn't love, but a strange infatuation. A sickness," Larry said. "The whole part about the person in love having their love returned is vital to the equation. How could anyone be stupid enough to believe they are in love with someone who doesn't love them?"

"Unrequited love," Lila said dreamily.

"Is hell," Larry said.

"I wouldn't know," Lila said with irony, and they all laughed.

Chapter 13

Lila packed her bags, her hands shaking slightly. How many times had she kept watch over a hospital bed waiting for the man she loved to die? At least she didn't love Roy. *Not yet,* a small voice said in her ear.

She stopped momentarily, letting her hands rest in the soft silk of a camisole, and let out a long breath. Killer sat on her bed, looking at her with those big, sad eyes as if he knew what she was thinking. And what *was* she thinking? Roy was a friend— Carl's friend, for goodness' sake. She'd decided weeks ago that she would not remarry for at least five years. *Then you'll be thirty-eight, and your biological clock is already ticking.* Lila scowled fiercely, and Killer whined, so she reached over and gave him a reassuring rub behind his batlike ears.

"I have to do this," she told herself and Killer. She knew herself better than to think she could stop herself from falling in love with anyone if she was headed down that path.

Finding love had always been so easy for her. She loved all men, older men in particular, and her husbands most of all. No, she didn't love Roy, not with the all-consuming passion that she'd had for Carl, but she could sense it coming, knew that if she stayed by his side and nursed him back to health, it would be inevitable.

Lila abandoned her suitcase and went to the window to look out at the Atlantic. Windsurfers were taking advantage of an unusually high surf, riding waves and doing flips beneath a brilliant blue sky. She looked across to her house and was arrested by the sight of Lawrence standing in his tower window looking down with such vivid intensity it was almost frightening. Lila followed his gaze and took a startled breath when her eyes rested upon Kat sitting on the seawall, her legs outstretched in front of her, her arms braced behind her. Kat lifted her face to the sun, then looked out to the ocean, drawing up her knees to her chest and holding them against herself. Lila looked again at Lawrence and smiled. He had it bad, she thought. He stood still as a statue, his eyes never wavering from the woman below, his jaw tight, his body taut. Then he turned abruptly, almost angrily, and he was out of sight.

Lila hadn't thought much of it when she saw the two of them on the couch. They'd both been through an ordeal, and she'd sensed they had become friends long before she arrived. But now that she thought back on it, Kat had seemed uncomfortable while Lawrence had seemed relaxed, content. "Oh, Lawrence. She's your unrequited love, isn't she?" she said softly and swallowed down the pain in her throat.

* * *

Lawrence turned away from the window because he wasn't in the mood for torturing himself today. What the hell was happening to him?

And why the hell wasn't it happening to Katherine? He knew she found him attractive, maybe even liked him. She probably would go for that summer fling now if he teased her into it. But he didn't want a summer fling with her. He wanted her to love him and beyond that, he really didn't want to think at all. He had never put the word *marriage* anywhere near the name of a woman he'd been seeing, not even in his mind, and he wasn't about to start now, he decided. They hardly knew one another. How could he be thinking, even in the most abstract way, that they could marry?

"Oh, God," he groaned and felt his stomach twist. He'd gone and done it. He'd thought of Katherine and marriage, and now that thought was going to stay there and haunt him, ridicule him for the rest of his life. Downstairs, he could hear Jocelyn giggling and Thomas's hearty laugh and then a long silence. Those two were long gone, he thought. Thomas looked at Jocelyn as if he'd die if she was taken away from him. And she looked at him the same way. After just a few days!

The joke of it was, if he could, he'd look at Katherine that way. But she'd probably just run screaming from the room or laugh and tell him to stop it.

He dragged his hand through his hair and tried not to think about how nice it was when she'd put her hand there, gentle fingers caressing his head. He had to stop this nonsense; he had to get away from her, or he'd truly go mad from wanting her.

And she hadn't a clue.

He let out a long, shaky breath and stared at his laptop as if it were the enemy, not his own heart. A pair of feet bounded up the stairs, followed shortly by a loud knock.

"Hey, Lawrence," Thomas said through the door. "That lawyer is back with a court order. I let him in. Is that all right, then?"

"Shit. Yeah." He opened the door as he pulled on his shirt. "Do me a favor, and go get Lila next door."

"The blonde with the big . . ." Thomas made a gesture near his own chest.

"That's the one."

By the time Lawrence got downstairs, the lawyer had begun cataloguing items in the living room, but he paused for a rather long time to stare at the painting above the mantel.

"Getting a good long look?" came a soft voice from the front door.

"Mrs. McKnight," the attorney said, his cheeks flushing slightly. "I was trying to determine whether to include this picture on the list for the appraiser. But I don't suppose your in-laws would be interested in it."

"No, I don't suppose so. You have a court order?"

The attorney pulled it out, and Lila hardly glanced at it before handing it to Lawrence. "You take this, will you? I have to get to the airport. I'll call tonight and tell you how Roy's doing."

With that, Lila walked out the door, hardly even acknowledging the same lawyer she'd looked like she might murder the last time he'd come knocking.

The lawyer looked a bit dazed by her departure, but went back to work. "I shouldn't be more than an hour. The children are mostly interested in cataloguing the artwork." His eyes darted up to the provocative portrait before resting on his clipboard as he cleared his throat. "And the antiques and personal items. Photographs and the like."

"You can let yourself out?" Lawrence asked.

"Sure."

Katherine walked in then, her cheeks flushed from the sun, looking so beautiful Lawrence had to look away or else let every feeling he had show in his eyes. "Hi. Just thought I'd stop by and say good morning before I head over to the B&B. You need anything? Laundry done? Dusting?" She grinned at him, and he forced a smile.

"Hey, what's wrong?"

He shook his head. "I've just got to get working on my book, and nothing's coming," he lied.

"It will."

"I wish I had your faith." Small talk—and awkward small talk at that.

"You know, Larry, you're not the shallow little rich boy you pretended to be. If you'd just put a small amount of your real self into your books, they'd have a soul."

He looked to the ceiling as if asking for help from above, but he was secretly glad she had moved away from polite chitchat. "You save one life, and she's nominating you for sainthood."

"Ha-ha. I'm just saying that there's more to you than beautiful women and fast cars."

Lawrence pretended to be wounded. "Please don't be so cruel. Fast women and beautiful cars are all I've cared about for seven years."

"I said beautiful women and fast cars."

"The other is so much more appealing," he said

with all the charm he could muster. And he thought, *No wonder she thinks I'm a jerk. I am.*

"I guess I'm glad to see that what most people would have regarded as a life-altering event has left you completely unfazed. I'll see you later."

Don't let her go. Don't. He screamed it inside his head even as he gave her a jaunty little wave. He turned toward the stairs hating himself, hating his agent, hating the world. And as he took that first step toward spending the rest of the morning staring at his computer and personal torture device, it came to him. He sat down on the third step, a look of wonder on his face, like a man seeing a miracle. And then he bounded up the stairs two at a time, threw open his laptop, and waited impatiently for it to boot up. And then he started writing.

Kat had just finished cleaning the last of Roy's four guest rooms when she heard the ding at the front desk that told her his new guests had arrived two hours earlier than check-in time. "I'll be right with you," she called down. She was wearing her ratty jeans, so she made a mad dash up to the top floor to change into a pair of clean capris before flying down to meet the guests.

Kat let the young couple check in and helped take their bags to their room on the second floor. "I'm Kat. Roy Baxter, the owner, is going to be in the hospital for a few days, so if something isn't to your liking, don't blame poor Roy."

Kat showed them the room and was about to head back to the third floor bathroom when the woman stopped her. "We thought the rooms had bath-rooms," she said.

"They do. Each guest room has its own bath. This one's yours," Kat said, pointing to the door opposite their room.

"It's not inside the room?"

Kat looked at the bathroom and then at the woman. "Um-m, no. It's across the hall."

"We thought it was in the bedroom."

Kat wondered how long she was going to have to stand in the hallway and have this discussion.

"Honey, it doesn't matter. We have our own bath. Who cares if it's across the hall."

"I do."

The man pulled the woman into the room with an apologetic look to Kat. "Well, do you want to stay somewhere else?" he whispered, but Kat heard him clearly.

"No. I guess not," she said to him. "It's fine. But I thought the bath was in the room."

Kat smiled while she envisioned herself stuffing the woman's head in the toilet. "Sorry."

The woman let out a huff and closed the door, and Kat chucked her the bird . . . or rather gave the door the bird. She realized she liked cleaning houses because most of the time, the owners planned for her to be there when they were not. No wonder Roy liked his martinis.

Kat finished cleaning the third story bathroom and went down to dust and vacuum the small lounge Roy had set up to make the place seem more like an intimate hotel. His apartment was in the back of the house, away from the view, Kat realized. The guests were allowed the run of the place, including the kitchen, large living room, and dining room, where Roy put out a basic breakfast of bagels, muffins, scrambled eggs, bacon, sausage, coffee, and juice. At least it seemed basic when Roy was doing it. She knew he had the muffins and bagels delivered daily, but the rest of it was going to be tough for Kat, who admittedly was not the best cook in the world. She felt like gathering the guests together and apologizing ahead of time that the level of service they'd been receiving would not be forthcoming.

Kat checked the guest book to make certain she knew who was where, who was leaving tomorrow, and who was coming in. That's when she realized she'd have to move out of the third-floor room the next day. "Damn." She'd just have to shuttle from one house to the other and let the guests know where they could find her. She was going to have to do that anyway because she'd promised Lila she'd take care of Killer, and she couldn't keep the dog at the B&B because she couldn't be sure to keep him out of trouble.

After breakfast and checkout, the guests were mostly on their own. Roy had a kiosk full of pamphlets giving people ideas of what to do and where to go. Nearly every restaurant in Oak Bluffs and Vineyard Haven had given him a menu to display.

Kat looked around the place and decided all was in order, despite the bathroom debacle, and went next door to check on things there. The first thing she saw was Thomas and Jocelyn making out on the couch like a couple of teenagers. When she walked in, they pulled apart slowly, both dazed and flushed.

"Sorry to interrupt," Kat said, feeling like she didn't belong in either house. "Have you seen Larry?"

"Last I knew he was up in his room working. Actually heard the keyboard being used," Thomas said, then looked at Jocelyn with a huge grin. "Jocelyn is coming to England with me. As soon as she can get a visa, she's coming over. We're to be married."

"You're kidding," Kat said and looked at Jocelyn to make sure he wasn't joking. "Wow."

"Yeah. My parents are freaking out," she said to Kat, then turned to Thomas, her voice all soft. "My parents are going to love you. They just have to get used to the idea of me being in England."

"Wow."

"I know it's fast," Jocelyn said, tearing her eyes away from Thomas. "But we've both been dating forever, and we're done."

"Done," Thomas echoed, giving her a kiss.

"You must think we're insane. We are insane," she said with utter joy. "What are the chances I would be on the island at the same time Thomas was? That I would see Lawrence and come over to talk to him and see him and—"

"Fall in love," Thomas finished. "Amazing."

Kat should have felt slightly ill by the display, but instead what she felt was complete and devastating envy. Why couldn't someone fall in love with her like that? Had anyone ever looked at her the way Thomas was looking at Jocelyn? It almost gave her the chills. She knew for a fact that Brian had never looked at her that way. And she had never looked at him that way either. It was as if the entire world had disappeared but for the two of them. Kat wanted to be cynical, to say to herself that it would never last. But she couldn't. Instead, she was awed by them. They weren't teenagers falling in "love" for the first time. They weren't victims of raging hormones, though Kat was quite sure they were playing a big role.

"Good for you," she said.

"Good for us," Thomas repeated.

"Are Emma and Clarice around?"

"I thought they were with you, actually. Weren't they on the boat with you when Roy had his attack?" Thomas asked.

"No. They decided it was going to be too boring for them. I hope they're all right."

"Those two are like cats. They always land on their feet."

Kat left the two alone, wondering when she'd abandoned the idea of a solitary vacation licking her wounds. What was the point of having a household of people if there was no one to talk to? Eyeing the phone, she dialed her mother and told her the sad news about Roy.

"Lila called me and told me all about it," Barbara said. "That Lawrence sounds like something."

"He used to be a doctor. Thank God he was on that boat." Kat didn't think she was breaking a confidence telling her mother Larry's secret since they were never going to meet.

"A doctor," Barbara said with emphasis. She was of the generation where finding a doctor to marry was every girl's ultimate goal.

"Used to be," Kat said. "Now he's a writer."

"Oh. A writer. I've never heard of him," she said, inferring he must not have much money. This from her mother, who thought a night at the Motel 6 was high living.

"Well, he's not John Grisham, but he's had a few

books published. Real serious stuff." Kat paused, wondering if her mother had learned anything else about Brian and his wife. "Have you seen Brian?" she asked, trying to sound casual.

"Actually, he stopped by here yesterday with some things of yours. A couple of CDs, a DVD, a sweater."

Kat furrowed her brow. "A sweater?"

"A big Irish wool cardigan. It's gorgeous."

Kat's gut churned. "I made him that sweater. I worked six months on the damned thing."

"Well, you've got it back now."

Kat wanted to tell her mother to burn it, but she'd loved that sweater by the time she'd finished. If it hadn't been so big, she might have kept it for herself. As it was, she couldn't remember Brian ever wearing it, though he'd claimed he had.

"You know, sweetie, you don't need a man to be happy."

"I know that. But it is nice."

"Only when he's nice."

Kat bit her lip for a second and listened to dead air.

"Mom?"

"Still here."

"Were you ever lonely? I was a kid, and it seemed to me you always had a boyfriend."

Barbara let out a low chuckle. "Kept hoping to find Mr. Right, I guess. Sure I was lonely, even with all those men. Probably because I had all those men. Wrong men can make a woman lonelier than no man. But I had you, so it wasn't so bad. You've got plenty of time, sweetie."

"Oh, I'm not worried," Kat said quickly. "It's just that I haven't been single in a long time. And there are these two people here who met less than a week ago and are getting married. That sort of stuff, plus Brian dumping me, is making me feel—"

"Like a class A loser?"

"I wasn't going to say that, but thanks, Mom."

Her mother laughed her rough smoker's laugh, and Kat decided to change the subject. "Did Lila tell you I might be staying on the island a bit longer because of Roy?"

"No, but I assumed you would since you're taking over the B&B. I wish I could help, honey, but I've already used up all my vacation time, and Sal would throw a conniption if I asked for more."

"Don't worry. So far I'm handling things okay, though I haven't had to make breakfast yet."

"You have to cook?"

"Yes," Kat said, sounding slightly ill. "Just eggs and bacon and stuff. I should be able to handle that."

"Just call if you need me," Barbara said. "I have to get ready for work."

Kat hung up and sighed. It was pretty sad when talking to your mom about your ex-fiancé and his new wife was the highlight of your day.

By mid-afternoon, Larry still hadn't made an appearance, so Kat decided to take him a sandwich. From the other side of his door, she could hear only the sound of typing.

"Larry? I brought you something to eat."

The typing stopped abruptly. "Leave it there, please."

Kat stared at the door. "The bread will get stale."

A chair scraped on the hardwood floor, and Larry

pulled the door open, looking slightly insane. His hair was sticking up at all angles, he needed a shave, his eyes were all glassy and bloodshot, and his shirt was more rumpled than usual.

"Hi," she said, offering the small tray. "You look like shit."

He gave her a crooked grin. "Thanks." He looked at her, then down to the food as if he'd never seen her or a sandwich before in his life. "I'm writing," he said vaguely.

"Yes. I could hear the typing."

Then he smiled at her, and her heart felt as if it were going to explode. "I'm writing," he repeated.

"Now you're eating," she said and pushed the tray to him. "You can't write if you pass out from lack of food."

"What time is it?"

"About two-thirty."

He rubbed a hand through his hair absently, giving Kat a big clue as to how it had gotten so messy. "Five hours," he muttered. "It flew by."

"Eat, Mr. Writer."

He grabbed the tray and gave her another brilliant smile before closing the door. "I'll be back around seven with dinner if you're still up here."

"Fine."

Two hours later, Kat looked out from the porch and watched as a huge yacht went by the house. She was drawn to it because it appeared to be some sort of tourist party boat. Loud music throbbed from the yacht as it slowly passed by, and the deck was covered with people. Above the music, Kat heard a woman's excited scream, the kind one lets out when she sees a rock star. There on the boat were Emma and

Clarice, clad in skimpy bikinis, jumping up and down and waving to Kat as if they were best buddies. They had found their fun apparently.

Three stories up, Lawrence was dimly aware of the music and women screeching. His fingers ached, his eyes burned, but his brain was on fire. His fingers could not keep up with the words streaming from his mind. It was incredible, a miracle. He didn't stop to reread anything—just forged on, writing, writing, not knowing what he was doing, not caring, really. His half-eaten sandwich lay forgotten on the desk next to him. He'd never written like this in his life. He'd always been very methodical, working on each sentence as if it was a piece of art. He examined each word, read over each paragraph again and again to make certain it said precisely what he wanted it to say. He'd always scoffed at writers who claimed to have written a novel in a weekend. Maybe so, but it was likely trash, he thought.

Now he understood the passion. This was different from anything he'd ever experienced. This, he thought, his heart beating hard in his chest, had a soul all its own.

Chapter 14

Open heart surgery. *God damn.* Roy hadn't been in a hospital since his wife died, and he still couldn't believe his heart was diseased. He didn't smoke, he had one drink a day like all those doctors were saying was okay now, he wasn't overweight, and he ate okay. He liked fried food too much maybe, but he was trim. Okay, so he didn't exercise; he was active enough taking care of the bed and breakfast.

"It's likely hereditary," his doctor had told him. Roy didn't want any "likelies"; he wanted to know precisely what had happened and why. He didn't like the hereditary part because that meant he was stuck with whatever he had. But the doctor was probably right. His father had died young, and he'd never known his grandfather on his father's side. He was too young to be old.

"Hey there."

Lila's soft, breathy voice drew him away from his morbid thoughts. "You didn't have to come," he said, knowing he sounded surly. He really didn't want her here, seeing him in his hospital gown all helpless.

"Yes, I did. I will not let you go through this by yourself," she said in what Roy suspected was her best stern voice.

"You planning to join me at the operating table?"

"I would if I could."

Yeah, she probably would, he thought. "Who's minding the store?"

"Kat." Roy winced. "She shouldn't do that much damage, and for certain she'll keep the place spotless."

"But I could be in here for a week or more," he said. "Kat can't handle that place alone that long."

"Sure she can. Don't forget—she ran her own business for years."

"What happened to it?"

Lila waved a hand dismissively. "She got sued for killing one of her client's dogs. No one ever complained about her professionalism."

"I suppose she'll be fine," Roy said grudgingly. "I don't have a dog." He hated this. Hated lying here waiting, hated having his business being run by someone else. Hated feeling old. Hated the fact that he might die far sooner than he'd thought. Hated that now he knew how his wife had felt, angry and sad and helpless. Hated especially Lila looking down at him and feeling sorry for him.

"You don't have to stay. Go back and help Kat out. You'll be doing far more for me there than here."

Lila sat on the room's only chair and folded her arms. "I'm not going anywhere."

"I don't want you here," he insisted.

"Too bad. You are not going through this alone."

He was startled to see her eyes well up, which made him feel like a jerk. When Lila cried, her features became exaggerated. Her eyes looked impossibly bigger; her mouth became even more red; and with her arms folded like that, certain other assets appeared rather larger as well.

"What if something bad happens, Roy?" she whispered.

"You don't want to be here for that. Seeing another person die is something you don't need right now."

"You can't be alone." Lila reached over and took one of his hands. "I want to be here. I'll go crazy back at your cottage knowing you're here by yourself. If you won't let me stay for you, let me stay for me."

How could a man say no to her? Roy was definitely a man, and he couldn't bring himself to send her away. Not with her soft hand in his, not with her eyes still sparkling from unshed tears.

"All right. Stay if you want."

Lila beamed him a smile and gave him a quick peck on his forehead. "Okay. Now you have to give me a shopping list. You'll need shaving equipment, books, magazines. Tell me what you want."

He wanted to be left alone, actually. But he couldn't tell her that either, because if he did, she might cry again and he sure as hell didn't want her to do that. Instead, he gave her a list of things he needed, and off she went, happy to be helping. Roy thought he'd be glad when she was gone, but the room seemed far emptier than it had when she'd been there. And he could still smell her damn perfume. Woman wore too much of the stuff. He breathed in slowly, let his eyes drift closed, and smiled.

* * *

"Larry?"

The typing stopped.

"It's almost nine o'clock."

"Thanks," he called through the door, and then she heard the typing again.

"You want anything to eat?" Type, type, type. "Larry."

She heard his sigh through the door. "No. Thanks."

Kat made a face at the door and headed down the stairs only to bump into Emma and Clarice, sunburned and obviously drunk.

"Hello," Emma said. "Did you see us on the yacht?"

"Hard to miss," Kat said, moving to the side to scoot around them and down the stairs.

"Where's Lawrence?"

"Working. He doesn't want to be disturbed," she said, hoping the two were sober enough to heed her warning.

"Working? We're meeting friends in Edgartown tonight, and we need him to drive us. He's the only one with a car, and we don't want to drive."

"Too drunk," Clarice said and giggled. "Wouldn't want to kill anyone by driving the wrong way. Bloody confusing the way you Americans drive on the wrong side of the road."

Emma moved past Kat in a loose-limbed way calling loudly for Larry.

Larry opened his door, not bothering to hide his irritation. "I'm working," he said.

"He's working," Emma said and giggled. "It's our holiday, Lawrence. You invited us here to be with you, and we haven't even seen you. We've seen more of your roommate than of you. You must come out with us," Emma said, putting on a big pout.

"I'm working, ladies. Katherine will take you out."

Both women turned toward Kat, who was frantically shaking her head.

"What a brilliant idea. You're sober, aren't you?"

"Very," Kat said dryly.

"Well then, it's settled. You can drive."

"I really don't want to go out tonight. It's late. Besides, I have to be here in case something happens at the B&B."

The two women looked at her as if she was quite mad. "It's not even ten o'clock," Clarice said.

"I have to take the dog for a walk right before bed," she said, thinking she had come up with a clincher.

"I'll take Killer for a walk," Larry said, surprising her. "Katherine. Take them. Please. I'll be here in case one of your guests has a problem. You'll probably see half of them out in town."

Kat gave him a look that told him he would pay dearly for making her take his drunken friends out to a bar. "I thought you didn't want them corrupting me?"

"This time I want your goodness to rub off on them. Please?"

"Let me at least change into something better," she said, unable to resist him any longer.

"There's a girl," Emma said. Kat figured she was the less drunk of the two, which wasn't saying much at all. "You never know, maybe you'll meet the man of your dreams tonight."

"Maybe."

* * *

He was gorgeous. The man of her very sexy dreams. And he was Italian. From Italy, not the Bronx, with deep brown eyes. Thick, wavy hair; and an accent that made her knees melt just to hear it. He was also so obviously looking for a one-night stand, it was almost comical.

"I'm not sleeping with you," she said.

"Who said anything about sleeping?" he said, his smile slow, his accent delicious.

Every once in a while, Emma would sidle up to her and give her a nudge as if pushing her toward Enzo's bed. Two more drinks, and she just might.

"Water, please," she said to the bartender. Enzo hovered behind her, using his entire body to entice her, and it was working. Kat had never in her life picked up a man in a bar, and she wasn't going to start now. But this sure was fun. He had a way of making her feel as if she was the most beautiful woman in the entire bar. Maybe his radar had picked up the desperate woman bleep emanating from her.

"You smell incredible," he said, his voice soft and low by her ear, making her shiver.

"Irish Spring," she said, putting the glass quickly up to her mouth before he could lean in and kiss her.

"You do not find me attractive, *si?*"

"You are very attractive, Enzo. And you know it."

"And you are *bellissima*. Beautiful."

Kat couldn't put her finger on just what her problem was. She was single, available, and not completely averse to spending a passionate night with a man who could have posed for Michelangelo's David. She could tell because he had his shirt unbuttoned to the navel. Just because she'd never in her life had a one night stand didn't mean she couldn't.

She sighed. She couldn't. And she knew why. If she took Enzo home, beautiful, sexy Enzo with his smoldering brown eyes and perfectly cut abs . . . Kat shook her head to get back on track. If she took Enzo home, Larry would know, and for some reason, that bothered her. A lot. It bothered her as much as it would bother her if Larry brought a woman home for a one-nighter. And of course, that meant she'd allowed her heart to get involved a bit more than she wanted to, given Larry's blasé attitude toward her.

"I can make you come," he whispered into her ear, and Kat thought if he did that again, she just might. She looked at him, and he was smiling because he truly thought he was winning this game. Kat might not be able to turn off her body, but she definitely could not turn off her brain or her heart. Kat smiled back, and Enzo flashed even more white teeth.

"I'm sure you can," she said. "But I'm not having sex with you."

He put on a little boy pout that probably had charmed a hundred women but was doing nothing for her. And then his face changed, the "ah-h-h" moment, so to speak.

"You," he said, pointing a long, well-manicured finger at her, "are in love. *Amore*. Ah, no wonder. I was thinking it was something wrong with me. But that is impossible, no?"

Kat laughed aloud. "You're something else, Enzo. No, I'm not in love."

He looked wounded again, then his face cleared. "You are one of those lesbians?"

"Enzo. No."

"Then it is *amore.*"

"You're that good, huh?"

"I am very good. You are the first woman I have met who told me to go away." He seemed awed by the idea. "He must be very handsome."

"Very."

"Who's handsome?" Emma asked, coming up behind her.

"Larry," Kat said without thinking.

"Who? Oh, Lawrence." Emma was scary drunk, and Kat could only imagine how toasted Clarice was.

"Where's Clarice?"

"She was looking a bit green so she went to the WC."

"She's being sick?"

"Oh," Emma said, pointing in the general direction of the ladies' room. "There she is now."

Clarice was walking in a curved line toward them.

"I think I better take my friends home now. 'Bye Enzo."

"*Arrivederci,*" he said. The way he said it, all drawn out and rolling those Rs, was almost enough to make Kat reconsider. She began walking toward the door, grabbing Clarice along the way, and looked back just to see if she was being a complete idiot. Enzo was already talking to another woman who'd been sitting at the bar near them, and Kat thanked the big guy above that she'd had enough sense to say no.

It was midnight before Lawrence stopped writing for the day. The only break he'd gotten was taking Killer out for a much abbreviated walk. He physically couldn't write anymore. His fingers were cramped, his neck ached, and he was hungry as hell. He made his way downstairs hoping there was something in the refrigerator other than leftover pizza. Despite his vow not to eat another bite of the stuff, no one else seemed inclined to actually cook a meal, including himself. No pizza, but there were three large bagels left over from breakfast next door that Katherine had put in the fridge. He downed two while standing in the kitchen before grabbing the last beer.

Lawrence heard the three women long before he actually saw them. He could tell Emma and Clarice were arguing loudly about something, but he couldn't quite make out the subject before Katherine managed to shush them as they were climbing up the porch.

"How was your night out?" Lawrence asked when they all came in the door, Katherine sort of pushing the other two women in front of her.

"Great," Katherine said. "I got propositioned by a gorgeous man from Milan, and these two threw up in your rental car. It was just lovely."

"You were propositioned?" Lawrence asked.

"M-m-m-h-m-m-m. The car's a mess."

"You obviously said no," he said, peering around her as if expecting to see her Italian. He was also losing the battle of trying not to let the image of some guy mauling Katherine get to him.

"He's leaving tomorrow, so I guess it would have been one of those long distance romances. I seem to be attracting that sort of attention lately," she said pointedly.

"Yes, well, I meant an entire summer, not some sordid one-night stand."

"A man of high moral fiber."

"I think I'm going to be sick again," Emma said, and Katherine led her quickly to the bathroom, where she was, indeed, very sick. Clarice didn't look much better, but at least she managed to make it to the second-floor bathroom before vomiting.

When both women were upstairs and more or less in their beds, Katherine came back down the stairs looking like she'd taken a large bite out of a very sour lemon.

"Did I tell you how much I appreciate you taking the women out for me?" he asked, trying to sound sincere.

"No. You didn't. Not that it would matter. Those two should be locked up in a detox tank for their own good. You would not believe the amount of alcohol those two consumed. And they were already drunk."

"Yes," he said, scrubbing at his unshaved face. "That's what passes for fun for those two."

"And if you think I'm going to clean out your car—"

"I'll do it," he said quickly, but just the thought of it nearly sent him into dry heaves. "Tomorrow. So. Tell me about your brush with Italy."

"Oh. Nothing. Just this guy who was coming on to me."

"And you weren't interested?" he said, feeling his entire body tense.

"Of course I was interested. You'd have to be dead not to be interested. Or a guy. He was beyond hot, and he had this incredible accent."

"I have an accent."

"And these brown eyes you could drown in. Like rich dark chocolate."

"I have brown eyes," he said, widening them so she could see the color.

"Actually, yours have gold specks, so they're not quite plain brown. And, God, he smelled so good."

"I . . ." He stopped because he was quite certain after a long day writing in his rather stuffy room that he did not smell very good. "I can smell good."

Katherine laughed. "This isn't a competition. You have your charms."

"Do tell."

She held up her hands as if ready to count off his attributes. "Um. You, um. You don't have bad teeth," she said as if happy to have come up with something.

He gave her a deadpan stare.

"You still have all of your hair," she said hopefully.

He drew a self-conscious hand up to his head. He knew she was just teasing, but this conversation was beginning to grate on his nerves.

"Are you telling me you don't find me at all attractive? You told me on the boat you thought I was beautiful."

"I was tipsy. And I said you were pretty."

"I see."

She began laughing. "Oh, come on, Larry. You know you're gorgeous. You don't need me to tell you."

"Perhaps I do," he said far more seriously than he'd meant to.

She gave him a thoughtful look, then smiled as if getting the joke. "Okay. You're very, very okay-looking."

"Good night, Katherine."

"Oh, come on. I was just kidding you. You and I

both know you're the best-looking man who's ever kissed me."

He stopped dead. "You kissed the Italian?"

Kat had a sneaking suspicion that he might actually be jealous so she pretended to think. "Well, do you mean did I kiss him or did he kiss me?"

"You met him tonight," he said, full of sincere outrage.

"Yes. I can understand your moral outrage given that you propositioned me within hours of meeting me. What really is the definition of sex anyway? It's all so blurred nowadays." She was having such fun torturing him.

"You . . . you . . ."

"I . . . I . . . what?"

"I don't know quite what to say to you," he said, sounding incredibly prudish.

Kat had had enough of his judgment. "You know what? I am just kidding. He didn't kiss me, and I didn't kiss him, but he invited himself over several times, and I said no every time. And you know what else? It's none of your business, is it, Mr. Summer Fling Man?"

His nostrils flared, and Kat could tell he was actually getting angry. "That was a mistake," he bit out.

"Was it ever."

"But not for the reasons you think. It was a mistake because I . . ." He stopped and swallowed. "I need to go to bed now. I'm tired." He began walking toward the stairs. "I'm sorry I judged you. I have no right."

Kat watched him walk up the stairs and felt terrible that what had started as fun banter had ended up as a fight. She didn't want to be angry with Larry.

"Larry," she called and ran up the stairs to where he was. "I'm sorry. I didn't mean to tease you like that. I guess I wanted you to know that you're not the only one who could leave a bar with someone." As she said it, she realized it was the truth.

"But you didn't leave with him."

"Naw. But I could have." She gave him a tentative smile. "But I didn't because I knew how devastated you would be," she said airily.

"Very considerate."

Kat put a hand on the stair railing and looked up at Larry. He had circles beneath his eyes, and his hair was more disheveled than usual. He looked exhausted.

"Have you heard from Roy or Lila tonight?" she asked, purposefully changing the subject.

"As a matter of fact, I called the hospital earlier and spoke with Roy. Apparently, he's scheduled for bypass surgery tomorrow morning. Lila is a mess, and he asked that one of us come and get her."

"Lila tends to be a bit of a worrier. I'm sure she means well."

"He actually didn't sound as if he meant it. I heard Lila yelling in the background for us not to come. At least I suppose it was her attempt at yelling. I think he was teasing her."

Kat wanted to linger and talk some more, but she was tired and had to get up with the sun to make the guests breakfast. That day's fare hadn't been completely inedible, but Kat noticed most guests had grabbed the bagels and muffins and stayed away from the sausages, which apparently were undercooked, and the bacon, which was dry and crumbly.

"Guess I'll head to bed," she said. "Good night." Something in his stance made her pause. "What?"

"Do you realize it's been more than a week since we kissed?"

"Really. We resisted that long?" Kat said, her tone teasing.

"Now why is that?"

"I suppose we both decided it would be better just to be friends. If I recall, you didn't want to complicate things while your friends were here."

"I never said that."

"Yes, you did. And then you kissed me. I think you're just looking for attention," Kat said, crossing her arms over her chest when she noticed his eyes had dipped to her breasts.

"I'm looking for a kiss."

"What happens if you go more than a week without kissing a woman? Your lips fall off?"

Larry laughed. She loved his laugh, all throaty and deep. "I shall die if you do not kiss me, milady."

Kat pretended to shiver. "O-o-oh, you do that so well."

"I also kiss well."

"You do. All right, then. Let's kiss and get it over with so I can get some sleep." She trudged up the stairs to the landing where he was standing, as if the last thing she wanted to do was press her lips against his strong, sexy mouth. Then she stood before him, arms straight down, closed her eyes, and pursed her lips.

"What are you doing?"

"Waiting for my kiss," she said without opening her eyes. It was hard to maintain pursed lips because she wanted to smile. She waited a bit more before opening her eyes.

He scratched his head. "Well, this isn't very spontaneous."

"I'm sorry. How's this?" She launched herself into his arms, her legs wrapped around his waist, making him stumble back to the wall and forcing him to hold her. His arms came around her, holding her against him as she put her hands around his neck and leaned back so she could see his expression. His eyes were smiling as they dipped to her mouth, and then he wasn't smiling at all.

Without a word, he turned so her back was to the wall and he let her legs slide slowly to the floor as he moved closer, pressing himself against her. Still, he hadn't kissed her, he just looked at her as if . . . Kat must have been imagining things because no one had ever looked at her quite that way before. Then he put a hand to the side of her face, the way sexy men did in the movies, making the beautiful heroine's face seem delicate and impossibly feminine, and Larry was doing that to her. His thumb moved along her cheek, then gently touched her bottom lip, and all the while, his eyes tracked his own movements as if he were fascinated by her. He moved his other hand to her face and pulled gently so that their lips met in the most soul-shattering kiss Kat had ever experienced in her entire life. He pulled back, and the smallest smile touched his mouth.

"Thank you, Katherine."

Kat took a deep breath. "You're welcome. Any time." *And while you're at it, you might lead me up to your bed because, honey, all it would take would be for you to crook your index finger at me, and I'd be there.*

His smile widened. "You know, I might take you up on that."

To Kat's great disappointment, he pulled back, and she resisted grabbing him and yanking his head down for another long, wet one. "Good night, Larry."

"Good night."

Kat watched him walk up the stairs, then resigned herself to another night alone in her bed. It never really bothered her before, not even when she and Brian were apart, but lately alone felt so darned lonely. Kat smiled when she thought back on what her mother had said about not needing a man to be happy. It was true. Of course it was. But couldn't she be happy *and* have a good man? She mentally crossed Larry off her good man list. He was handsome, intelligent, a great kisser. A phenomenal kisser. But what he wanted was a summer fling, and Kat knew she couldn't do that. She liked Larry, but she didn't believe for an instant that he truly thought she was any more special than any of the other leagues of women he'd been with. Besides, he seemed to be hung up on that unrequited love thing.

No. Larry was a great kisser and was probably fantastic in bed, but he was not the man for her. Kat sighed, wondering if she could ditch her emotions and just go for the pleasure. It would be nice, she thought, stretching out naked beside a guy like Larry. Those magic hands, those incredible lips, endless muscles, furry chest.

"Damn," she said as she pulled on the oversized T-shirt she slept in. If only she didn't like him so much, then having sex with him would be so much easier. Kat laughed out loud at that ridiculous thought, even though it had become strangely true.

Chapter 15

Roy lay in a hallway outside the operating room, scared out of his mind but too sedated to throw off his IV and make a run for it. Lila had said goodbye to him in his room, telling him firmly in that wispy voice of hers that she'd see him in a few hours. He probably would see her. But as routine as open heart surgery had become, people still died on the operating table. Doctors encountered problems they hadn't detected through examination; hearts were weaker than suspected. He might die, he thought, and he couldn't garner even a good bout of panic anymore thanks to the drugs they'd given him to relax.

He closed his eyes briefly and opened them when he felt a hand on his arm. "Sara, you're not supposed to be here," he said, then realized he'd never said a truer statement. How could his wife, looking young and beautiful, be standing next to his bed smiling down at him? Her long brown hair skimmed his hand as she leaned toward him, her eyes crinkling up at the corners just the way he remembered.

"I just thought I'd see you off," she said.

He frowned. "See me off to where? Am I going to die?" he asked, figuring she might know since in his best recollection, she was already dead.

"Supper's in the fridge. I've got to get the baby at my mother's."

His eyes drifted closed as he fought to stay awake. "We don't have a baby, honey. We never could."

"We have a baby. She's just not here yet. You'll see. She's beautiful."

Even in his drowsy state, he realized how impossible this conversation was. "Sara, honey, you're dead."

Her smile widened. "I know that, silly." And then her smile disappeared, and she leaned down and kissed him on the forehead. "But you're alive."

Roy finally succumbed to the weights that were pulling on his eyelids. He wanted to talk some more to his wife; he wanted to hold her, to bury his face in her hair, but he couldn't fight the drugs any longer. When he felt a touch on his arm again, he forced himself to open his eyes just a little.

"Mr. Baxter," said a nurse, "we're going to wheel you into the operating room. How are you feeling?"

He tried to ask her where his wife was, but he couldn't seem to move his lips. Instead, the only thing that came out was a grunt.

"Okay. Here we go."

The next thing he remembered was waking up on a respirator and wishing he could yank the thing out of his throat.

"Sh-h-h. The nurse said they'll be back in a few minutes to take it out. Can you make it that long?"

Roy looked over, saw Lila, and managed to nod. She put a hand on his arm in almost the precise place his wife had right before the operation. With a startling realization, he knew he must have been dreaming or having a drug-induced hallucination. But seeing Sara had seemed so real. He swore he had even smelled her shampoo. Prell. She'd always used Prell.

"You did really well, Roy. Thank God they brought you in because they found an aneurysm."

Roy widened his eyes.

"It would only have been a matter of time," she said, and her eyes welled up. Lila, he thought, was far too soft. She hardly knew him, and here she was crying at the thought that he might have died.

"Ma'am, you're going to have to leave while we remove the respirator."

"Okay. He's definitely ready. He tried to take it out himself," she said. Then Lila bent down to him and pressed a kiss against his forehead. "I'll see you in a little while." Her lips were soft and warm like the rest of her, and he decided then and there to stop fighting it. If Lila wanted to fuss over him, to make certain he wasn't alone, he'd let her. At least until he could get back to normal.

"He's fine," Lila said, her hand squeezing the phone. "He's awake, and they're taking out the respirator as we speak, which is really a big hurdle."

"That's terrific," Kat said.

"Is everything good there?"

"I'm actually getting the hang of this breakfast stuff. This time the sausages were actually edible, although I still have to work on the bacon and eggs."

"I knew you could do it," Lila said. "Roy's going to

be in intensive care for another day. Depending on how he does, he should be home within a week or so. Are you sure you can handle things?"

"Roy's really organized with his books. I should be fine. Tell him all is well, but I want him back here as soon as possible."

"I will." Lila slowly hung up the phone and closed her eyes. She was exhausted. The night of the operation she hadn't slept at all, and she'd come to a realization. She could not, would not go through this again with someone she loved. She'd vowed to stay single. She'd buried three husbands, and she'd be damned if she did it again. Lila knew her heart could not take it one more time. Just being here with Roy, who she didn't even love, was tearing her apart. She'd help him through the worst of it. She'd make sure he was ready to run his business, and then she'd go back to California and live safely alone.

If she wanted a child, she could adopt one or visit a sperm bank. Lord knew she could afford to support herself and a dozen children with all the money she had. Lila was not a spender, and she'd found she had a talent for making good investments and hiring the right people to make certain those investments kept going. She could live independently for years and years. She didn't need a husband, and she didn't want one.

Lila knew that wasn't true. She loved men, but she refused to lose another one. Her heart was mush, her soul shattered. She had to stay away from all men who endangered her, and that would have to include Roy. He didn't fawn over her like most men. She'd never caught him staring at her breasts or getting all tongue-tied around her. He didn't flatter her or put her on a pedestal. But she liked Roy, and she had a sneaking suspicion that despite his gruff demeanor, he liked her, too. Which meant they were both halfway in love, and that was very, very bad.

A nurse buzzed herself out of intensive care and walked over to her. "Are you Lila?" She nodded. "Mr. Baxter is asking for you."

Lila wanted to tell the nurse to go away, but she nodded and walked through the doors with her. This is the last time, she thought, that I walk toward a hospital bed and worry about a man. Then she walked around the corner, sidestepped a large piece of equipment, and saw Roy, partially sitting up with a smile on his handsome mug.

"Hey, beautiful."

And Lila knew at that moment, she was doomed.

That morning, in Lila's island cottage, two women were in far more pain than Roy, and they only had themselves to blame. Kat had been up for hours when Emma and Clarice came gingerly down the stairs looking like two overused whores.

"Stop breathing so loud," Emma told Clarice. They both clutched their heads and went directly to the living room couch where they sat down.

Kat was dust mopping the hardwood floors, full of energy and health, which made the two women on the couch frown at her fiercely.

"Must you act so chipper?" Clarice asked.

"I must," Kat said, then jogged out to the porch and banged out the dust.

When she returned, they were leaning back on

the couch, holding hands for mutual strength. "Have either of you two taken anything? I think I saw some Alka Seltzer in the medicine cabinet."

"I'm not certain my stomach can handle anything just yet. But I suppose it's worth a try," Emma said, and Clarice nodded.

"I'll be right back with two hangover cocktails."

"Please don't mention alcohol," Emma said with a moan.

Kat was in the kitchen mixing two tall glasses with cold water and Alka Seltzer when Larry walked in looking slightly less rumpled than he had last night. "Good morning," he said and kissed her on the cheek.

Surprised, Kat moved back slightly. It was one thing to succumb to an ill-conceived goodnight kiss in the middle of the night, it was another to accept a casual kiss first thing in the morning.

"I can't help it," Larry explained. "My mouth has a mind of its own."

"Do me a favor and take you and your mouth out to the living room with these. Your two friends look like death."

He grabbed the glasses and left with a big, silly grin on his face. Kat looked to the ceiling and shook her head before putting away the medicine and following him out to the two suffering women. Clarice held the cool glass up to her head before forcing herself to take a sip. "Oh, God, this is foul," she said.

Emma drained her glass, then looked like she'd just made a mistake. She clutched her stomach and squeezed her eyes shut while her breathing came out in short gasps. Finally, the wave of nausea apparently passed because she relaxed.

"This is all your fault," Clarice said, looking at Larry accusingly. "I never drink this much when you're out with us."

"That's not true," Larry said on a laugh. "You drink me under the table every time. If you ladies will excuse me, I have a book to write."

"Lawrence, you must take care of us. You keep abandoning us for your work." Clarice managed a pout even though it probably hurt her head to do so.

"I'm sorry. Truly. But this book is different."

"You mean it's good?" Emma said and laughed aloud. She paid for her cruelty because she immediately clutched her head in agony.

"See what happens when you are mean-spirited?" Larry said without rancor. He turned to Kat. "If you could manage to bring me something to eat around midday, I would greatly appreciate it. I know how busy you are."

"I'll see if I can fit making a sandwich in between making beds, washing linens, cleaning toilets, and scrubbing floors."

"Marvelous."

Kat gave him a face. "It wouldn't hurt you to take thirty minutes to make yourself a sandwich. It will probably help the creative juices."

"Fine," he said, walking toward the stairs with Kat following behind. "But if you were to bring me a sandwich, I might pay you handsomely."

Kat narrowed her eyes. "Are you bargaining with something other than money?"

"Perhaps."

"Make your own sandwich, Larry," Kat said, but she liked the way he was teasing her. What woman could resist that kind of charm and the veiled promise of another kiss that might just make her toes curl?

Kat fully intended to make Larry's sandwich because she had a feeling he'd keep working right through lunch. But she got so busy at the bed and breakfast she lost track of time. New guests were coming to two of the rooms, so they had to be completely stripped and cleaned. The main rooms needed a dusting and vacuuming every day; the bathrooms also needed cleaning. By the time she was finished, the new guests had arrived, and they chatted for a while. An older couple—they must have been in their sixties—they were truly distressed to hear Roy was in the hospital. Apparently, the couple had been coming to the island and staying at Roy's for ten years.

"I get updates every day, and I'll let you know how he's doing. In fact, I'll make sure he gets the message that you're here and asked after him."

Then the woman asked if they could use the phone to order flowers for Roy's room. "I can't believe it," she said as she looked up the number of a Boston florist. "Roy's so young to be going through this." She looked at her husband, worry in her eyes, and in that moment, Kat saw such a flash of love it almost hurt.

By the time Kat was finished checking everyone in and making certain everything was running smoothly at the B&B, it was nearly three o'clock.

He couldn't still be working, she thought as she made her way next door. As she climbed the stairs though, she could hear the sound of his fingers banging on his laptop in sporadic spurts as if he paused to think, then let his fingers fly over the keys.

When she knocked, there was one more spurt of sound, then silence as he walked toward the door.

"Is it lunchtime already?" he asked, then frowned when he saw she didn't have anything in her hands.

"You haven't eaten? Larry, it's three in the afternoon."

He shook his head. "It can't be that late," he said, then leaned back to see his bedside clock. "Apparently, it can be that late. I'm ravenous. Let's go eat."

"I'm not really all that hungry, but I'll watch you eat," Kat said. "Pizza?"

"Please, no," Larry said, looking slightly ill.

"How about fish and chips? I hear you Brits love the stuff."

"You know, it's not my personal favorite, but right about now, I could eat a mountain of the stuff."

"Or an ocean," Kat said, jabbing him in the ribs as if she'd just said the funniest thing. "Get it? Ocean?"

They were headed down the stairs when someone knocked on the front screen. Kat could see the shadow of at least two people standing on the porch and wondered if the lawyer had returned with a friend for some reason. Before Kat could reach the door, however, two men and a woman walked right in.

"Oh, my God, will you look at that?" said the woman, her hand going up to her throat as she stared at Lila's portrait. She was slim and older, and she had the type of blond hair women get when they've gone completely gray. "You can't be serious."

"Hello?" Kat said. "Can I help you?"

"Who are you?"

"I'm Lila's niece. She's letting me stay here for a few weeks. Who are you?" Kat asked, but she had a sneaking suspicion she knew exactly who they were.

At least one of the men was the spitting image of how Carl must have looked thirty years ago.

"We own this property," the woman said.

"Stacy, cut it out. We're Carl's children. I'm Henry; this is Ted and Stacy, the youngest and still a spoiled brat."

Stacy gave Henry a scowl. "We're here because we were unhappy with the list of items our lawyer faxed to us. It seems that many items are missing, and we wanted to see for ourselves. Is Lila here?" she asked as if just saying her name gave her a bad taste in her mouth. "Her housekeeper said she was."

"Lila is visiting a friend in the hospital," Kat said.

"A rich, old friend, no doubt," Ted said beneath his breath, and Henry gave him a subtle shake of his head.

"Actually, she's with Roy Baxter from next door," Larry said. "He had a heart attack and needed surgery."

"Roy Baxter? He still lives in that old house?" Ted said, smiling. "He's going to be all right, isn't he?"

"He came through the operation just fine."

"Lila knows Roy through Carl," Kat said, ready to defend her aunt because she could already see Stacy's mind whirling with the information Lila was with another man.

"Come on in," Larry said, ignoring Kat's fierce frown. "I'm Lawrence Kendall. Your father was a great friend of my father's. Before he died, he loaned the cottage to me."

Stacy stepped in front of Larry, her eyes wide. "You're not the Lawrence Kendall, the writer, are you?"

Larry smiled. "Actually, yes, I am."

"Oh, my God," she said, staring at him as if he'd just sprouted a halo. "Do you two know who this is?"

"I believe he said Lawrence Kendall," said Ted dryly. Clearly, thought Kat, Ted was the comedian in the family.

"Yes. I think you're wonderful. My reading group studied your latest novel. Are you here writing?"

"Thank you for the compliment, and yes, I am here writing," Larry said, and Kat couldn't believe how full of himself he seemed.

"Larry had writer's block," Kat said, and she gave him a big grin.

He cocked an eyebrow at her that told her he knew what she was doing. "Yes, but I'm well over it now."

"You must have dinner with us at our hotel. You two don't mind, do you?" Stacy asked her brothers, who both shrugged their complete indifference. Kat had a feeling the two of them had been dragged along by their outspoken sister.

"I can't believe I'm standing here in our house talking to Lawrence Kendall," she gushed.

Larry didn't even have the grace to look embarrassed. He just drank up the admiration like a dry plant in desperate need of water.

"Technically, isn't this house Lila's?" Ted asked, and Kat had to stifle a laugh.

"Not for long," Stacy said through clenched teeth. Then she gave Larry a big, toothy smile that showed her poorly done bridgework. "You don't mind if we look around a bit, do you?"

"Not at all," Larry said and shrugged helplessly when Kat gave him a nudge.

"I'm really not sure that's a good idea," Kat said, sounding far less certain of herself than she wanted to.

"Who are you again?" Stacy asked.

"My housekeeper," Larry quipped, and Kat could have murdered him right on the spot. Stacy dismissed her with a quick look, then walked deeper into the house. "I wish we could remove that immediately," she said, referring to Lila's portrait.

Even though Kat agreed the picture was overlarge and very possibly the tackiest thing she'd ever laid eyes on, she felt she had to defend her aunt. "I think my aunt looks beautiful," Kat said and got ready to dodge the lightning bolt.

"Yes. I'm sure you do."

Now it was Larry's turn to stifle a laugh. "You're out of your league here," he said in a whisper as he passed by her. Kat's hand snagged his upper arm, and she pulled him aside.

"Just what is that supposed to mean?"

"They've got forty years of practice on you. Small, petty people should be smiled at, their egos stroked. Then they'll go away thinking they've won something."

"I don't like being nice to people who aren't nice to me," she said, knowing she sounded as unsophisticated as a ten-year-old.

"That's your biggest flaw and your most wonderful quality." He tapped her on the nose, put his hands behind his back, and sauntered over to Carl's children. Kat let him go. He was right—he was better at handling people like Stacy. She already had two strikes against her because she was related to Lila.

The three spent two hours at the house, one of them on the front porch where Kat, feeling put out, served them cheese and crackers and wine. She wanted to dislike them all, but the men were actually friendly and extremely likable. They spent the afternoon reminiscing about growing up at the beach house; playing with Roy; endless summer days doing nothing but surfing, swimming, and trying to get laid—except for Stacy.

"Do you bring your own children here?" Kat asked, and the group got quiet.

"I spent one summer here, but the kids were bored," Henry said. "They missed their friends. It wasn't like it was when we were kids."

"So do you all want the house to visit or to sell?" Kat said, knowing she was breaking an unwritten rule by being direct.

"Hate to sell the place," Ted said. "But I live in Florida. I'm not going to come all the way up here every summer. And God knows the kids have no interest. They couldn't afford the taxes here."

"It's really none of your business what we do to the property once it's rightfully returned to us," Stacy said, giving her brother a glare for responding to the question.

"I just think it's sad that a wonderful old place like this should be empty. You all sound like you loved it. Wouldn't it be hard to sell?"

"Personally, I don't care what happens to it," Stacy said. "It can burn down for all I care just as long as that woman doesn't get it."

"Don't be getting all emotional on us again, Stace," Henry said, and he leaned toward Kat and Larry. "Daddy's little girl."

"I know what you think of Lila, and I also know that there's nothing I can say to change your mind about her," Kat said, using all her resolve not to scream at the woman. "But she's my aunt, one of my closest friends, and I love her."

Larry gave her a wink, and Kat felt immensely better. Then Stacy surprised her. "I'm sorry. I didn't mean to be insensitive."

Kat had to let her off the hook then. When the conversation turned to world travels and places they'd all seen except her, Kat wandered over to the B&B to make sure none of her guests needed anything. She was glad she did because one of the second-floor guests had taped a note on the front desk indicating that a toilet was clogged and they couldn't find the plunger. It took Kat fifteen minutes to find the thing in the garage, and she made short work of the clog. She peeked next door only to find them all still jabbering away. Larry sat back, an ankle propped up on his knee, looking casual and elegant and morbidly bored.

By now, Kat was hungry, and she knew Larry must be ready to faint from hunger, so she decided to save him.

"Larry, are you ready to go?"

He nearly jumped up, but he politely told the group he'd have to take a rain check on their dinner invitation.

"You two are dining together?" Stacy asked, pointedly looking at Kat.

"She's not really the housekeeper," Larry said.

"I see."

Kat was pretty sure she didn't "see" anything, but the way she said it definitely put Kat in the whore category. Larry grabbed her hand and dragged her off the porch before she could say something she'd probably regret later.

"Thanks for saving me," Lawrence said. "That woman is the most tedious person I have had the misfortune of meeting. I shudder to think that is the type of person who enjoys my writing."

"The men were okay."

"Henry was a bit of a stiff," he said, liking the way Kat's hand felt in his.

"They sure didn't keep their dislike of Lila a secret." Katherine sighed. "The thing is, I understand how they feel. On the surface, Lila fits the profile of a gold digger. You really have to know her, to have seen her with her husbands to fully appreciate how much she loved them."

"To be honest, I thought she was just after his money. Then again, I never saw her with Carl. Most women are attracted to money."

Katherine rolled her eyes. "Here we go again."

"Take it from a man who had money and now does not. Do you see any women here chasing me?" He looked around as if searching for them.

"No."

"Before the well began to run dry, I could have my pick of beautiful women. The fact that I'm a writer is good for a couple of dates. And then they find out my books haven't sold and the reason I charge everything is because I don't have any money, and that's the end of it."

"You are so bitter," Katherine said, shaking her head. "Bitter, bitter, bitter."

Lawrence laughed. "I am."

They walked on for a while, and Katherine dropped

his hand. He couldn't very well grab it back, so he shoved his hands in his pockets.

"Do you think they'll get the house?" she asked.

"I know nothing about the American legal system. But it seems to me if Carl specifically gave the house to Lila, they don't have much of a legal argument."

"How are you doing with your book?"

Lawrence smiled. "I'm actually almost done. I have to go back and edit, of course. But the meat of the story is done."

"Wow. That's incredible. Do you like it?"

"I think I do," he said, knowing it was a vast understatement. It was, by far, the best and most personal book he'd ever written, but it was so different than anything else he'd written, he was unsure how his publisher would receive it.

"After it's done, you go back to England?"

He stopped walking and looked out at the Atlantic as if he might see the coast of England looming in the distance. "I suppose I will."

"Oh. You'll be glad to be home."

Katherine posed it as a question, one he was uncertain of how to answer. "I do miss England."

"But?"

"But I don't really have a home there. I gave up my flat, and I had been living with my brother and his family. They have a huge country estate, so I wasn't in the way, and I was hardly home. I'm afraid I've become a bit of a mooch. Here I am, after all."

"I have a great apartment. At least I thought it was great until Brian bought a house with his new girlfriend." Katherine shrugged. "I don't know what I'm going to do when I go back home. I wish I could just stay here, but that's impossible. I don't think there are too many jobs available on the island once the season is over."

It was on the tip of his tongue to ask her if she wanted to come to England with him, but he stopped himself just in time. What a bloody idiotic thing that would have been.

"Sometimes, I wish I was ten years old and could start all over again. I'd do better in school, get a scholarship, go to college, and do something with my life."

"I did all that, and look where it got me? On the same island as you, homeless and living on the edge of disaster."

Katherine laughed, throwing her head back, showing her straight, white teeth. When she smiled like that, her entire face changed. She became completely beautiful, the kind of woman men stopped and stared at. He knew because that's exactly what he was doing.

Chapter 16

The next three days were a long blur for Kat, who seemed to spend every waking minute either cleaning; cooking; walking Killer, who seemed to have developed a bladder problem; or answering phone calls at the B&B. Roy was completely booked through Labor Day weekend, so she had to refuse at least twenty people looking last minute for a place to stay. From what she'd heard, most of the hotels had been booked solid for weeks.

Roy ran an efficient business, but she knew he didn't spend the time she did cleaning the place. It wasn't much of a skill, but Kat knew how to keep a clean house. When people complimented her on the inn's meticulously kept rooms, she couldn't help but feel proud. After living through the failure of a long-term relationship and a business, she had to throw herself a few crumbs for how well she'd been able to handle running the B&B.

Larry became so involved in his writing the only time Kat saw him was when she brought a meal to his door. In fact, she really didn't even *see* him most of the time. He didn't even bother stopping, just called for her to place it outside and he'd get to it when he could. Once she brought dinner only to see lunch still sitting outside his door.

"You know, I don't fix you meals for my health, buddy. You're going to starve to death, and then who will finish your book?" she yelled through the door on the second day. His answer was a flurry of typing, so she dropped the tray outside the door and tried not to imagine what the room must look like.

Emma and Clarice were none too happy with him either. Their holiday ended in just two more days, and they grumbled constantly that he was unavailable to them. And the famously in love Thomas was worse than Larry in their book.

"Lawrence has never been like this," Clarice complained. "Lawrence was always the life of the party, and Thomas was the one who organized it."

But Kat was too busy to even think of entertaining the two women. At least they'd toned down the drinking after that one night at the bar.

"You work awfully hard for someone who's not a maid," Emma commented after three days of complete drudgery. "Are you sure you don't want to come out with us?"

Kat declined, claiming honestly that she was too tired to go out. Waking up every day at five-thirty in the morning to prepare breakfast was beginning to take its toll. But Kat realized the reason she didn't complain or resent the fact that her relaxing vacation had turned into a work marathon was because she was truly enjoying herself. Other than the one client who complained about the bathroom being across the hall, Kat had met some wonderful people. She'd taken to sitting on the porch at night with a glass of wine, and often some of the guests would join her. Some of the people were incredibly fascinating, and Kat began to have an insight into why Roy had run the B&B for so long.

Kat looked at the clock and realized it was likely no one had fed Larry that evening. The man was so obsessed she half-believed he'd write until he was dead, skeletal fingers tapping at the keyboard while whole meals sat untouched around him. Kat made him a quick plate of pasta and a salad and headed up to his room, stopping outside to listen. She heard nothing, so she tapped gently on his door.

"Larry?" Kat pressed her ear against his door and thought she heard soft snoring, so she opened it a crack and peeked in. He was lying flat on his bed, wearing only a pair of boxers, sound asleep. Kat was about to close the door when she caught sight of several days' worth of dishes piled about the room. Grimacing, she walked quietly into the room and began straightening up. After three trips downstairs carrying dirty dishes, Kat made one more pass to make sure she'd gotten everything. Then she looked at Larry, sleeping with his mouth slightly open, and smiled. In the soft twilight, he looked like a fallen gladiator, except for the candy cane-striped boxers. He had three days' growth of beard, and his hair was damp from a recent shower. She took her time looking at him, feeling only slightly guilty to be gaping at his near naked frame as he slept. She'd seen him in his bathing suit, of course, but she'd been too self-conscious to give his body the stare it deserved.

He was so unlike Brian, who'd been hairless and on the thin side. Larry was big, just short of being a beefy, football player type. He was lean without seeming thin, and his chest was so wonderfully hairy she was dying to run her fingers through it, rest her cheek against it.

Kat let out a little sigh, wishing she'd had the courage for that summer fling. Instead of crawling into bed with him like she wanted to do, Kat gently took a sheet and lifted it over him, covering up his beautiful body. She was about to turn away when he grabbed her wrist.

"God, Larry, you scared the hell out of me," she said, hoping he hadn't been awake too long and seen her staring at him and drooling like some sex-starved female.

He didn't say a word, just pulled her down so she was forced to sit on the bed beside him. Then he wrapped his other hand behind her neck and drew her down to his mouth. Neither made a sound as they kissed, but when Larry thrust his tongue into her mouth with sudden intensity, Kat couldn't help but let out a moan. And then his hand was on her breast, his thumb moving against her nipple, and she moaned again.

Kat laid her hand on his chest, loving the feel of him, the crisp hair, the solid muscle, the velvet skin. He pulled her over him with one fluid motion so she was lying next to him prone on the bed. But during her flight, she felt his arousal hard and huge, against her stomach.

Kat sat up and looked down at him and smiled, but he just stared at her, his eyes slightly glazed. "You are awake, aren't you?" she asked. The corners of his mouth lifted just slightly, and he pulled her down for another kiss, wet and wonderful and incredibly sexy. He moved his hands beneath her shirt; they were hot on her skin as if he were fevered. They were strong, maybe from all that typing, and not quite gentle. This was too good, she thought, as he moved his mouth from hers to her neck. If she'd have been standing, she would have melted to a puddle on the floor.

Skin. She needed more skin, she thought as she pulled off her T-shirt. He unsnapped the front of her bra and pulled her down so he could suck one nipple. His other hand slipped beneath her shorts and cupped her behind, drawing her close against his erection.

"Oh, God, Larry," she said as he moved to the other breast. Kat had always had sensitive breasts, but Larry was apparently especially skilled at that part of lovemaking. She felt hot and liquid and more aroused than she could ever remember being. Kat moved against his penis, and he finally groaned, a low guttural noise that almost sounded like he was in pain.

Then he kneeled so he was between her legs, and Kat wanted to tell him that maybe they should think about a condom, but he pulled down her shorts, then her panties and kissed her navel. And then he put his mouth on her, his tongue, and Kat clutched at his head and spread her legs, throwing her head back as she squeezed her eyes shut. Nothing, ever, should feel this good, she thought. Nothing, ever, could feel this good again. He was slow and wonderful, and when she came, she called out and pressed his head even tighter against her.

Larry kissed his way back up her body, lost his boxers, and smiled down at her, and still, he said nothing.

"You can. I'm on the pill," Kat said, and reached down and wrapped her hand around his penis, stroking him with her thumb. He hissed in a breath, and he trembled as he knelt between her legs, his back arched, his fists on either side of her head. He bent down and rubbed his cheek gently against hers, and it was so intimate, that gesture, Kat nearly believed she was something special to him and she hated that thought because it made her wonder if she was.

Just enjoy, she shouted silently.

Larry gave her one more kiss before he plunged in, letting out a sound that for some reason tore at Kat's heart. When Larry came, his mouth was against hers, his hands on either side of her face. He withdrew, but he held her against him, face to face, his chin above her head. Slowly, his embrace loosened, his breathing deepened, and Kat knew he'd fallen asleep. It didn't bother her—she knew how tired he'd been, and frankly, she didn't want to face him right now. Kat eased out of his arms and off the bed and headed toward his bathroom, which was still damp and soapy-smelling from his shower.

She took a quick shower, just long enough to steam up the mirror. With one hand, she cleared a spot on the glass so she could see her reflection, then stopped and stared. "Oh, my God," she whispered, finally allowing herself to think about what Larry and she had just done. She was looking at her reflection when a horrible realization came to her. She was looking into the eyes of a woman who'd foolishly fallen in love with her summer fling.

Chapter 17

Kat had lived long enough to know two things. First, she was not going to tell Larry making love was a mistake even if it was, on some level, the biggest mistake she'd made in a while. She refused to be a cliché, and it seemed to her that every book she'd read and every movie she'd seen had the heroine folding like a wet noodle and telling the guy it was a mistake. Second, she wouldn't tell Larry she loved him even though she was pretty sure she did. If there was one thing she did know it was to never, ever say it first. She didn't allow herself to think that no one would ever say, "I love you" if they followed her second rule.

After that, she didn't know quite what she was going to do. She couldn't stay in the bathroom all night staring at her shocked face. Maybe she could sneak out, and he'd forget it ever happened or think he'd been dreaming. Or she could do what she really wanted to and climb back under the covers and hope he'd turn to her in the night and proclaim his undying love. She threw a hand over her mouth to stifle a sharp sound of hysterical laughter.

Kat wrapped a towel around herself and shut the light off in the bathroom before going back into the bedroom. It was almost dark outside, giving the room only the slightest bit of light to see by. She tiptoed over to the side of the bed where Larry lay, his arm still outstretched from where she'd made her escape. As she stood there looking at him in the fading light, her heart physically hurt. More than anything, she wished she could snuggle next to him and know that when he woke up, he'd be happy to see her and not regretful, or worse, painfully casual. It was that last thought that had her picking up her clothes quietly and padding back to the bathroom to get dressed. And then she went down the stairs dreading the next day.

Kat needn't have worried because Larry went about business as usual. The first part of the morning she was so busy she didn't have time to obsess about the fact that Larry hadn't bothered to come on over and at least say good morning. Apparently, she was going to have to be the brave one. She went up to his room with breakfast and heard his keyboard going again, bit her lip, then knocked, refusing to put off talking about what had happened or at least somehow acknowledging it.

"Just leave it outside the door," he called, and something in his tone told Kat he was just having fun with her.

"Okay," she said, all chipper, and noisily dropped his tray. And waited.

In two seconds, the door flew open. "Oh," he said, recovering remarkably quickly. "I'm starving." He bent down to pick up the tray, but Kat put her foot on the corner of it. He let out a sigh, facing the inevitable morning after, and Kat's heart sank just a little.

"I suppose you want to talk about what happened."

Her heart slipped to about her navel. "Not really. Just thought after sleeping together, you could at least get your breakfast in person instead of yelling through the door."

He rubbed his hand through his hair, making it stick up even more than usual. "Yes. Well. It was just fine."

"Fine." He was looking somewhere over her shoulder, and Kat was tempted to turn around to see what was so damned interesting there.

"Of course, more than fine. You were there, after all."

Kat narrowed her eyes, wondering if this was just a stiff British thing or a jerky Larry thing.

"That was me. There with you."

"All right then. Thanks for breakfast." He bent down to pick up the tray, and this time she let him. She realized something just as her heart plummeted to her feet—he hadn't met her eyes once. Even as he turned and closed the door, his eyes never got higher than her nose. She stood there, staring at the door, wondering who the bigger idiot was, her or him. She voted for him. Then changed her mind. Fine? It was fine?

"Fuck you," she said softly, too much of a coward to yell it the way she knew Larry deserved. And then went next door to clean toilets.

* * *

Lawrence closed the door and put the tray on the bureau before pressing his forehead against the door and raising his fists to either side of his head. "What an ass," he whispered. "Fine. More than fine. Shit." Making love to Katherine had been perfection. Why couldn't he tell her that? He'd never had a problem telling a woman she'd been wonderful. Hell, he'd have dragged most women back into the bedroom for another go.

But not Katherine.

Because he was scared to death if he let her into his room, she'd know what was in his heart, and he just wasn't ready to do that. So he'd brilliantly insulted her instead. For the first time in his life, Lawrence was unsure about himself and a woman. Kat had left right after making love. What the hell did that mean?

He knew what it meant when he did it. It meant he wasn't interested. *Thanks for a good time, honey; see you around.* And when he'd leave, he'd feel the most overwhelming sense of relief, almost as if he'd escaped a mad criminal.

Most women wanted to hang about and talk and make love again. In his experience, that's exactly what they wanted. They wanted to be held and stroked and talked to. But Kat had left. *Taken a shower* and left long before morning. He knew because he'd woken up just before midnight, reached for her, and realized quickly that she was gone and had been for quite a while.

There was a distinct possibility he'd read her quick departure wrong. He'd seen something in her eyes when he told her making love was fine, but he couldn't tell if she'd been angry or hurt or insulted.

Fine. How the hell did a man come back from that brilliance? For the first time in his adult life, he wished he was more like Thomas. That poor slob was declaring his undying love the night after he'd met Jocelyn. He'd been a walking, talking fool, but he was bringing her home to England to be his wife, and he certainly seemed happier than Lawrence had ever seen him. Why not find Katherine at this moment and tell her he loved her? Why not?

Because if Katherine had loved him, she wouldn't have left. Then again, he loved her, and he'd told her sex was "fine."

"Christ," he said loudly and stared at his laptop. It drew him, wiping everything else away. He couldn't think about love and Katherine. He had to finish this damn book. He'd never had such a rough draft, and he was fairly shocked by some of what he'd written. It was good. By far the most riveting book he'd written, but it needed work, and when he was working, he couldn't think about Katherine and how much he loved her and how much of an ass he was.

"Fine. He said fine."

Dead silence.

"Lila? Are you still there?"

"Yes," she said, sounding hesitant. "Oh well, honey, it can't all be fireworks all the time."

"That's just it. It was. At least for me. Why do men have to be such jerks?"

Lila laughed. "Because they don't have a clue that they are being jerks. It's one of the things I love about them."

"He knew. I just don't know why he would purposely be mean. I also know that it was better than fine for him, too." Kat paced in Roy's kitchen, peeking out once in a while to make sure none of the guests was nearby.

"I'm sure it was, honey."

"It's not like I don't know what I'm talking about. I know mediocre sex when I have it. Brian was definitely mediocre, although I didn't know it at the time. But this was . . ."

"Not mediocre?"

"Definitely not mediocre," Kat said on a sigh. "I'm done talking about Larry. What do you want me to do about your in-laws if they show up again?"

"I can't concentrate on that right now. I can't get all worked up about something that's completely out of my control. My lawyer will deal with their lawyer, and a judge will make a decision."

Kat couldn't believe what she was hearing. "But you were so upset. You came all the way from California because you knew they'd sent a lawyer. By the way, your stepdaughter is a real piece of work."

"She sharpens her nails at night. I don't know what to do about them. I actually liked the brothers at one time, but now . . ." Kat could hear a soft breath hit the receiver. "It's all so ugly. I'm glad I'm here with Roy so I don't have to deal with that mess. How are you doing businesswise? Roy's a nervous wreck about not being there."

Kat relaxed, glad finally to be talking about something that was actually going well. "It's great. I've got the breakfast thing down pat. And you can tell Roy I ordered scones, too. Half bagels, half scones. I noticed that we always had a bunch of bagels left over, but people really chow down on the scones. Maybe he should try some croissants, too."

"May be too fancy for Roy, honey."

"Roy thinks croissants are fancy? Then I don't think he's going to like the fresh flowers I put in the rooms. Don't tell Roy, but the fake silk ones were sort of . . ."

"Tacky?"

"A little. I know it's more expensive, but the arrangements last nearly a week, and I'm sure the guests think I'm putting in a fresh bouquet every day. I rotate them from room to room. Pretty crafty, huh?"

"You sound like you're actually enjoying it."

Kat smiled down at her hands, still a bit raw from doing some pots and pans without her trusty rubber gloves. "Actually, I am. And I was thinking of something. Just a passing thought."

"You want to run my house as a bed and breakfast?" Lila gushed. The two of them were almost always on the same cosmic level. "That's an incredible idea."

"You think so?" Kat said, feeling her excitement grow. It had been something she'd been thinking of, a little bit of a fantasy, for the past couple of days. "Of course, it won't work if the in-laws from hell get the house."

"They won't according to my lawyer. It's not as if Carl didn't leave his children anything. They got nearly all his liquid assets, as well as his antique car collection and the Malibu house. I only got the little house in Coronado and this place."

"Only."

Lila laughed. "Carl's will was very specific," she

said firmly. "We'll have to add an apartment on to the back of the house for our use, but there's plenty of room. You could live there year-round, and I could visit in the summer."

Kat let Lila gush on. She loved her aunt, but Lila tended to get passionate about something and just as quickly lose interest. Kat didn't want to get her hopes too high. But it really would be wonderful, she thought, living on the island, running a small inn. "Let's just wait to see what happens with the house. Any idea when everything's going to be resolved?"

"I agreed that they can have whatever they want from the inside. After all, the furniture must have some sentimental value to it, and I'm really not all that attached to the furnishings. My attorney says if he can get this before the probate court this week, it could be resolved before the end of the month. It all depends on how hard they fight."

"I can't believe how compromising you're being, Lila." She could still picture Lila, her face as fierce as her baby-doll looks would allow, charging after the lawyer and throwing him out of her house.

"It's Roy." Kat could almost see Lila smiling softly. "He has wonderful memories of the McKnights and growing up with the whole family. Including Stacy. He likes them," she said, sounding slightly amazed. "If they want the furniture, they can have it. I really don't think the brothers will want to fight it for too long."

"But the sister is a different story," Kat said.

"A very different story. She hates me."

"You did steal her daddy."

"I stole her husband first."

* * *

Lila loved drama, and she could just picture Kat's face.

"You didn't. He's so young."

"Very funny. I didn't really steal him, and it wasn't my fault at all. They guy was drunk, and he captured me in the kitchen during a family get-together, and, well, Stacy found us in a compromising position. I should have called the police and charged him with assault. I actually threatened to, but that only made her more mad." Lila laughed. "You should have heard Carl laugh. He stood in that kitchen door and laughed his ass off, and of course, that only made Stacy more angry. Carl never believed for a second that I was participating. He was such a doll."

"And Stacy never got over it."

"Her husband was a class A jerk, and she probably knows it. But it's a lot easier to hate me than to hate the husband that keeps you in a penthouse apartment in Manhattan. Anyway, the bottom line is I'll probably win and you can have your bed and breakfast. How's my baby?" Lila asked.

"Killer's fine," Kat said. "But he misses you."

"Give him a kiss from me," Lila said before ringing off. Life was so strange, she thought. Two weeks ago, she never would have dreamed of turning that house into a small inn that strangers would live in, but now it didn't matter. A small line formed between her blue eyes. *Why didn't it matter?*

The answer came to her, and she didn't like it. Funny, it should feel good not to be completely devastated by Carl's death. But Lila felt as if part of her, part of Carl was now gone forever. She missed him, was still devastated, but she was moving on. Just as she always did. She just hadn't thought it would

happen this time because Carl had taken with him
such a huge part of her heart. She walked down the
hospital corridor that had become so familiar to her
and turned into Roy's room.

She stood there a moment looking at him before
he turned and saw her. He was a good-looking man,
she realized, feeling almost stunned by an embarrassing rush of pure lust. *Oh good God,* she thought,
bracing one hand against the doorjamb. Lila had
never been attracted to good-looking men. Oh, she
appreciated them, was attracted in an abstract way,
but she had never felt a strong sexual rush before.
And now she did, and it nearly blew her away.

Sex had never been a high priority for Lila. It was
nice, sometimes better than nice, but she was a re-
alist. She loved older men, and sometimes, older
men had problems in that department. Viagra was
lovely, and she just adored the physical nature of her
marriages, but she'd never in all of her marriages
felt body-flaming lust.

He wasn't doing anything special, just sitting up in
bed, his reading glasses perched low on his nose as
he read a book. But Lila had the sudden urge to tear
off her clothes and his, and she just couldn't figure
out why. Roy lifted his head and smiled.

"You coming in or just going to stand there watching me read? I'm sure it's fascinating."

Lila gave him a scowl, then headed straight for his
little blue pitcher of water and poured herself a cup.
Roy wasn't even that nice to her. He didn't fawn over
her and compliment her. He hardly gave her the
time of day, and here she was swilling down a cup
of water to keep from jumping up on his hospital

bed. She put the cup down a little roughly, disgusted and confused with herself.

"Where've you been?" he asked as if he were only making conversation and wasn't truly interested.

"I just talked to Kat. She's really loving running your place, you know."

Roy scowled.

"I was wondering if you thought you could stand a bit of competition?" Lila smiled as what she was saying began to register on his face.

"Hate to put her out of business," he said. "She's a good kid."

"I think she's going to give you a run for your money. Besides, if Kat's living there, it will give me more reason to come back every summer. I wasn't really planning to, you know."

"I know."

"Carl wanted me to. Told me I had to, in fact."

Roy sat up a little straighter. "Did he now?"

"I don't know why. I suppose he thought it would be good for my spirits to come back." She smiled at him. "He was right."

"You haven't spent hardly any time in the house. You've been stuck here with me. This place isn't good for anyone's spirits."

"We'll be home before you know it." Roy gave her the strangest look before fiddling with his IV.

"Is that bothering you, Roy? I can call a nurse."

"Naw. I'm fine."

But Lila could tell he was lying. She just didn't know why.

Chapter 18

Let him starve to death, Kat thought, staring up at the clock. It was past eight, the sun nothing but a red-gold glow in the western sky, and Larry hadn't eaten since she'd dropped lunch outside the door without so much as a word. She simply knocked loudly and walked away. As far as she knew, he hadn't been out of his room since.

The McKnights had stopped by to say goodbye, and Stacy was horribly disappointed not to see him. But when Kat told her he wasn't available because he was working so hard on his next book, she rubbed her hands together in excitement. "I can't wait to read it," she gushed. "Tell him I said so."

"Sure."

"And don't get too comfortable here," she said, losing her smile as her eyes touched upon Lila's portrait.

"Come on, Stacy. We've done everything we have to do, and we've got to catch that ferry," Henry said.

"We should have chartered a plane, you cheapskate."

"I like riding the ferry. Reminds me of when we were kids."

Stacy rolled her eyes, but Kat could see the affection she had for her brothers. She didn't like the woman at all, but at least she wasn't a complete shrew.

They left, walking along the boardwalk toward the Oak Bluffs ferry landing, not pausing to look back at the house they most likely would never be invited into again. Maybe they could be paying guests, Kat thought with an evil little smile.

Larry's friends were leaving tomorrow, and Kat would be glad to see the end of them. They just added to her workload because she was pretty certain both women firmly believed she was the maid. Just that day, they had looked at her turkey sandwiches on wheat as if they were some distasteful, exotic foreign cuisine.

"What is this?" Clarice asked, flipping up a corner of the bread to peek beneath.

"Turkey."

"Don't you have anything else?" she asked, staring at it.

"Not unless you both bought something at the grocery store," Kat said with exaggerated patience.

"I really would prefer something different."

"Sorry, ladies."

Later, the two women stopped by and complained again about Larry and how they'd both ruined their holiday by coming to this "God-awful island."

"We should have gone to New York or L.A.," Emma said. "At least we could have gone shopping.

If you see Lawrence, tell him we're not happy with him and that we'll be at the View." Clarice rolled her eyes as if the View was the last place on earth she wanted to be.

"I'll tell him," Kat said, knowing she'd be glad to see the last of them. Tomorrow, she would be alone with Larry, and it would stay that way until Lila and Roy came back. Kat wasn't sure whether she was glad or not. She wasn't even sure if she was still angry with him. After all, he'd never promised anything other than a summer fling. She was the one who'd gone and gotten all emotional about it. It was like being angry at a snake for swallowing a mouse whole. It was in his nature to be emotionally unavailable. He'd been polite, perhaps even a bit regretful for being such a snake, so how could she fault him?

Easy, she thought as she looked at the clock again. She'd be damned if she went and checked on him again. The last time she'd done that, she'd ended up in bed with him. Finally, after pretending to read for about ten minutes, she heard some rustling above her head as he emerged from his seclusion. That's when her novel got extremely interesting. Her eyes were glued to the page as he made his way slowly down the stairs. She knew the instant he saw her because one bare foot hesitated just the slightest bit before continuing onward.

"Good book?" he asked, his voice sounding husky and unused.

"Yup."

He bent his head so he could read the title. *"Wanting What You Get?"*

"Yeah. Good title, huh?"

"Katherine."

She held up one finger as if trying to finish a particularly riveting scene. Finally, she looked up, pretending interest in whatever it was he was going to say. But before she made that look, she hardened her heart. She would not melt with one look at his ruffled hair, his unshaven jaw, his sleepy brown eyes.

"I'm sorry."

Kat sure as hell hadn't expected that, and her hard heart sort of melted a bit, especially when she looked into his eyes and saw that he *was* sorry. "About what?" she asked, even though she knew.

"I'm sure you know—the whole 'it was fine' thing. Wasn't very good of me, and not at all true."

Now that heart was just a little ole puddle sitting in her chest, not so much from what he was saying but from how miserable he looked as he said it. "Really?"

He sat down next to her and stretched out his legs, putting his hands behind his head. "Really."

"Not that I'm a needy person or anything, but could you retract that 'it was fine' statement officially?"

She saw the corner of his lip lift. "Retracted."

"Not good enough."

"It was amazingly wonderful," he said, turning his head to face her. "You know that."

"I thought it was," Kat admitted. "Until the 'it was fine' statement."

"I've retracted that."

"Hm-m-m. Yes, so you have. Now that we have that out of the way, how's the book going?"

"I've only two more chapters to go through, and I'm done."

"That's great, Larry," Kat said, even though selfishly, she didn't think it was so great. With the book done, Larry wouldn't have a reason to stay on the island. He'd head home, fond memories dancing in his head of his American summer fling, while she'd be left here with a heart that would be badly bruised. Not broken—she wasn't as far gone as that. But she knew when she said goodbye, it was going to be tough. "What's next for you? Going back to med school?" She was joking, but he stiffened by her side. "I was just kidding."

"I thought I'd stay on here for a few weeks," he said slowly. "Until I hear from my agent. When I get home, I'll have to live with my brother and his wife. And their three children." He gave a mock shudder. "I'd like to put that off as long as possible."

"I forgot you don't have a home."

He looked at her, and she could tell he was slightly bothered by her statement. "I have a home. I just don't have my own home."

"I stand corrected."

"Anyway, I thought I'd stay on here if that's all right with you."

"Oh. Sure."

"A less than enthusiastic response," he said dryly.

Kat gave him a playful punch to the arm. "That's not what I meant. I meant that it's really not up to me whether you stay or not. Carl gave you the house for the summer, so by rights, you can stay here until Labor Day."

"It's just that . . ." he stopped and pulled his elbows together as if squeezing his head.

"It's just that what?"

"You'll be here," he said, his voice low.

"That's a problem?" Kat said, hating the way her

stomach felt. If she wasn't careful, this slightly in love stuff was going to turn into something full-blown and irreparable.

"Hell, yes, that's a problem," Larry said, throwing himself off the couch. He stood before her, hands outstretched at his sides as if he was angry with her, which made absolutely no sense at all.

"Why?"

"Because," he said as if that single word was enough explanation. He took a deep breath. "Because you and I . . . You. And. I." He let out a swear.

"Would it be easier if you wrote it down?" Kat asked, half-teasing.

"No. You and I have an attraction," he said finally, as if dragging out words that were stuck deep inside.

"You don't say."

"I'm not joking," Larry said, getting irritated.

"Well hell, Larry, it's obvious we're attracted to one another. That's not necessarily a bad thing. It's just something we're going to have to watch."

"Watch."

"We have to decide whether or not to act on it," Kat said, wondering why this man who'd talked so casually about having a summer fling before he'd even known her could be so tongue-tied now.

"Let's think on it," he said. He sounded and looked like a businessman about to buy an office building, albeit a disheveled, exhausted businessman.

"I'm glad you've decided to be so thoughtful about casual sex and not demand marriage like Thomas did," Kat said, a smile on her face.

Something dark flashed in Larry's eyes, and for a second, he almost seemed irritated. Then he returned her smile, dazzling her with it. "I'm always thoughtful about casual sex," he said, turning on his charming self.

"Liar," Kat said, studying him. *Fear.* That's what she'd seen in his eyes. Fear that she was going to make more of their little tryst than there was? She could tell she was right when he smiled again and seemed to relax. "Listen, Larry. I won't say what happened was a mistake because it wasn't completely. You were half-asleep, and I was there, and it just happened. Let's not ruin the rest of our summer by dwelling on it."

Lawrence was amazed he was able to not grab her by her arms and shake her until she admitted that making love to each other was the most brilliant thing they'd ever done. Casual sex, she'd said. Don't let it ruin our summer, she'd said.

"Do you really think I would let something like sex ruin anything?" he asked, putting on the charm even as his throat felt as if he'd swallowed a cricket ball. Good God, how the hell had he let this happen to him? He wanted to crush her to him, to press her against him so tightly she couldn't draw breath to tell him to stop. No, that wasn't it. He wanted her to love him the way he obviously and wretchedly loved her.

He should be happy. He was about to complete the best work, by far, he'd ever attempted, but all he could think about was her heat, her warm, soft, wet places. He wanted to bury himself inside her again and again, and she was sitting there on the couch, smiling up at him, completely oblivious to the fact that she was ripping him in two. And that, if there was a God, was the way it was going to stay.

"I better get back to work," he said, even though that was the last thing he wanted to do. In truth, he wanted to spend the evening with Kat, walking around Oak Bluffs, eating ice cream and fried clams and chips.

"Clarice and Emma were looking for you. You do know they're leaving tomorrow? They told me to tell you they were headed to The View. That's the place down by the marina. You should go. They're not very happy with you, you know."

Lawrence hesitated, knowing his friends would be extremely angry if he didn't go out with them before they left. He knew he hadn't been what his friends were expecting when he'd called them weeks ago and begged them to end his monotony. That had been before Kat, before his obsessive writing spree.

"Would you like to come along?" he asked, hating the surge of expectation that flooded him. "I may need help dragging them home."

"Only if you promise neither of them will throw up on me."

He tried not to be excessively happy that she was coming along, but he couldn't help it. What was he going to do when he was back home and living with his brother's family? He was going to go mad. "Before we find them, would you like to ride the carousel tonight? Give it another go? There won't be too many more chances before the summer's over."

"Sure," Kat said, and the smile she gave him made him physically hurt.

It was nearly ten o'clock by the time they reached the center of the town, which seemed more crowded than usual. Everyone seemed to be walking in the same direction, and the air was filled with an almost palpable excitement.

"Oh," she said, grabbing his arm. "The Illumination. Oh, yay." She was acting like a child, pulling him in the same direction as the rest of the people.

"What is the Illumination?"

"I've never been on the island when they've had it, but I've heard about it. Everyone puts lanterns on their porches. You know, those Japanese paper lanterns. Lila told me it's beautiful."

"What about the girls?"

"They'll still be there when we get there." She dragged him, and Lawrence willingly went along. Suddenly, they were away from the noise of the main strip and were standing in what appeared to be an enchanted fairy world. Each brightly painted Victorian cottage was lit by beautifully ornate Japanese lanterns strung along the front porches. The owners of the homes sat on the porches, talking quietly while people walked by.

"Beautiful," Katherine called to an elderly black woman who sat alone on her porch.

The woman nodded a thank you and smiled as she rocked the night away.

"Isn't this neat?"

"Very," Lawrence said, looking down at her. Katherine wasn't the most beautiful woman he'd ever been with. But she had an almost indefinable beauty. It was her smile, the way her eyes lit up in an almost innocent wonder at what she was seeing. She grabbed his hand and pulled him along, and he wondered if she was even aware that she was doing it. Some of the streets were narrow, allowing no cars. In the center of the houses was a large pavilion where musicians were putting away instruments and sheet music.

"This is the Tabernacle. We missed the concert. Darn it. I've got to start reading the paper. It's a sing-along." She sounded so sad to have missed it, like a child who's missed talking to Santa.

"Do you sing?"

"Badly. But it would have been nice to have heard it. It's so different here. Like stepping back in time." They both paused to look around, and indeed, it did look like something unrealistically idyllic. Families strolled the grounds, children played tag, elderly people still sat in the chairs chatting away, and in the background were the gingerbread cottages glowing in the darkness.

"There are some villages in England like that, ones that seem to have avoided the twenty-first century entirely."

Katherine dropped his hand, and he felt the cool night air in its place. "I'm thinking of staying here," she said. "I don't have anything back home."

"What do you have here?" The minute he said it, he wished he hadn't because she looked so incredibly sad suddenly.

"Nothing," she said, shrugging and looking into the darkness behind the Tabernacle. "Except that maybe someday, there'll be more than that."

By the time they got back to the town center, the carousel was closed, but Kat didn't mind so much. She was just glad she'd been able to see the Illumination before heading to The View. The bar was on top of a restaurant and was so named, obviously, because of the incredible view of the harbor. It was packed with tourists, including Emma and Clarice, who'd managed to snag a spot at the bar. The smell of fine perfumes was mixed with coconut suntan lotion, which went perfectly with the summer whites, capris, boat shoes, and suntanned skin. It was a lively, noisy crowd, a different planet from the quiet beauty of the Illumination.

"Fancy meeting you here," Emma said brightly, then frowned slightly when she saw Larry had brought Kat. Emma wore a cream silk halter top and chocolate brown capris, making Kat feel slightly frumpy in her baggy cargo pants and simple knit tank. Kat could tell Emma was confused about their relationship. That made two of them, Kat thought, looking around the crowd while Larry and his friends talked. She was stunned to see Enzo, her Italian from Milan, looking at her intensely from across the bar with his sleepy and sexy dark eyes, and even more stunned when he smiled and started heading her way.

"*Bellissima,*" he said, flashing his beautiful white teeth.

"I thought you were leaving a few days ago," Kat said, full of good-natured suspicion.

"The women are so beautiful here I decided to stay." He looked at her with meaning, and Kat would have laughed out loud if he hadn't seemed so serious. He moved so close to her she had to crane her neck to look up at him. Kat tried to move away, but it was so crowded, there was nowhere for her to go. Frankly, Enzo, as beautiful as he was, was losing his charm. "You are alone. Again."

"Actually, I'm with some friends." Kat turned and

found herself alone. "They were right here," she said, looking around for the three friends.

"Perhaps they mean to give us privacy."

Kat looked pointedly at the crushing crowd surrounding them.

"Not so private, *si?* I still have my hotel."

"Enzo, I'm really not interested," she said, less than enthusiastic about his persistence. The first time he'd come on so strong, it had been flattering; this time, it was just annoying. Then Kat saw Larry fully engrossed in a conversation with a beautiful redhead, and she could almost feel the razor-sharp daggers flying from her eyes. At least she wasn't blond, she thought darkly. Larry threw back his head, laughing, and she felt the hot burn of ugly jealousy.

"She is *bella,* no?" Enzo asked, following her eyes. "But not for me." He shrugged.

"Oh? Why not?"

"She has a tattoo. Right here," he said, pointing at his chest. He wrinkled his nose and shook his head.

"You don't like tattoos," Kat asked and tortured herself by looking at Larry again. He was a beautiful man, and he looked so right with that beautiful woman. Kat knew she wasn't a dog, and she wasn't lacking in self-esteem. She liked herself just fine, thank you, but she wished Larry was talking to someone who was slightly shorter, slightly fatter, and with a bad complexion.

"It is not feminine," Enzo pronounced definitively.

"Well, I'm afraid I'm not for you either. I have a tattoo of a heart and flower right here," she said, pointing to her hip. "It's really big."

He narrowed his eyes as if he knew she was lying.

"Hey, Enz, what's up?" a man said, clapping Enzo on the back. The friend was American, and he gave Kat a quick look. "Man, you've got to leave this alone. Heather's looking for you, and if she catches you again, man, you're dead."

Enzo gave his buddy a sharp jerk of his head, but his friend just laughed. "He's not Italian," the friend said, turning to Kat. "Maybe his grandfather was, but this guy is about as Italian as I am." Then to his friend: "Heather's getting pissed in a big way."

"You rat," Kat said, horrified both for her and for whoever Heather was.

Enzo gave his friend another dirty look, then shrugged and smiled. "Works almost every time," he said in a perfect American accent.

"You are sick." Kat was embarrassed she'd been taken in and slightly mad at Enzo, but he was so disarmingly chagrined she couldn't get too worked up.

"He's been doing this since we were in college. The man has a gift," his friend said, grabbing Enzo's arm and pulling him away. "He's really not a bad guy."

"He's a shithead," Kat called good-naturedly after them. Kat turned away from them and picked up her mug, downing a nice big swallow. The first guy who'd come on to her in a big way was a complete fraud, and she'd nearly fallen for it. Thank God she hadn't slept with him.

"Was that the Italian?" said a cultured, deep voice in her ear.

"No. He was full-blooded American ass."

Larry laughed. "According to Shelly, that guy has hit on every woman in Martha's Vineyard. Or at least every tourist."

"Shelly? Was that the redhead?" Kat asked, then inwardly winced because she'd obviously been watching him.

"Shelly is Jocelyn's best friend. She's flying to England for the wedding. According to her, I'm the best man, and she's the maid of honor. Though Thomas hasn't mentioned it to me yet."

"Wedding? They've actually set a date?"

"According to Shelly, they're getting married the first week of September, if you can believe that."

"But that's only in two weeks. How can they put a wedding together in a foreign country that quickly?"

Larry shrugged. "Thomas is extremely wealthy. If anyone could do it, he can. He'll probably fly her entire family over. That's the way he is."

Kat took a sip of her beer, digesting that information. "So you're definitely going home then. If you're the best man, you've got to be at the wedding."

"So it would seem."

"You'll probably have to fly out early to do all your best man stuff."

He smiled. "Are you trying to get rid of me?" he asked.

Kat felt foolish for feeling as ripped apart as she did. What did she think? That Larry would fall madly in love with her and stay on Martha's Vineyard with her? That he'd beg her to go to England with him? Suddenly, she didn't want to be in this bar with all these happy, slightly drunk people. It was as if the noise level had grown exponentially, as if the air conditioning had suddenly failed.

"I've just gotten used to having someone around," she said. "I feel the pathological need to take care of people. And you are very needy." The truth was she was going to miss him, and she wished she wouldn't. "I'm going to go back to the cottage. It's crazy in here," she said, putting down her half-full beer.

"I'll come with you."

"No. What about your friends? They'll be mad at you."

Larry took her arm and pulled until she was facing him. "I really don't care," he said. "I'll go with you."

Kat really wanted to be alone. She felt like she was going to cry any minute and didn't feel like having an audience. Larry, his warm hand wrapped around her upper arm, led her out of the bar and into the warm and humid night air. He led her away from the crowd waiting to get into the place, pulling her until she was forced to jog.

"Larry."

Then he stopped and put his hand behind her head, lowered his, and kissed her until she was forced to hold on to his shoulders or else fall to the ground. "I thought we were going to resist each other," Kat said softly, her lips still against his.

"I'm finding that quite impossible," he said and pulled her against him.

"Get a room," someone said as they passed by, and Kat and Larry laughed.

"Well, should we?" he said, and Kat pulled away slightly, torn in a way she'd never been before. She wished she was one of those women who could sleep with a man just for the sheer joy of it. But her heart was already too far gone, just as she'd known it would be if she made love to Larry. She'd known it, and she'd done it anyway, and here she was thinking maybe she could get away with making love again.

"I don't think so," she said slowly, and Larry dropped his forehead gently against hers and let out a long breath. "Is that okay?"

"Not really," he said, chuckling deeply.

They walked home in near silence, both caught up in their own thoughts. A fine mist began to fall, and just before they reached the cottage, it turned into gentle rain. Larry grabbed her hand, and they ran across the street and up to the porch.

"I was beginning to think it never rained in New England," Larry said, shaking the rain out of his hair with his hands. The result was a curling mass that was so adorable Kat had to kiss him. It was the strangest thing—the two of them couldn't exchange a simple kiss. Every time their lips touched, it was as if they were both drowning and the only way to breathe was to wrap their bodies around each other and hold on tight. His hands always ended up on her bum, pressing her against him, and hers somehow ended up beneath his shirt where she could feel the smooth, muscled heat of him.

"You are the best kisser," Kat said, moving her hands from his back and up his chest. He hissed in a breath and pressed her closer, against his obvious erection.

"Katherine. I want to make love to you."

She looked into his brown eyes and couldn't stand what she saw there, the raw heat, the want. "I'm not good at casual sex," she said.

"It's not so casual. I like you quite a lot." But he said it so casually Kat felt her heart bruise a little.

"And you're leaving in about a week to England." Kat pressed her head against his chest.

"Are you afraid you might fall in love with me?" he asked softly.

Lawrence held his breath and waited for her answer. He got it when she sprang away from him.

"God, no. You don't have to worry about that." She let out a funny little laugh.

A normal man who'd just received such a crushing blow might retreat, but Lawrence was not a normal man. He was a man who found himself in love for the first time with a woman who didn't love him, and he wasn't about to let her go so easily. He had a week to get her to fall in love with him. One week was not nearly enough when she seemed to be so hell-bent on not falling in love.

"It takes me months and months to fall in love," she said airily, then looked up at him as if seeing if he believed her.

"Then we're safe," he said. "If you're in no danger of falling in love, I don't see the harm in a one-week tryst."

"You don't." Katherine bit her lip, looking utterly lovely. "What happens, hypothetically speaking of course, if I do fall in love with you? Should I tell you?"

"Absolutely."

"Why?"

He couldn't very well tell her it was because he was already madly in love with her. That wouldn't do at all. "So I know how nice to be when I say goodbye."

Katherine gave him a look of sheer disgust. "You're just as bad as Enzo," she said, and he hadn't a clue what she meant. "Okay. What if you fall in love with me? Will you tell me?"

"Of course not," he said. "In any event, I don't think either of us is in any danger. It's only a week."

"One week. No strings."

He thought about that one, knowing whatever he said was going to be a lie. There'd be strings, ones that stretched across the Atlantic and wrapped around his heart. "I might ring you up once or twice," he said. "Just to say hello and such."

Katherine appeared to think about it. "We'll see," she said and walked through the front door. Lawrence followed, not happy with the way that conversation had gone, and he wondered if he should just go ahead and tell her how he felt.

"Lawrence," Thomas boomed out as he walked into the living room. He was sitting on the sofa with Jocelyn, his arm slung around her as she snuggled into his side. "You're my best man. The wedding's in sixteen days."

"Congratulations," Lawrence said, giving his friend a hearty handshake. "And welcome to the clan." He bent and kissed Jocelyn on the cheek. "I'm sure you shudder in your sleep to think how close you came to missing out on this bloke," he said, referring to himself.

"Every night," Jocelyn joked.

"I'm flying out tomorrow night, and Jocelyn's following in a week. I'd like you there about the same time; all the planning, you know," Thomas said with underlying nervousness, as if Lawrence wouldn't be there, as if his bride might actually change her mind.

"As it is, half my friends won't be able to be at the wedding because they don't have passports," Jocelyn said. "It takes forever to get one now."

"We're planning a big party back here at Jocelyn's home after our honeymoon for all her friends and family who won't make it to the wedding. Be sometime in the fall."

"Your mother must be going insane," Katherine said.

"No, she's thrilled. She's as nuts about the English as I am. Plus, it's not every woman who gets to be married in a cathedral and has her wedding reception at a manor."

"Bloody social climber," Thomas muttered, and Jocelyn pretended to strangle him.

"He thinks this was entirely orchestrated by my mother," Jocelyn said, laughing.

Lawrence drew Thomas aside. "What day do you really need me there?" he asked quietly, sparing a look at Katherine, who was talking wedding plans with Jocelyn.

"I'd like you to fly back with me tomorrow, but I know you can't. I'm going to have to do nearly everything, you see, because it's happening on my home turf. Mother can help, of course, but I need you there."

"How about in a week? Will that do?" Lawrence looked again at Katherine, who was laughing at something Jocelyn said.

"Is that how it is then?"

Lawrence looked back at Thomas a bit startled. "What?"

Thomas jerked his head toward Katherine. "Your roommate. I thought the two of you had been spending an awful lot of time together."

"Must be something in this damn island water,"

Lawrence said, lowering his voice even more. "I've fallen in love."

Thomas looked startled, and Lawrence knew he was about to say something loud and embarrassing, so he grabbed his arm hard before he could. "What?"

"She doesn't know," Lawrence whispered.

"Why the hell not?"

Lawrence wished he'd never said a word. "Because she doesn't feel the same. Not nearly the same."

Thomas nodded and let out a long ah-h-h. "Well, that's a bummer, as Jocelyn would say. Are you sure about her feelings?"

"Very."

"That's too bad. Because I'm finding this all rather exhilarating. But I can't imagine what it would be like if Jocelyn said no. Rather devastating, really."

"That's about it," Lawrence said, looking up again at Katherine and feeling the crushing weight of looming failure.

Chapter 19

"I want you to read this," Larry said, holding out a two-inch-thick ream of paper.

"No." Kat looked at the manuscript as if he was holding out a live snake. "I'm sure you're very good, Larry, but I'm not your typical reader. I read romances, romantic thrillers, romantic comedies, and historical romances. Is this a romance?"

"There is a bit of love in it," he said warily.

"And I bet it ends tragically."

"Not tragically exactly. No one dies. Please, Katherine. I've sent it to my agent already, so it's not as if your opinion will stop me from going forward."

"Is it like your other books? Literary?" She felt foolishly stupid and hated that feeling. Just because she hadn't graduated from college didn't mean she was stupid.

"It's a story," he said. "I truly would like you to read it. Being one of the masses and all."

"Ah, the huddled masses you hope will make you rich." Kat smiled and took the manuscript, putting it on her lap without looking down at it. Larry hovered in front of her as if waiting for her to begin reading. "You want me to start now?"

"If you've the time." Which meant he did want her to.

"Can I be honest without you getting all mad?"

"No." Then he smiled, kissed her cheek, and jogged up the stairs. Kat sat on the couch holding the stack of pages in her lap and tried to think of something she needed to do. Unfortunately, the bed and breakfast was clean, no new guests were coming in that day, and she had nothing—for once—to do for at least four hours.

With a heavy sigh, she began to read, deathly afraid she was going to hate it, find it boring, or worse, riddled with words she'd need a dictionary to understand. She began to read.

Lawrence waited nearly three hours before venturing down the stairs. He'd overnighted the manuscript to his editor yesterday, and he pictured him sitting at his desk with its stack of other unread manuscripts, his on the bottom of the pile. He'd been so certain of the book when he'd finished it, pressed "Ctrl S," and saved it for the last time before taking it to be printed out. He'd even been certain of it when he expressed it to his editor and agent. But now he felt almost sick to his stomach. This book, which didn't even have a title yet, was so far different from anything else he'd ever written, and it would be a complete and utter failure. His editor would hate it. His agent would pretend to like it, then suggest he write something else. Worst of all was Katherine sitting downstairs reading it. For some reason, it meant more to him what she thought than anyone else. Maybe he'd missed the mark. Maybe what he'd thought was a universal theme of lost dreams and conquered fears would fall flat. He'd thought his other books were fine examples when he first finished them. But months later when he would read them back, he'd think they were crap. Three hours. She must have read a great deal by now, he figured. Or maybe she'd fallen asleep, put into a coma by his endless, pointless dribble.

Lawrence walked to the door, flung it open, and went purposefully down the stairs, telling himself it didn't matter whether she liked it or not. It didn't matter because it was finished, and he'd be damned if he made any major changes at this point.

He came upon her in the living room, the manuscript, half-finished, lying next to her, and saw immediately that she'd been crying.

"What's wrong?" he asked, dreading what she was going to say. She was crying because she was afraid to tell him it was dreadful.

"It's your book," she choked out. "It's horrible."

"Horrible?" he said, his voice sounding unnaturally high.

Katherine gave him a watery laugh. "Not horrible like that. This is one of the best books I've ever read. I mean it's horrible what this bitch is doing to poor James."

He leaned over to see where she was in the manuscript. "I didn't mean for her to come off like a bitch," he said a bit worriedly.

"No, no. But why doesn't she know that he loves her? How stupid can she be? It's horrible what he's going through. And why doesn't he just tell her that he loves her?"

Lawrence sat down next to her, trying to hide a smile. "Some women are simply obtuse."

"Please tell me they end up together. I can't stand this. I know this isn't a romance and probably won't have a happy ending, but they've got to end up together."

He studied her a moment, more convinced than ever that he'd made the right decision in not telling her his feelings. "Wouldn't it be awful for him if they do end up together, and she never falls in love with him?"

"She will," Katherine said, looking adorably certain of his fictional characters' love.

"This isn't *Gone With the Wind*," he said.

"I hated the way that ended. Rhett loved her, she loved him, and off he goes into the fog. What a horrible ending." She shook her head. "No, it wasn't. It was a wonderful ending. You're right."

Lawrence chuckled. "Why don't you just finish the book? There's a lot more to it than the love story."

Kat gripped the pages in her hands. "I want to ask you something. How much of this is autobiographical?"

"Very little," he said.

"The abuse? You know, when James is a kid. Did that happen to you?"

"No. A friend of mine though."

"Oh. Good. I mean not good that your friend was abused, but good that it wasn't you. I wondered about that." Katherine fingered the pages, rippling them over and over. "I really like James," she said finally. "Larry, this book rocks. That's from a middle class viewpoint, of course. So you should be happy about that."

"I didn't write this for the middle class. I wrote it for me."

Katherine smiled, and he couldn't resist her another second. He leaned over and kissed her. "Have you given my suggestion any thought?" he asked, moving from her mouth to her neck.

"A bit," she said, tilting her head and sighing. "I wouldn't want to be like Carol in your book though. Leading you on."

"You inspired the character," Lawrence said, and though she couldn't see his expression, she knew he was smiling.

"Lawrence, really," said Emma, entering the front door and giving her friend a scornful glare.

"I really don't mind," Katherine said, then to his complete delight, pulled him closer to give him a rather long and enjoyable kiss.

"I don't think it's fair for him to take advantage of you, dear," Emma said with complete seriousness. "It's fine for one of us. We know how Lawrence is."

"And how am I?" Lawrence asked, even though he really wasn't curious about her analysis.

"You are completely wonderful and devastatingly detached," she said just as Clarice joined her. Emma looked to Clarice. "Isn't that true?"

"You've both dated him?"

"I wouldn't really call it dating," Clarice said pointedly. "And no, only I have had that pleasure. But Emma has witnessed enough battered hearts to attest to my statement."

"She's right. Lawrence steps on hearts the same

way most men step on bugs. It's all unknowing, but it happens just the same."

Lawrence was aghast. As far as he knew, he hadn't left a single broken heart behind. He'd ended every relationship he'd ever been in long before there had even been a threat of love. "Name one person whose heart I've broken," Lawrence said, incensed.

"Mine, for one," Clarice said airily.

"What garbage," Lawrence said.

"You did," Emma said, putting an arm around her friend, who looked completely wholehearted to him. If anything, Clarice was the expert at breaking hearts. "She was so miserable after you two broke up she only dated men with blond hair for a year."

"For the record," Lawrence said, looking at Katherine, who seemed far too interested in this conversation. "Clarice and I never slept together."

"We almost did," Clarice said. "If that's not dating, I don't know what is."

"It's nothing," Lawrence said.

Clarice looked at her perfectly manicured hands. "I suppose you're right. We're much better friends now than we were then. That's why we stopped by, actually. Our flight out of Boston is in four hours, and we've got to get going to the airport here." She gave a little shudder as if remembering their flight to the island on the small plane.

"I'll see you in a little more than a week," Lawrence said.

"Oh. The wedding. I still can't believe Thomas is gone to us," Emma said.

"He's not dead," Lawrence said, laughing.

"He might as well be. The next thing you know,

he'll be having babies," she said as if that was completely distasteful. "Thank heavens we still have you. Once you're home, things can get back to normal."

"We all might be married someday," Lawrence said.

"Not you, Lawrence. And thank God for it. I can't imagine you with a boatload of brats." The two women had a good laugh over that thought. "But Thomas," she said, full of scorn.

"He seems happy," Kat said and was gifted with a look of derision from both women.

"Thomas cannot be happy with one woman. Some men can, I'll grant you that. But men like Thomas and Lawrence cannot."

Kat realized that Larry wasn't arguing, wasn't saying a word at all. "Why not?" she asked, barely stopping herself from looking at him.

"It's in their genes," Emma said as if that somehow explained everything. It didn't, and apparently, Emma could tell.

"They both had cheating fathers," Clarice explained, looking at Larry. "And mothers."

Kat realized Larry's book was more biographical than she had thought, because the character was scarred by the that fact both his parents had been unfaithful. And James, the hero, loved Carol but was morbidly afraid of marriage and all that went with it.

"Well," Larry said, pressing his hands to his thighs and standing. "Now that we've aired all my dirty laundry, I'll see you two off. When does the taxi arrive?"

Just then, a car horn sounded. "Right now. Could you two please help us with our bags?"

"Sure," Larry said, quickly walking toward the stairs and their rooms as if he couldn't wait to see the last of the two women.

As they went up the stairs, Kat looked over to Larry. "You're all full of secrets, aren't you?" she teased.

"One more nasty than the next," he muttered.

"Someday, I'd like a full accounting, please."

Larry gave her a quick smile, but she could tell the two women had bothered him.

"Hey," she said, putting her hand on his arm. "My father is the water meter reader and I never met him. See? There's some of my dirty laundry."

"It's not true," he said, pulling out the handle to one large roller bag.

"Your parents didn't cheat?"

"Oh, no, that's the sordid truth. But for the record, they're still married and seem happy. I meant the part about Thomas and I being unable to stay with one woman."

"How do you know when you've never tried?" Kat asked, a teasing note to her voice.

"I just have a feeling that I'd stay with someone forever. Death 'til you part and all that."

"How very middle class of you, Larry."

"Yes, well, I'm learning."

Kat laughed. "I think they were just being nice. Warning me about the skirt chaser in our midst."

"Clarice and Emma are never nice. Especially not to the help," he said, then scuttled out of the way when Kat took a friendly swipe at him.

They helped the two women into the taxi and said goodbye. And good riddance, Kat thought.

"Where's Thomas?"

"He took an earlier flight."

Kat watched the taxi disappear around the corner, dreading the day she'd watch Larry's taxi leave. "When do you go?"

"In a hurry, are you?"

"No, I'm not. I just might miss having you around."

"Is that right?"

"You are a pretty good kisser."

"Only that?"

She got a devilish look in her eye. "As I remember, you've got a nice package, too."

"Package?"

Kat blushed. "You know," she said as she looked pointedly between his legs.

He looked momentarily startled, then smiled. "Thank you," he said, sounding all formal. They still stood outside the house in a tiny slice of sunlight that peeked over the roof of the house.

"When *are* you leaving?"

"In one week."

He was leaving in seven days, back to England. It seemed so far away, so foreign. If he was heading back to Boston or even New York, Kat might see a glimmer of hope for their relationship. But he was going to be living across an ocean, seven plane hours away.

"One week," she repeated.

"I have a proposal," he said, still sounding formal, but she could hear a smile in his voice. "What do you say you make a decision regarding my suggestion for a summer fling. We know each other better now, so I hope it won't be so objectionable."

"No strings," she said softly.

"How about one?" he said, surprising her.

"Oh?"

"Say one of us desperately misses the other, I say it would be all right for that person to fly to the other person."

Kat knew that would never happen. She wouldn't get the courage to fly to England, never mind pay for the ticket, and she just couldn't imagine Larry being so desperate for her that he'd hop a plane back to the States. But she nodded anyway, trying to fool herself into thinking that maybe this could turn into something more than a summer fling, something that hopefully they'd both look back on with fondness.

"All right," Kat said. "One desperation flight allowed."

"You're not taking this at all seriously."

"I'm supposed to take a summer fling seriously? Isn't that an . . ."—she fought for the right word—"oxymoron? A serious fling?"

She tried not to get mad when he raised his eyebrows in surprise that she knew the word oxymoron.

"Shucks. Was that there word more than two syllables? What the heck and tarnation was I thinkin'?" she asked, mugging like an idiot.

"Very amusing."

"A-muse-in'. Now don't that mean funny?"

"All right already," he said, giving in to laughter. "I'm a snob, and I admit it. I apologize."

"You ought to." She returned to her own accent and crossed her arms, pretending to be a bit mad still.

"I believe I did. The fact that you like my book is enough evidence for me that you are extremely intelligent and discerning."

Kat smiled. "You are something else, you know that? Maybe that's what I like about you. You're not like any other man I've ever known."

He put a hand over his heart and looked heavenward. "She said she likes me."

"Don't press your luck though. I could turn on a dime."

Chapter 20

Roy got out of the taxi, looked at his house, and goddamn if he didn't feel ready to cry. Any illusions he'd had that he could pack up and leave this island were wiped out in that moment. Once or twice in the past few days with Lila hovering over him, he'd flirted with the idea of maybe spending some time with her in California after she left, but now he knew he just couldn't do it. The island was in his blood, the sea air as much a part of him as the food he ate.

"Missed the old place," he said after he paid the taxi driver.

As if reading his thoughts, Lila said, "Ever think of leaving the island? You've been here your entire life."

"Sure I did when I was younger. I thought I'd suffocate if I had to spend my life here like my parents did. But here I am, nearly sixty years old, and I'm still here. Don't think there's anything that would make me leave." He said it purposefully because he sensed that Lila was beginning to think of him as more than just an old friend. Maybe he was wrong. Maybe it was just wishful thinking because he knew exactly what he thought of Lila. He couldn't stop thinking of her, and he'd probably regret for the rest of his life not taking things further. But he couldn't keep a woman like Lila happy. Hell, she'd brought more shoes with her for what was supposed to have been a one-week stay than he'd owned in a lifetime. She wore expensive clothes and designer perfume and dripped with jewelry as if she were attending some sort of ball. Lila would hate island life, particularly the long, dreary months of winter. Roy only dreaded winter because of the horrible loneliness that descended, but he loved the quiet of those months, the way the sea looked, the gray and browns of the landscape, the way the island took on a different feel. He liked going into town and seeing only people he knew; he liked being able to drive to Edgartown in five minutes versus the half hour it took in the summer, thanks to tourists.

"Thanks for your help, Lila," he said stiffly, then turned to go into his house, leaving Lila standing on the sidewalk looking almost comically bewildered.

"You cannot handle the bed and breakfast alone, and you know it," she said, hands on her lusciously curved hips. God above, why did He make her so damned sexy? By doctor's order, he couldn't do anything about it anyway, and a month ago, it wouldn't have mattered. But Lila was a powerful aphrodisiac with her full lips and soft and sexy everything.

"Kat will help. From what you said, she's done a fair job of it."

"Kat is on vacation, and that poor girl who just had her heart broken," Lila said, pointing a fierce finger at the house next door, "hasn't had a moment to mourn. She's been so busy taking care of her English houseguests and your business I'd be surprised if she's had a single moment to herself."

Roy pulled his brows together and wished he could insist that she was wrong. But she wasn't. And the horrible truth was that he was so tired he could barely stand. He couldn't believe a couple of taxi drives and a short plane ride would do him in, but apparently, it had. "All right," he said gruffly. "Suit yourself."

"A thank you would have worked as well," she said, brushing past him in an obvious huff. Roy didn't say a word, just watched her sashay up his porch steps, his overnight bag clutched in her hand. And damn if his poor, worn heart didn't pick up a beat, and that mouth that was far too used to frowning twitched a bit into what might have been a smile.

Lila stood inside the doorway waiting for him, so he made certain his smile was gone.

"What in holy hell?" he asked, his words trailing off. His rather austere interior had been transformed into a florist's shop, and the painting he'd had on the wall of men working on a rain-washed fishing boat had been replaced with another picture of a child playing on the beach that he recognized from the attic. He'd put it there after his wife had died because it had been her favorite painting and he simply couldn't bear to look at it.

"I'll put everything back," Kat said, walking into the reception area from the kitchen. "I'm sorry, Roy; I know this is your place, but that painting of men gutting that shark was just so gruesome. It's right here." She pulled it out from behind the front desk, removed the beach scene, and put it back up. It *was* gruesome, he thought begrudgingly, and too much a reminder of the fact that he'd been sawn open just a few days ago. He valiantly suppressed a shudder.

"Ew-w-w," Lila said, looking at the picture, then closed her mouth as if she could stop the remark from escaping. Now that he thought about it, he could remember some of his female guests staring at the picture with looks of faint disgust. The guys had liked it though.

"Put the other one back up," he said. "I'm getting sick of that old shark anyway."

"It really is a nasty picture," Lila said.

"It's got character," he argued, even though the sight of it was making him slightly ill.

"It's ugly," Kat said flatly, hurrying to take the picture down before he changed his mind. "And half your business is women, and it's the women who decide where they are going to stay. If you keep stuff like that up, Roy, I'll put you out of business in a season."

Roy gave her a good-natured glare. "We'll see about that, missy."

"Then you really want to do this, Kat?"

"If Roy doesn't mind a little competition."

He let out a growl, and Kat laughed.

"You look worn out, Roy. Why don't you go on back and rest," Lila said, getting that soft, doe-y look in her eyes he was beginning to dislike. He didn't want to fall for her, and when she looked at him like that, the only thing he wanted to do was rest his weary head against those beautiful breasts of hers. He wished he didn't feel so tired because he wanted to be left alone; he didn't want to need her, never mind want her.

"Maybe for a little while. I suppose the more I rest,

the quicker I'll recover, and then you can go home."
Lila narrowed her eyes as if she knew exactly what
he was doing.

"Take your time, Roy," she said. "That's what the
doctor said." She smiled at him as if he was the most
pleasant man on earth, which made him scowl even
more. He looked at Kat, and she was smiling, too.
God help him.

Lawrence waited until ten o'clock before giving
up and going to search for Katherine. Now that
they'd officially agreed to a fling, his body had been
putting him through sheer torture. It seemed as if
everything she did, from bending down to pick up a
leaf tracked in by someone to reaching up to swipe
at a spider's web, was a calculated move to seduce
him. He'd never in his life experienced anything
quite like what he was going through right now.
He'd never been consumed by thoughts of making
love to a woman. He'd never planned it, never been
made nervous by it—except, perhaps, the first
time—and never, ever walked around with a raging
hard-on. He even found himself staring at her ear-
lobe as if that was the sexiest, most erotic part of a
woman's body he'd ever seen.

"I'm mad," he said aloud, looking at his frenzied
expression. He needed a shave, he realized, and to
comb his hair. Maybe a shower, even though he'd already showered that day. A cold shower so he
wouldn't make a fool of himself. So he showered
and shaved and towel-dried his hair, then went in
search of the woman who truly was driving him
insane.

He found her on the couch, fast asleep, her lips parted slightly, her short hair swept back, revealing a small scar on her forehead that he hadn't seen before. He knelt down next to the couch, hoping to have a few moments to look at her, but she opened her eyes, and he felt his world tilt.

"Where did you get this?" he asked, touching the scar with his fingertip to distract himself and her from his obvious lovesick gaze.

"Skateboarding."

"You were a tomboy?" he asked, smiling at the image of a little girl with smudged cheeks and bandaged knees tearing down a hill.

"Yes. And I wanted to be a princess when I grew up, and the two philosophies didn't really jibe. I had a mad crush on Scott Burton, and he liked to skateboard."

"Ah. And did he turn out to be a prince?"

"Actually, he ended up making millions in Silicon Valley. He married a supermodel, got divorced, and announced he was gay at our ten-year reunion."

He leaned down and kissed her lips. "Fascinating."

"You know, there's a part of me that still believes I could be a princess. You don't have any royal blood, do you?"

"Sorry. That's Thomas's department. We got rich the American way, I'm afraid. Through greed and speculation. My father was a genius at business, and my brother has followed in his footsteps to a spectacular degree."

Katherine sat up and patted the couch next to her, inviting him to sit down. "You were the black sheep of the family?"

"Only when I quit my job. Until then, I was the

darling of the family, the altruistic one who gave up working for the family business to become a physician. My parents were disgustingly proud of me. Made my fall a bit more dramatic. And then, of course, came the women and cars and wastrel life."

"Sounds horrible," she said, teasing. She drew up her knees, wrapping her arms around them. "I wish I could have had some years of debauchery. The best I can do is skinny-dipping in Lake Spoofed after shotgunning three beers."

"Shotgunning?"

"That's when you poke a hole in the bottom of a beer can, then open the tab. The beer sort of squirts down your throat. I only did it once, and I wasn't very good at it. Half of the beer went down my shirt. Very lower class, even for me."

He kissed her again and breathed in. "I'll put it in my next book."

"Larry?"

He pulled back and looked at her, trying desperately not to show how far gone he was. "You know, I don't even mind you calling me that anymore." He was goofy in love, and part of him wondered what would be the harm in telling her, just blaring it out: *I love you. Will you marry me?*

"It is your name," she said, smiling with only her eyes.

"I'd love you to meet my mother solely so you could call me Larry in front of her."

"Your mother is a snob?"

"She taught me. And my father taught her."

A noise at the door distracted them, and they were both surprised to see Lila at the door. "Killer," she said, her face full of joy as she scooped up her dog.

Killer was so happy to see her that his little body wiggled dangerously in her arms. Lila gave the dog some love, then looked over to Larry and Kat, her look of joy turning to anger. "That man is going to die, and he'll do it alone," she said, stomping into the room with her three-inch heels. "He kicked me out. He knows how weak he is, and he kicked me out."

"We do have room now," Katherine said, and she was rewarded with one of her aunt's less than convincing scowls. It was as if her face could not pull off an angry look.

"And you," she said, pointing a finger at Lawrence. "How dare you tell my niece it was just 'fine.'"

"Lila!"

Lawrence looked at Katherine with complete disbelief. "You told your aunt?"

"Every gory detail," Katherine said, throwing up her hands. "She's my friend, and I was upset because of what you said."

"But I take it you didn't tell her about my apology."

Katherine bit her bottom lip. "No. I guess I didn't."

He turned to Lila. "I apologized."

"So," Lila said, "are you two . . ."

"We're friends," Katherine said firmly.

"Well, I'd say we're more than friends," Lawrence said blandly. "We do plan to have wild sex before I leave, don't forget."

"I haven't forgotten," Katherine said through clenched teeth.

"They call it shagging in England, don't they?" Lila asked.

"Indeed."

Katherine let out a puff of impatience. "Will you two please stop talking about this?"

Lila laughed. "We're just teasing you. There's nothing wrong with two consenting adults engaging in a bit of wild sex. You have my blessing."

"I didn't ask for it," Katherine said, burying her head against a pillow.

"I don't know how she ended up such a prude," Lila said, sounding and looking way too much like Marilyn Monroe.

"I'm rebelling against you and my mother," Katherine said, still amazingly talking through lips that hardly moved. Lawrence couldn't tell if she was truly mad or simply having fun with her aunt.

"Anyway, don't mind me. Carry on with whatever you were about to do." She winked at Katherine, and the younger woman groaned.

After Lila left, Katherine said, "You do know that we can never have sex as long as she is under this roof."

"Then we'll have to send her packing."

"I have a better idea," Katherine said before jogging out of the room. He thought for a panicky moment that she was hiding in her room, but minutes later, she returned with a bundle of blankets. "To the beach, my prince," she said and headed out the door.

It was harder than Kat could have imagined, finding a spot on the beach that was private enough for her. After walking what seemed like a mile in soft sand that was unfortunately laden with the odd rock or two just to make things interesting, Larry lost his patience.

"Here. Here is perfect."

"If it wasn't for your British accent and your handsome face, I'd just walk back to the cottage right this minute," Kat said, not meaning a word of it. The truth was it all seemed too contrived, too let's have sex now and be done with it. True, she'd been the one to grab the blankets; that had been spontaneous. But this slogging down the beach trying to find a place that was isolated and free of other couples with the same thing on their minds was beginning to feel desperate. It didn't help that she knew Larry was losing his patience.

"Katherine. I'm going mad here," he said, grabbing one of the blankets she held and laying it down where he stood, dropping their shoes beside it. Then he lay down and let out a swear. "Rock." He moved the blanket a bit more. "There. That's better. Come join me."

"Are you sure there's no one around?" Kat asked, making her eyes hurt as she gazed up and down the dark beach.

"So what if there is? They can't see us. We can't see them."

Kat hugged the blanket to her. "I know."

Larry stood and put a hand on each of her upper arms. They seemed amazingly warm, and she shivered. "What's wrong? We can go back to the cottage if you like. We don't have to do this now." She could tell by the grip on her arms that this was the last thing he wanted to say.

She let out a small breath. "I want you, Lawrence Kendall, more than any man I've ever been with. I really, really like you, and I need this to be more than two people screwing."

"Do you mean a threesome?"

She laughed and gave him a little shove. "Bastard."

"Katherine."

"What?"

"I . . ." He rested his head against hers. "I'm losing it," he whispered, and he wrapped his arms around her, hugging her, pressing her so close it was nearly painful. She could feel his entire body, his strong chest, his muscled arms, his hard erection, his beating heart. God, she could even feel that. She wished she could blurt out how much she loved him, wished she was brave enough or foolish enough. What was the worst thing that could happen?

He could gently push her away, could thank her, tell her he was flattered. And she'd be devastated.

So instead, she held his head in her hands, feeling the strength of him, the raw maleness, his short hair, his surprisingly smooth face, and strong jaw, and kissed him hard and with all the passion and feeling she knew. She didn't even realize he was kissing her back the same way; she didn't care. All Kat knew was that if she couldn't say out loud how much she loved him, she'd somehow let him know with her body.

When he reached under her shirt, she pulled it off for him. When he tugged at the buttons of her cargo shorts, she slipped them off, too. The night air was warm and humid, holding just a hint of the cool nights to come. Her nipples hardened when the night air touched them, and they were exquisitely sensitive when his mouth closed on one, when his tongue drew her into his mouth. She reached down and touched his penis through his khakis, and he let out a low moan and reached down and held her hand there as if he was afraid she might let go.

"Katherine," he breathed. He was shaking, his entire body, as they dropped to the blanket. He lay over her, his mouth tugging at one nipple, one hand on the other breast, the other moving beneath her panties to touch her.

"Oh, God," he said when she was wet and hot, and Kat spread her legs and lifted her bum so he could take off her panties.

"I'm naked," Kat said with a smile, "and you're not."

"Isn't this how you Yanks go about it?" he asked, kissing her, bringing his tongue into her mouth. "I think I like it like this."

"You need to be naked, too."

"Do I?"

"Yes. Otherwise, I can't touch all the good parts. Like here," Kat said, and pushed her hand down his flat belly and touched his penis. He unbuttoned and unzipped and, within moments, was pantless. "Much better. Now the shirt, please."

With one fluid motion, the shirt was gone. "Is there anything else I need to know?" he asked as he knelt down beside her.

"Yes. This." She leaned down, took him into her mouth, and his entire body jerked.

"That's quite nice," he said with some difficulty. "Very."

Kat kissed his navel; then his chest, his wonderfully hairy, muscled chest; then his neck and jaw; and finally reached his mouth. "You are beautiful," she said, and he shook his head.

"I wish I could see you. I wish the sun were shining, and I could see your expression when I do this," he said and touched her between her legs. "I wish I could watch you come."

"Oh, blah, blah, blah," she said, pushing him down on the blanket. "All words and no action."

He laughed aloud, spun her around so he was on top, and entered her, solid and smooth and as if he'd done it a hundred times. "I've never laughed while making love, you know."

"Me neither. It's nice." He moved, and she hissed in pleasure.

"More than nice."

"Sh-h-h." She put her finger over his mouth, and for a long time, they were silent, hearing only their harsh breathing, the sound of the ocean coming ashore, their bodies meeting. He reached down between them and made her breath catch as he moved his finger back and forth. Kat held on to his bum and squeezed, urging him silently to move faster, to make her come. And then Kat let out a cry as she came, her body stiffening, her skin on fire with pleasure from her breasts to her toes. Larry moved frantically, then buried his head against her shoulder, holding her against him as if he was still afraid she might back down. His heart beat almost scarily fast as she held him, making him suddenly seem all too human and flawed.

"You okay?" she asked, still feeling his strong heartbeat.

"I'm definitely okay," he said. He was silent for a long moment, then lifted his head and kissed her. "I never made love on a beach."

"Me neither." She thought a bit. "I've never made love outside. It's nice."

They heard voices, and Kat stiffened, but Larry just pulled the blanket that was half-covering them up high so they were like two little kids playing tent. When the couple had long since passed by, they stayed there under their blanket tent, holding each other.

"So," Kat said to stop herself from whispering that she loved him, "this is what a summer fling is like. Not bad." See? She could be sophisticated about all this.

He rolled away slightly, and she wished she could see his expression. "I wish I'd never said those words to you," he said, sounding almost tired.

Kat rubbed her hands up and down his arms, sensing that he'd been bothered by her attempt at sophistication. "It's not just a summer fling," she said. "Not to me." It was as close as she dared come to letting him know how she truly felt.

Chapter 21

Roy felt surprisingly strong the next day, so he helped Kat prepare breakfast. He didn't say a word about her croissants or her flavored coffee, but he had to stop her when she attempted to make the scrambled eggs. She was about to pour in way too much milk, and he suspected she was going to scramble the hell out of the poor eggs.

"Let me," he said, and Kat gladly gave up the bowl.

"Your customers really missed you," Kat said. "And not just because you do eggs and bacon better either. Almost everyone asked where you were. You should read the guest book."

"I will when I get a chance," he said, whisking the eggs. "Where's your aunt?"

"Lila's in her house fixing her own breakfast. You want me to send her over?"

"Nah. I'm surprised she's not over here hovering over me, that's all."

"Lila does love to hover," Kat said, chuckling.

"I appreciate what you've done here," Roy said. It was a vast understatement, but Roy never had been very good at thanking people. Made him uncom-

fortable. He didn't like to feel he owed anyone anything, which was why he was glad Lila wasn't over
there helping out. She'd done way too much already. Not that he didn't appreciate it.

"It was no problem. In fact, I learned that I have
a knack for it. At least, I think I do."

"You do. Place looks nice. Needed a woman's
touch, I guess."

"You should have Lila help you decorate then.
She's amazing. By the way, she's not responsible for
that portrait of her over the mantel."

Roy let out a sharp laugh. "That I know. Carl was
nuts about her."

"Most men are," Kat said as she left the kitchen
with a fresh pot of coffee. He heard her say a bright
good morning and realized that as good as his place
was, it did need a woman to brighten things. His customers were lucky if they got a gruff good morning
out of him, never mind a smile. Of course, thoughts
like that brought forth an image of Lila entering the
dining room with her brilliant smile and incessant
cheerfulness. He shook his head firmly. Wasn't
going to happen, and he was a foolish man to think
it would.

"I see you're feeling better this morning."

He flushed as if Lila had come in because she'd
read his thoughts.

"Doing fine," he said and couldn't bring himself
to look at her.

"Looks like you have everything under control."

She sounded almost uncertain, and he finally
turned to her and wished he hadn't. She was so goddamn beautiful it nearly hurt his eyes to look at her.
Lila smiled, those soft lips curving upward, revealing

perfectly straight, perfectly white teeth. She was dressed all in white, every curve defined by whatever figure-forming material her dress was made out of. And she wore silver three-inch heels.

"You headin' to a ball or somethin'?" he asked, suddenly feeling mean and not knowing quite why.

Her smile didn't falter a bit. "I knew I was coming over here," she said, all cheerful. He scowled, and he swore her smile grew even brighter.

"You know, Roy, you keep frowning like that, you'll get wrinkles."

With that, she left him alone in his kitchen with his perfectly scrambled eggs and crispy bacon.

"Let's go to the carousel," Lawrence said, grabbing her hand and pulling her out the door. It was six in the evening, Kat's work at the bed and breakfast was finished, and he knew she couldn't give him any more excuses to stay away. For some reason, that's exactly what it seemed like Kat had been doing all day, but maybe it was just his imagination. He'd been going nuts all day, wanting to drag her up to his bedroom, wanting to drag her anywhere just to get another taste of the incredible passion they'd shared the night before. He was a goner, he knew that, so he decided to enjoy the ride for as long as it lasted.

Katherine laughed and went along willingly, which helped his ego tenfold. They crossed the street to the boardwalk, and she put her arm across his back, and he flung his across her shoulders. They fit well like that because he was taller than she was. He hadn't realized how much taller until they walked together. The top of her head reached to perhaps his mouth, so he turned and kissed her hair just to see. She leaned her head briefly against his shoulder as they walked, and he felt so damn happy he grinned like an idiot.

"Hardly a line," he said as they walked up the steps to the carousel. He walked over to the ticket counter, his nose filled with the scent of the freshly popped popcorn that they also sold there. The carousel was going, music blaring loudly above the noise of a few arcade games tucked in a back room. Most of the horses were filled with kids trying to grab the rings from the metal arms.

When it was their turn, he gave her a lingering kiss. "For good luck," he said, and she held up both hands with fingers crossed. She was ridiculously serious about this, which he found rather charming.

They rode the damn ride twice, with Katherine fiercely grabbing at the rings that appeared, gathering up as many as three at a time, but someone else got the brass ring. "I'm cursed," she said, laughing. "I'll never get that brass ring."

"And what if you do get it? Then the challenge will be over. What will you have to live for?"

"You get a wish," she said. "And a free ride."

"Ah. A grand aspiration then." He kissed her because he couldn't stop himself. His cell phone rang, and he pulled away reluctantly, planning only to shut it off when he recognized his editor's number. "It's my editor," he said, his stomach churning nervously. There were only two reasons his editor would call so quickly—either he loved the book, or he hated it. He wouldn't be getting a phone call from him this late in the evening if it was a typical effort. "I'm taking this," he said. "My editor." Katherine's eyes widened, and he smiled briefly before answering.

Kat watched nervously, hovering close enough to hear every word Larry uttered and watching his face closely.

"Yes, I did. Truly." Larry listened for a while, and nothing in his face told her what he was hearing, be it good, bad, or indifferent. His expression was intense, as if whatever the editor was saying was critically important. Which it likely was, Kat realized.

"I'll pass that on to my agent. Thank you, Bill. I'll be in touch." Larry closed his phone and looked at her, still not giving her a clue as to what had been said. Then he broke out into a huge grin. "He loved it. Was practically gushing. He didn't even think I wrote the damn thing."

Kat launched herself into his arms, and he held her, pressing her head against his shoulder and turning slowly around. Kat could see people smiling at them as they walked by, and she wondered what they were thinking about the two of them. "I told you it was wonderful," she said, peppering his scruffy face with kisses.

"You did, didn't you?" He put her down but kept holding her. "He said they planned to actually promote this one. A series of interviews, radio, television, an ad in *The New York Times*. A bloody book-signing tour."

"Wow." Actually, Kat thought all authors got stuff like that, but Larry truly seemed thrilled, joyous even.

Just then, his cell phone rang again, and this time, he didn't hesitate to answer. "Ryan. Yes, yes. I just got off the phone with him. Right. I know, unbelievable

. . . Well, read the damn thing so you have something to talk about with Bill . . . I'm leaving for New York Tuesday. Nice that I'm still on the East Coast. The timing is perfect because I was about to head back home in about six days. I'll see you there, then."

Leaving? Tuesday? That was in just two days.

Larry rang off again, his face glowing with happiness, his entire being electric, as if he could hardly contain himself. The man she loved was happy, and all she could think was, *He's leaving Tuesday.* She sure didn't want to bring him down, so Kat kept a big smile on her face. Tuesday was much too soon. She'd thought they'd have another six days together.

"Wow. New York. You're a big shot now."

He stood on the sidewalk, looking off to somewhere, maybe a vision of his name on *The New York Times* best-seller list.

"Hey," she said, giving his arm a tug. "You too much of a big shot for me now?"

Larry looked down at her in a distracted way she'd never seen before, and it scared the hell out of her. He finally answered, but it was a cursory answer at best. "Of course not," he said, then he smiled again, and she knew he was thinking of those phone calls, and she felt as if he was already on that plane to New York.

Suddenly, Kat felt foolish and desperate, and she realized something horrible. She'd hoped, deep down where she hadn't even acknowledged it, that Larry would fall in love with her in the next week. That he'd beg her to marry him and they'd happily live on Martha's Vineyard while she ran the bed and breakfast and he wrote best-selling books. Instead, she would become a pleasant interlude in the life of a jet-setting playboy. Now he was leaving the day after tomorrow, and he wouldn't be coming back. She'd go on with her life, and in a few years, he would become a nice memory, and please God, not a painfully embarrassing one. She just had to keep her wits about her, not dissolve into any hysterical tears, not give him a hint of what she'd been secretly dreaming.

"Of course, just because my editor and agent loved the book doesn't mean anyone else will," he said.

"It was one of the best books I've read, Larry," she said honestly.

He tore his gaze away from the waterfront and looked at her. "It's because of you, you know. If I hadn't met you, I couldn't have written that book."

Kat was flattered, but she suspected he was simply throwing her a few bones, already laying out an easy exit path for himself. "Glad to be of help," she said lightly, letting him know she thought he was full of crap.

"You don't believe me."

"Not really. But I appreciate the thought."

He gave her the oddest smile then. "Someday, you'll know," he said, and she gave him a skeptical look. "I better make plane reservations. And pack. I don't think I'll be able to make it back here before I have to leave for the wedding."

"That's okay. We can say goodbye on Tuesday." She was trying valiantly to make it sound as if she didn't care, as if her heart wouldn't be broken by the ease of his departure.

"The timing couldn't be worse," he said, honestly looking frustrated.

"But you just told your agent that the timing was perfect because you're still here," she pointed out ruthlessly.

"For seeing my editor, sure. But I don't want to leave you. Not yet." He looked and sounded like he meant it, but his body was thrumming with an unusual energy, and Kat knew he couldn't wait to get back to the cottage and plan his departure. This chapter, apparently, was ending, and he was giving it a soft touch, making the hero seem not so ruthless and unfeeling.

God, she read way too many romances because when he said things like, "I don't want to leave you," it gave her stupid hope. And Kat wanted to beg him not to let her think that she meant more to him than a summer fling. She'd rather he just leave than pretend he didn't want to go. It was clear from watching his face when he was talking to his agent that he wished he was already in New York. Kat didn't want to be a small person, and she *was* truly happy for him, but that didn't mean she couldn't feel a little sorry for herself.

"Katherine. Look at me," he said, touching her shoulder.

She did, keeping her expression clear, happy even.

"I don't want to leave you."

She smiled. "That's nice," she said, hugging him quickly before she lost her grip and started bawling. She had a very distasteful image of herself clinging frantically to his ankle and him dragging her along as he tried to reach the taxi. When she pulled back from the embrace, she couldn't read the expression on his face. He seemed slightly stunned that she was being so cheerful. He was probably used to women weeping and clinging to him. Well, maybe she knew what an idiot she was, but she'd be damned if he knew. "I wish you were staying another six days, too."

"That's not quite what I meant," he said vaguely. He dropped his hand from her shoulder suddenly as if he'd forgotten he was still touching her. He shook his head slightly as if trying to wrap his mind around a difficult problem.

"You're okay with my leaving."

"Sure. I mean, you were going to go anyway," she said, feeling her throat burn slightly, so she stared at a passing family, an overflowing trash can, anything to distract herself enough to keep from crying. "I am going to miss you, though." *Keep it light, girl; that's the way.*

"Well, then."

"You want to go anywhere else?" Kat wanted to go home, fling herself onto her bed, and sob silently into her pillow.

"No," he said softly. "You know, you're much better at this summer fling business than I gave you credit for."

She turned her head slightly away from him because damn if her eyes weren't watering. "Thanks." She let the wind off the ocean dry her tears long before they fell.

Chapter 22

Lawrence sat at the edge of his bed and stared at his empty suitcase, which he'd laid open thinking he might as well start packing his things. But half his clothes were in the laundry room on the first floor, and he just couldn't trust himself to be anywhere near Katherine. He'd actually wondered briefly about asking her to go with him to New York until she'd seemed so completely unaffected by his leaving early.

He just didn't get it. When they'd made love on the beach, he'd felt so certain that he was staring into the eyes of a woman who loved him. Nothing had ever been as good as that, as *making love* to a woman. He'd used that phrase a hundred times and never realized what it meant until last night.

She was his Carol, after all. In his book, the two characters never did resolve their differences, and he gave no hint that they ever would. Katherine loved the book but wanted him to put the couple together in the end. She wanted a happy ending, and he thought she just didn't get it. Happy endings didn't happen very often in real life, and his two characters didn't seem to want that. And so he'd written about their pulling apart, loving each other but not knowing how to overcome the pain they'd caused one another.

"You know I love your book," she'd said. "But if you'd just get the two of them in a room to talk things over, they'd be okay. Real people talk about how they feel. Other than that, it was a masterpiece." She'd laughed and kissed him, and he told her that in the end, his characters had found each other again after the closing of the book and fallen back in love.

"And lived happily ever after. Right?"

Lawrence squeezed his eyes shut at the memory, clenching his jaw painfully. Bloody hell if he didn't feel like crying.

Just get the two of them in a room to talk things over.

"Okay. You want to talk, we'll talk," he said aloud.

He strode down two flights of stairs and went directly to her room. He wasn't certain exactly what he was going to say, but they were going to talk.

Kat lay alone in her bed wondering if her pride was worth the pain she was feeling right now. She had two more nights to be with the man she loved, and she was in her room all weepy while he was two floors up, alone and probably celebrating his success.

She'd stopped crying a while ago, and a look in the mirror told her she didn't look that obviously heartbroken, just in case Lila stopped by to say good night. Kat hadn't seen her aunt all day, but she'd assumed she was over at Roy's helping out.

"Katherine. We need to talk."

Kat stared at the door, her heart beating madly in her chest. She dashed to the mirror just to make sure she didn't look as if she'd been crying. "Come on in."

He stood in her doorway, looking as disheveled and unshaven as usual, and she wished she didn't think he looked gorgeous that way, but she did. He also looked slightly angry.

"I'm coming back," he said. "To see you."

"Oh?" Kat held her breath.

"I plan to invoke the clause of our summer fling."

"The one about being desperate to see the other person?"

A smile tugged briefly on his lips. "The very one."

"You plan to be desperate?"

He sagged slightly and brushed a hand through his hair. "Katherine, I already am. A bit. I'm terribly afraid that I'm in love with you."

Kat sat down on her bed because suddenly, her knees couldn't bear her weight. "Why does that make you afraid?"

He swallowed visibly. "Because I've never been in love before, and it's scaring the hell out of me, if you must know."

Kat furrowed her brow. "But what about that woman you loved—"

"You little idiot, I was talking about you."

"You hardly knew me then." She twisted her hands in her lap. "That was weeks ago."

"I know. That's why I think it's good that I have to go away. I have to make sure I'm not completely mad."

"Make sure it's real?"

He walked over to her and knelt beside her. "Yes. Does that make sense to you?"

"You think you love me?"

"I'm pretty certain that I do."

Kat smiled and wondered why her heart still felt like it was breaking. Maybe it was because he was leaving, and she was afraid that if he walked out that door, he would never come back. "I'm pretty certain that I love you, too."

"Carol and James need to be together," he said seriously, and it took a couple of seconds before she realized he was talking about the characters from his book.

"You mean Carol is me?"

"In a way."

"But I thought she was a callous bitch."

"I thought so, too," Larry said dryly.

Kat put a hand over her mouth, horrified. "I didn't know." Then she got a little mad. "Why didn't you tell me?" She answered her own question. "Of course. You didn't know how I felt. How could you?"

"Precisely."

"And you were afraid that I didn't love you and . . . Now I get it."

"It was pure torture," he said, smiling. "Here I was, falling in love, and you kept reminding me that the only thing we could ever hope to have was a summer fling."

"That's because that's all I thought you wanted."

He grinned and kissed her. "All we needed to do was talk."

"See?" Kat said, pulling him onto the bed with her. "I was right."

"No more talking though."

"No more," she agreed and lost herself to his kiss.

* * *

They lay entangled and naked, a cool ocean breeze drifting over their hot bodies. Kat had never felt so completely connected to another human being in her life, which amazed her since she'd been about a month from walking down an aisle and marrying another man. She held Larry just as tightly as he held her, two people on the same page. Neither one was wondering when to stop holding on; neither one was wondering if they'd just made a mistake.

He kissed her on her mouth, then groaned and kissed her again, making Kat feel as if he couldn't get enough of her, making her feel beautiful. A small bit of panic tried to push its way through to her, a voice that reminded her he was leaving for weeks, but she pushed it away and concentrated on his firm lips. He was big and bulky and hairy, and he made her feel soft and feminine.

"I don't want to get up from this bed," he said softly.

"But you'll have to. Eventually."

"Yes." He squeezed her tighter, his hand stroking her body from the nape of her neck, down her back, to the top of her calves. "You feel so nice," he said. "I think I'm going to miss you a great deal."

"Do you want me to go with you to the airport?"

"No. I want you to stand on the front porch and wave to me from there. Goodbyes in airports are far too dramatic."

Kat laughed. "And standing on the front porch isn't dramatic."

"It's prettier," he said, and she didn't argue. He was leaving in two hours, and she didn't want to let him go. The past two days had been miraculous, as if she knew for the first time in her life what being in love was like. He was like a drug, one that would be abruptly taken from her and one she knew she was going to need for a long time. And one she was afraid she'd never get again. Last night, after making love, they'd drifted asleep. She'd woken up, almost surprised to find this wonderful man sleeping next to her. She'd looked down at his face, his beautifully masculine face, and tried to memorize every detail, the way his beard was thickest on his chin, the small, barely visible cleft there, the way his brows grew thick and straight, the small lines near his eyes. He smelled wonderful; he felt even better.

She'd let herself go far, far more than she'd wanted to, and she swallowed down the wad of fear stuck in her throat. Because even though he'd said he loved her, even though he said he was coming back to her, he didn't talk about a future, not even in the vaguest of ways. He didn't mention her visiting him in England; he hadn't said anything about their spending time together during the holidays. And of course, he hadn't mentioned marriage. It would be too soon for two rational adults to talk about that kind of lifetime commitment after only a few weeks together. So what if Thomas and Jocelyn were getting married after less than a month together? They were an anomaly or very possibly clinically insane.

Still . . .

Kat breathed in, trying to capture part of him to hold with her forever. She didn't even have a picture of him to gaze at with longing. Smiling, Kat pushed him away and ran to her bureau, pulling out her small digital camera.

"Smile," she said, and he quickly pulled up the sheet to cover himself.

"Hey, I'm not that kind of guy," he said, laughing.

"I wanted something to remember you by."

His smiled faded. "I'm coming back. As soon as I can. I told you that."

"I know," Kat said, turning away and putting her camera back in her drawer. She believed at that moment he meant every word he said. But that didn't mean he was coming back. She spun around and plastered a big I'm-not-concerned smile on her face. "And if you don't come back, I'll hunt you down." She jumped on the bed and straddled him, her hands pushing down on his shoulders as if she really could outwrestle him.

"And then what will you do?" he asked, his eyes darkening and getting that sexy look she already recognized. She could feel his erection and gave him a grin before moving slightly and coming down onto him as he hissed in his breath.

"I'll subdue you," she said, moving up, then down slowly. "I have the power over you."

"Yes, you do," he choked out.

"And you'll have to do as I say."

"I surrender."

She leaned down and kissed him, and he placed his hands by her hips, guiding her, slow and languid at first, then pumping in a sudden frenzy as if he no longer had control at all. He arched his back, coming with a groan, and afterward, Kat sat there, feeling his erection soften, her hands on her hips.

He gave her a sheepish smile. "Sorry," he said.

She leaned down and kissed him. "My turn," she said.

"My pleasure," he said, guiding her body upward. Kat let out a gasp. "Hardly."

Kat finally sat on the porch of the Martha's Vineyard cottage the way she'd dreamed about when Lila had first proposed that she take the cottage for the summer. She held a glass of wine in one hand, an unopened book in the other as she gazed out at the Atlantic, her vision blurry from unshed tears. Somewhere at Logan Airport in Boston, Larry was sitting on a plane getting ready to go to New York. He'd said he'd call when he was there, and Kat figured he would. And then he'd call from England and they'd talk, and he'd get on with his life and she'd get on with hers. A couple of weeks would pass, and he'd call and maybe mention coming to see her. They'd have less to talk about but still claim to love one another, and then the phone calls would grow further apart, and each time they talked, their common experiences would seem distant and trivial, and finally, the calls would stop altogether. And that would be that.

Or he could fly back, beg her to marry him, and they'd live happily ever after.

Kat blinked and forced the tears that had been hovering in her eyes to fall, splashing onto her cheeks, then drifting down to her chin. She wiped her face with the shoulder of her T-shirt.

"Hey."

Kat looked up to see Lila coming out of the cottage, and she smiled, knowing her aunt would know why she was crying. "Just sitting here feeling sorry for myself," Kat said.

"Well, stop because we have a lot to talk about." Lila held out some legal-sized papers for her to see.

"The house is officially mine," she said. "Which means if we want to turn it into a bed and breakfast, we've got a lot of work ahead of us."

Kat launched herself into her aunt's arms. "Congratulations," she said, hugging her. "How'd this happen?"

"They dropped the petition," she said, shrugging. "No explanation. But Roy suspects they knew they didn't have grounds and didn't want to waste any more money fighting the will. It's not as if their father didn't provide for them, and I think that's why they dropped it. Carl was a brilliant man," she said, ending on a wistful note.

"So you really want to turn the house into a bed and breakfast?"

"Sure I do, honey. I just want to make certain that we don't do anything irreparable to the old place. We need to add a few bathrooms and put an addition in the back for the living quarters for you. That's where you come in. As far as I'm concerned, this is your baby. I'm the owner and you're the manager-slash-operator. I don't want anything to do with this, except the money." She smiled. "Less your salary, of course."

"Of course." Kat sat down and hugged her knees. She wasn't sure how she could be so happy and so sad at the same time, but there it was. She felt her aunt's hand on her shoulder and looked up at her.

"If it's to be, it'll happen, honey."

"I know. I just wish he wasn't going to be so far away. I feel as if I don't have any control over the situation."

Lila laughed. "You don't. You didn't control his falling in love, did you?"

"No. In fact, I hurt my cause more than anything."

"And you don't have any control over whether he falls out of love. Right?"

Kat furrowed her brow. "I know you're right, but I still feel helpless. I really love him." Kat swallowed hard. "He turned out to be such an amazing person." The man who wrote that book was frighteningly intelligent and emotionally deeper than she could have thought. The man who wrote that book wouldn't be married to a cleaning lady.

There. She'd said it, if only to herself. Lawrence Kendall, former doctor, brilliant author, would never in a million years have fallen in love with her if they hadn't been forced to share this house. He wouldn't have approached her in a bar; he wouldn't have met her in any of their respective circles. They were worlds apart, and not just geographically. Maybe dukes married scullery maids in romance novels, but they didn't in real life. Heck, in books, the scullery maid was almost always an heiress hiding out, not some lowly servant anyway.

Chapter 23

"You can't be serious. What do you really know about this girl?"

Lawrence looked at his brother with surprise, wondering when he'd become such a snob. Then again, John had married a girl from an excellent family, one who their father had accepted without question. Lawrence had no doubt that his brother loved Laura, but he'd made damned certain she was the right kind of woman before he'd allowed himself to fall in love.

"I know I love her," Lawrence said, settling himself down in his brother's library. The family money was most evident in this room, which was filled with priceless artwork and an even more precious collection of books. Their money wasn't old, but John's style of living was a close facsimile of it.

"What sort of family does she come from?"

"John, if you've decided to take on the role of parent, you can stop. You're two years older than me, and frankly, you're beginning to sound like an ass."

John laughed. "I am, aren't I? Having said that, what sort of family does she come from?"

Lawrence sighed. "Her mother works in a small diner. Her father's whereabouts are unknown. In fact, I believe the father's identity is unknown. But Katherine is an intelligent, beautiful woman who makes me laugh. She doesn't take me too seriously, either. I like that about her most. She's not impressed by me."

"She doesn't feed your ego? God help her," John said dryly. He paused, taking a long, thoughtful breath, and Lawrence braced himself for some brotherly advice.

"Please don't take offense by what I'm about to say. I spoke with Thomas before you came home, and I have some concerns about this Katherine woman. She's a housekeeper?"

Lawrence fought a twinge of anger and smiled, though it didn't reach his eyes. "Her aunt owns the house I was staying at. Carl gave me permission, and her aunt was unaware of our agreement when she told her niece she could have the house for the summer."

"But she actually was a housekeeper."

Lawrence pressed his jaws together. "Yes. She *owned* a cleaning company."

"I know what I sound like."

"Do you?"

John smiled. "Actually, yes. But there are reasons people with the same backgrounds, be it religious, political, economic, or whatever, seek each other out. We fit together. We have common interests. Common friends."

"God, do you know what you sound like?" Lawrence asked, losing a bit of his temper.

"Yes, I do. But there are certain truths that I want

you to think about before you take this relationship any further. How will she get on with your friends? With your family?"

"I hadn't thought about it, and frankly, I don't care."

"But someday, you might. Someday, when the glow of love is gone and she says or does something to embarrass you, you might find yourself hating her."

Lawrence looked at his brother sharply and wondered if his brother was talking about himself.

"I appreciate your concern, John. And I want you to know, even though it is none of your business, that I specifically did not mention a future with Katherine because I wanted to be certain of my feelings for her. She wants children."

"And?"

"And I've always said that I didn't."

John suddenly looked grave, and Lawrence suspected his brother knew why he didn't want children, particularly girl children. "You've changed your mind?" he asked quietly.

Lawrence shook his head. He was still intoxicated by Katherine's memory, by her smile, her sexual abandon, her complete and utter faith in him as a man. He wasn't prepared to make such a life-altering decision yet. Children. The thought of them had always scared the living hell out of him. What if one got sick or hurt? Or died? He knew he wasn't strong enough to face such a thing.

"No, I haven't," he said, and he wondered if he ever would.

* * *

Lila quietly placed the last of the dirty breakfast dishes in the dishwasher, hoping Roy wouldn't storm in and pretend he was angry she was helping out. At least she thought he was pretending. Either that, or he truly was annoyed by her presence. Lila had entered new territory. No man she'd met had found her annoying at all. Most men leered at her or at least admired her and wanted her around.

"I could have done that," he said from the doorway, sounding gruff as usual.

"Yes, but now you don't have to," she said, smiling brightly. He never seemed to look at her anymore, another thing Lila wasn't used to. Men looked at her, and she enjoyed the attention; she always had. She liked the way their eyes followed her when she crossed a room, the way they'd jump up and open a door for her or pull out a chair.

"After Labor Day, we've only got a few customers, and you'll be heading back to California, I suppose," he said, looking at his hand as he moved it back and forth across the countertop.

"I'll probably leave in about a week," she said and looked for some kind of reaction from him. He tapped his finger twice, two sharp sounds in the otherwise silent room.

"All right, then."

Stunned, Lila watched him turn away.

"Roy."

He turned, looking surprised that she'd called out to him.

Lila tilted her head in a flirtatious way that on another woman, might have seemed contrived, but on Lila, it was an innate and effortless gesture. "You've been acting very strangely the past few days," she said.

"Not used to a woman in the house. All these flowers are making me nervous. I'm not used to someone being underfoot, helping out." He held up a hand to stop her from interrupting. "Now, don't take that the wrong way. You know I appreciate all that you've done for me."

Lila folded her arms beneath her breasts and was slightly satisfied to see his eyes drop briefly to her cleavage, which she knew was showing nicely. Flirting might be natural for her, but she wasn't above using the assets God blessed her with to get her message heard. "You're running scared." And then, just because she was feeling particularly cruel, she leaned forward against the small kitchen table, giving him a show of her womanly charms that would have made a weaker man drool. Again, his eyes did a quick dip.

"I don't know what you're talking about."

"You *are* attracted to me," she said softly.

"So? Every man on the planet is attracted to you," he said, this time staring openly and with clear hostility at her breasts. "You flaunt yourself to every Tom, Dick, and Harry that walks by. Your pants are too tight; your shirts are too low; your shoes are too high."

Lila felt her cheeks heat with anger, and she stood up and thrust her fists onto her ample hips. "How dare you?"

"I'm just telling the truth, and you know it."

Lila didn't argue because it *was* the truth, but the way Roy said it made her seem like some kind of slut even though she simply enjoyed men's attention. Just because she was proud of the body she'd been given didn't mean she was trashy.

"You're an intelligent, sweet woman, which no one knows because they're too busy looking at your other assets."

Lila's anger faded slightly.

"I don't know how Carl put up with it."

Like that, the anger was back. "Because he was man enough to know that I loved him and only him. Frankly, he liked the fact that other men envied him."

"You're not a prize to put on display," Roy said, and Lila could tell he was about to lose his temper.

"He never treated me that way," Lila said, shocked.

"Of course he did. He was an old man with a beautiful wife who liked to show everyone just how beautiful she was. He got the prize. He wanted everyone to see he could keep a beautiful young woman happy. I liked Carl. I considered him a friend, and I know he truly loved you. But Carl was a man who liked to flaunt what he had, and he had you."

Tears welled up in Lila's eyes. "That's not true. Carl never . . ."

"Of course he did. He beamed when he was in public with you. He loved the attention as much as you did."

Lila shook her head. "He loved me."

Roy walked over to Lila and put his hands on her shoulders. "Yes, he did. As much as a man can love a woman. He loved the entire package. He loved showing you off and showing himself off. That doesn't make him bad or you less. It's the truth though."

Lila looked past Roy through blurry eyes, knowing in her heart that much of what Roy was saying was true.

"You shouldn't hide who you are, Lila, but you're more than this," he said, looking at her body.

"I know."

He smiled, but it was a sad smile, as if he didn't believe her. "You are the warmest, kindest soul I know." And he kissed her. It wasn't a kiss filled with passion, but it was probably the most wonderful first kiss she'd ever experienced. He pulled back and gave her another of those strange, sad smiles, and Lila had the horrible feeling it was also a last kiss—a kiss goodbye.

Kat looked at the clock. It was noon on the East Coast, five o'clock in England. She could no longer look at the time without mentally calculating what time it was where Larry was. She wondered what he was doing, whether he was going to call, whether she should call him.

He'd called from New York, sounding so wonderful and so normal. He'd said he loved her twice, and she'd said it back, her heart welling up with hope. Then he'd called her from his brother's when he'd first arrived, saying he was tired, saying he loved her and wished she was with him. He'd called the next day and the next, and then he didn't.

Kat looked at the clock, then the phone, feeling sick inside. It had only been two days since he'd called. Larry was probably busy with family and friends and preparing for the wedding, which was tomorrow. She was sure he hadn't had time for a two-minute phone call. Didn't have time to pick up a phone—one second—and dial her number—ten seconds. Nope. Larry hadn't apparently been able to squeeze eleven seconds of time out of his busy schedule to call and say, "Hello. I love you. I miss you."

Kat grabbed up the phone and looked at her carefully written out calling instructions. Then she picked up the calling card for international calls and dialed, plugging in seemingly dozens of numbers before she heard the sound of a phone ringing across the Atlantic.

"Kendall residence."

Kat nearly panicked to hear the sound of what she assumed was a servant answering the phone. "Larry, um, Lawrence, please."

"I'm sorry; Mr. Kendall is not at home. May I take a message for him?"

"Oh. Sure. Could you tell him Kat called?"

"Kat. Certainly."

And the servant rang off, leaving Kat feeling depressed and with the impression that her message wouldn't get to Larry. She didn't like the way the woman had said, "Kat."

Four hours later, the phone rang. Nine o'clock England time, she thought as she reached for the phone.

"Katherine."

"Hi, Larry. You got my message?"

"Actually, no. I've been busy with wedding plans. Didn't realize the best man had to do so much."

Kat could hear the clamor of a public place in the background, complete with throbbing music and crowd noises. "Where are you?"

"At the rehearsal party. Wedding's tomorrow."

"Is Thomas nervous?"

"God, no. He's never been more certain of anything in his life. It's downright nauseating."

Kat laughed.

"I probably won't have time to call you tomorrow with the wedding and all."

"Okay. Have fun."

"Yes. I . . . I love you, Katherine."

Hesitation. Oh, God, it was happening all ready.

"Me, too. Bye."

Kat hung up, her heart hurting so badly she felt as if he'd already made the final phone call saying things wouldn't work out after all. Tears streamed down her face as she stared blindly at a painting of a seascape that hung above the phone. She'd never noticed before, but just below the desolate lighthouse in the painting was the figure of a woman facing the sea. Waiting for her love to come home. Waiting in vain, she thought, stifling a sob. Just then the phone rang again, and Kat cleared her throat, hoping that whoever was on the other end wouldn't detect her tears. If it was her mother, she knew she wouldn't be able to fool her.

"Hello?"

"I miss you like mad, you know. And I love you like mad."

Kat's grin nearly hurt her face. "I know."

"You don't know."

"I'm trying."

"God, I wish I was there with you." He said it fiercely as if he could will her to believe it.

Kat closed her eyes, feeling her heart unbreaking. "I miss you like crazy, too."

"Good. I'll call when I can. Right?"

"Right. I love you, Larry."

And this time when she hung up, she felt as if all was well in the world.

Chapter 24

The wedding had gone well, as well as any of those things can. Remarkable since the couple hadn't known each other for even two months before exchanging vows that tied them together for a lifetime. At least that was the plan. Lawrence was cynical about love, but being in the midst of that emotion made him less so, and he actually found himself believing in a fairy tale ending for Thomas and Jocelyn.

The only annoying moment came when Thomas, well married and a bit drunk, pulled him aside and offered him some advice on Katherine.

"I'm telling you now, do a background check on her. What do you really know about this girl other than the fact she was a maid?"

"She owned a housecleaning business. She's a bastard, her mother's a waitress, and as far as I know, she's penniless."

"She does have that wealthy aunt," Thomas said, and Lawrence half-expected to hear dramatic music in the background foreshadowing disaster. "And how did that aunt get wealthy?"

"By marrying wealthy men," Lawrence said, knowing where Thomas's line of questioning was headed. He couldn't have been more transparent.

"Absolutely. See? It could run in the family."

"As far as I can tell, Katherine has no designs on my severely limited fortune. As a matter of fact, she is perhaps the least materialistic woman I've ever met." The conversation they'd had about his Burberry pants had been very telling.

Thomas put a heavy arm around his shoulder. "Just check. I did, you know, and look at us."

"I take it Jocelyn passed muster."

Talking out the side of his mouth, he said, "She's got nearly as much money as I do. Both parents are lawyers, and her father even made a run for state office. Jocelyn signed the prenuptial agreement without batting an eye and then presented me with one of her own. I think that's when I knew I was truly in love." He put on a silly grin.

"Was there ever a doubt?"

"Actually, no." His eyes found Jocelyn leaning toward his mother to hear her. "She's first class. Look at her. Even my mother loves her, and that's no easy feat. And she's an American."

"She's very nice," Lawrence said.

"Perfect."

Lawrence took his friend by the shoulders, turned him, and gave him a little push toward the bride. First, his brother, then Thomas. He wondered if the two of them had gotten together to conspire against him. He looked down at his empty glass and jiggled the ice a bit, wondering whether he should have another. One more, and he might be as drunk as Thomas was now. One more, and he might call Katherine and ask her to marry him.

Better not have one more. Not just yet.

* * *

Lila found Kat at the kitchen table, papers with drawings of what looked like an amateur attempt at house design littering the top.

"Hey. I'm just trying to figure out this bed and breakfast stuff. I think we can pull this off if we turn one of the bedrooms upstairs into two bathrooms, one for this room and one for this. Does that work for you?"

"Sure."

Kat looked up. "Are you even paying attention to me?"

This time, Lila looked down at the drawings. "Is there enough room for two baths? That's the smallest bedroom."

"If we just put in a shower, we can do it. We can make the master suite the deluxe room. That gives us three rooms on the second floor, and the attic would be a fourth that could be used as a family suite. We could fit a queen and a couple of twins up there. But we need to add another bathroom. I'm still not certain what to do down here, if anything. Other than take down that picture of you."

Lila sighed. "Works for me."

Kat put the pencil down and faced her aunt. "What's wrong?"

"Do you think I flaunt my body?"

"Yes."

Lila pursed her lips and took a deep breath. "I mean in an overt way. In a way that's designed to attract attention."

"Yes." Kat knew she was bothering her aunt, but she was answering honestly.

"But that's just not true."

Kat rolled her eyes. "Lila, look at you. You're a walking, talking sex advertisement. I'm not saying you're doing it in a sleazy way, but you are doing it. Look at your hair. It's not really that blond. And look at your skirt."

Lila brushed her hands down the skirt, which ended about midthigh. "What's wrong with this skirt?"

"I guess it would be okay for a sixteen-year-old, but it's a little short and a little tight for you."

"What else?" she asked through gritted teeth.

"You're getting mad. I think I'll stop here."

"Please go on."

Kat gave her aunt a sideways glance. "Keep in mind that I dress extremely conservatively, so you have to take all this with a grain of salt. You really do dress provocatively. I know you like to show off what you have, but sometimes, just sometimes, you dress a bit over the top."

"I do?"

"Sometimes."

Lila slumped down into a kitchen chair. "That's what Roy said, among other things."

"Really. Such as?"

"He said basically that I was a trophy wife. That Carl loved me, but he also loved to show me off."

"And that you liked being shown off?"

Lila shook her head. "I honestly never felt that way. But I suppose that's the way it looked. Maybe that's how it was."

"Why would Roy say something like that anyway?" Kat said, getting a bit angry at Roy for making her aunt sad.

"Oh, I was flirting."

"With who?"

Lila smiled. "With him. Giving him the lean." She stood and demonstrated, making Kat laugh.

"And he saw right through you, right?"

"Like a pane glass window."

Kat began straightening up the papers when she stopped dead, slowly raising her head to stare at her aunt. "Why were you flirting with Roy?"

Lila pretended to find her drawings suddenly fascinating.

"Lila?"

"Fine. I like Roy. A lot."

Kat let out a breath of resignation. "He's much too young for you," she said and laughed when Lila took an ineffectual swing at her.

"You know, I think Roy is the first man I've ever met who hasn't wanted to drag me into a bed."

"How do you know he doesn't?"

"I know. He finds me more annoying than anything. No one has ever found me annoying."

Kat laughed again. "Lila, you've been way too lucky in love." Then she put her hand over her mouth, remembering that Lila had buried three husbands.

"Oh, don't worry. I know what you mean," Lila said, waving away her horror. "I usually can get a man to fall in love with me before the last course is served. But maybe all this time, they've just been falling in love with this," she said, indicating her body.

"It's very possible that what they felt at first was lust, which later turned into love. I know Carl loved you. Everyone could see how much that man adored you."

Lila's eyes filled. "I know he did," she said firmly. "I know he did."

"He did. Maybe Roy's just jealous of the attention other men give you."

"I know he's jealous," Lila said offhandedly. "But there's something more there. Something deeper. He makes me feel . . ." Lila trailed off. "As if I'm missing something. As if . . ."

"As if?"

"As if he's disappointed in me."

It was a cool morning, the grass was still wet from an all-night drizzle, and Lawrence's two nieces and one nephew were trying to play croquet. It was beginning to deteriorate into a game of horseless polo, though, the way the two oldest were beginning to hit the ball. Lawrence sat on his brother's patio, a cup of coffee on a table beside him. He liked watching kids play, the way they talked to each other, the illogical way they solved problems. Sophie was the youngest, and at four, she just couldn't understand why she couldn't play as well as her older brother and sister. He watched her frustration with amusement, wondering when or if he should step in and talk to the other two about giving their little sister some sort of handicap. Sophie solved it herself.

"I get two hits," she said, then whacked her red-striped ball an amazing distance. She walked over to the ball with determination, but instead of hitting back toward the field, she whacked it even farther away, much to her big sister's disgust.

"Sophie. Wrong wa-a-ay-y-y."

"Don't care," came her answer from around a small hedge that separated this part of the yard from the pool. Then came the sound of the mallet hitting the ball again.

"I told you she was too little to play," Maybelle said sternly to her younger brother. "She always ruins every game we play."

"Maybe you should just ignore her and let her do what she wants. She's having fun," Lawrence called.

"But she's not playing by the rules," she explained patiently. "She never does." Maybelle was ten and, apparently, a strict rule follower. "And if she's hit the ball in the pool again, she can just get it herself."

Lawrence smile faded abruptly, then he leapt up from his chair. The pool. His heart slammed violently in his chest as he ran toward the pool, picturing Sophie floating face down and lifeless as the bobbing ball floated just out of reach. As he threw himself around the hedge, he saw her standing by the pool, a dripping ball in one hand, the skimmer net in the other, a look of triumph on her face.

"I got the ball," she said, holding it up.

Lawrence collapsed to his knees, his breath coming in shallow gasps, as if he'd run a hundred miles instead of just a few yards.

"In the pool again," Maybelle said with clear contempt. "That's it. You're not playing with us anymore."

Lawrence could hear the children arguing but couldn't make out the words over the roar in his ears. He stayed on the grass, hands clutching his knees, head bent, trying to regain control of himself.

"Uncle. Uncle?" Lawrence saw a pair of pink Nikes

standing by him. "Donald, run inside and tell Father Uncle Lawrence is dying."

Lawrence shook his head and actually let out a laugh. "No. Not dying," he managed.

"Stop, Donald. Uncle is not dying," came Maybelle's authoritative command.

Lawrence slowly got to his feet and looked down at Sophie's big blue eyes, full of innocence and a tiny bit of fear. "Don't you ever go near that pool by yourself again, young lady," he said, pointing a shaking finger at her.

Instead of dissolving into tears, Sophie lifted her chin. "You're not the boss of me," she said.

"He is when I'm not around, Sophie," John said as he walked out of the house and toward his family. "You apologize to your uncle."

Looking slightly chastised, Sophie mumbled an apology, then ran back to the other part of the yard to continue playing. The other two children hovered near the adults until their father shooed them away as well.

"What happened?"

Lawrence felt suddenly embarrassed. "Sophie fished her ball out of the pool. I thought she might have fallen in." He took a quick breath. "I panicked."

"She's not allowed to be by the pool by herself," John said, looking more annoyed than anything. As if he didn't realize how quickly Sophie could have fallen in, how she could have drowned. "She's a good swimmer, but still, we have our rules. I'll talk to her." Lawrence could feel his brother's eyes move from his daughter to him and sensed the moment when John knew something more was wrong. "Are you all right?"

His entire body was bathed in sweat, his knees felt weak, and he knew if he held up his hand, it would shake. And in that moment, standing in his brother's back garden, Lawrence knew without a doubt he could not marry the woman he loved more than anything in the world. "She wants children," he said softly, and his brother knew what he meant and put a comforting hand on his shoulder.

Summer was officially over. Even without a calendar, anyone living on the island would be able to tell. It wasn't only that the traffic was gone and school buses had appeared. The island had a different feel to it, a calmer, quieter feel that the locals welcomed the way children welcomed Christmas. It was as if the entire place let out a long sigh of relief that the tourists were gone.

To Kat, who had never been on the island other than during the summer months, it was a startling change. Wonderful and yet sad in a way. The passing of the seasons always brought a bit of melancholy, a clear marker that time was passing and nothing could stop it.

Kat looked out at the Atlantic with a renewed sense that what she was doing was right. She'd called her landlord and made arrangements to rent her apartment permanently to two of her friends. Her stuff would go into storage, and her mother would ship to the island the few items that meant anything to her. Her mother had been unusually unfazed by Kat's announcement she was staying on the island, and Kat wondered if she was involved with someone she knew her daughter wouldn't approve of.

She'd be busy this winter converting the cottage into a bed and breakfast. She'd have to go to the Home Depot in Falmouth and pick out fixtures and tile and everything else she'd need. Lila had practically given her a blank check to spend money, so she was going high end all the way. She'd hired an architect to design the addition for living quarters out back, something that would blend with the existing house. She'd also contacted a web design company to construct a website for the inn. Kat couldn't wait until her first customers came in, all windblown from the ferry, looking happy to have discovered such a wonderful place to stay.

Kat walked back into the house to work on the list of items she would have to buy on the mainland, glancing at the clock on the mantel. It was nearly nine in the morning, and just seeing the time made her heart pick up. Kat loved when the phone rang before noon because it was almost always Lawrence. Nine o'clock here, two o'clock there, she mentally said. His phone calls had continued with wonderful regularity. She loved talking with him on the phone. There were no long dead spots in the conversation, no struggling to come up with topics to discuss. They were as natural on the telephone as they had been in person, and Kat was finally starting to believe that she and Larry just might have a happy ending after all.

When the phone rang that morning, nearly three weeks after Larry had left to go to New York, Kat flew to the phone. "Oceanside Bed and Breakfast," she said just to be funny.

"Katherine."

Kat's heart dropped. She could sense from the

way he said her name that something awful had happened. "What's wrong? Are you all right?"

He laughed, but it wasn't a happy laugh, and she squeezed the phone even tighter. "I love you," he said.

"I know. Tell me what happened."

"I love you." It sounded horribly, impossibly like he was trying not to cry.

"Larry. Tell me."

"I don't want children."

Kat's entire body relaxed in that horrible way that happens when you know something awful is about to take place, but there is nothing, absolutely nothing, you can do about it. "I know," she said.

"I want to marry you, but I don't want children."

And just like that, she was crying. "Oh, Larry."

"I'm sorry."

"Don't say that. Don't say anything. I need to think." Even as she said those words, she knew she could never change her mind about wanting children. It was something she had wanted, dreamed about, for as long as she could remember.

"I'm sorry," he repeated, and she knew he was trying desperately not to cry.

"So this is it?" Oh, no, Larry. Say it's not. Say you're crazy in love with me again and you want a little daughter who looks just like me, and I'll tell you I hope our son looks like you. Stop, Larry. Stop. Stop. Stop.

"Sorry." And he rang off.

Chapter 25

Two weeks after Larry's phone call, Kat woke up feeling drugged and sluggish. She glanced at the clock lifelessly. Eight in the morning. She should get up because the contractor would probably start banging away in about a half hour anyway. She hated the constant banging. She hated the isolation of the island. She hated that Lila was still here looking at her as if she were a lost puppy. She hated just about everything.

Most of all, she hated Larry because he broke her heart. Hated and loved him. God, she still loved him.

She could hear Lila moving about the kitchen and grimaced. When was she going to go back to California? She ought to either leave or stay, but Kat wished Lila would stop hovering around her as if she might swim into the cold Atlantic and swim and swim until she slipped beneath the waves forever.

"Blah, blah, blah," she said to herself, even impatient with her self-destructive, depressing thoughts.

Kat heard the contractor's truck pulling in front of the house and peeled off the covers. Might as well take a shower. She hadn't yesterday, and today, she was feeling kind of funky. This breakup had really knocked her down, she thought as she made her way to the bathroom. "Really broke my heart this time," she said aloud just to hear her voice. "Really got me good. Not showering every day. Talking to myself. Going over the deep end with errant thoughts of suicide." Kat chuckled a little, and that scared her because nothing she'd been saying had been particularly funny.

She took a long, hot shower and emerged feeling much better. She needed a haircut, she thought, looking into the mirror at her wet, tangled hair. Kat tilted her head, finger-combing her hair a bit. Maybe she should grow it, make a change. Maybe she should color it, go really nuts, make a clean start. She should go red, one of those really obnoxiously obvious reds that people looked at funny. Maybe black. Maybe anything to change from the person she'd been when her heart had been ripped from her chest by a man saying over and over, "I love you."

She truly believed Larry loved her. She could torture herself by saying he didn't love her *enough*, but he could say the same, couldn't he? *She didn't love me enough to make it just the two of us*. Wasn't that just as fair as her saying, *He didn't love me enough to share me*?

It was so nice to be brokenhearted and rational.

Kat walked into the kitchen, her hair still slightly damp. "I was thinking of going red," she said to Lila.

Lila took a sip of her coffee and studied her face as if trying to picture red hair on top of her head. "That might work," she said finally. "I thought about going red once, but my stylist talked me out of it. Louie's going to die when he sees my hair. My roots have roots."

"Why don't you just have your hair done here?"

Lila looked at her as if she'd gone quite mad. "Here? I have to go to Louie. Even if I fly home just for that. Which I am planning to do, you know."

"You're flying home to get your hair done?"

"No. I am flying home though. I miss my place, and so does Killer." The dog shivered by her feet as if she couldn't bear the anticipation of going home.

"Are you going for good or just for a few weeks?"

"For good," she said with such forced nonchalance Kat knew her decision had not been easy. She gave her niece a smile. "I trust you to supervise what's going on here. The contractor said the guest rooms and new bathrooms should be ready by Christmas, then he'll start working on the addition."

"If we get zoning approval."

"We will," Lila said. "The neighbors don't have a problem, and that's usually the biggest hurdle."

"Thank God Roy doesn't mind the competition," Kat said, looking closely at Lila when she said his name. "By the way, what did Roy say about you leaving?"

"He doesn't know," Lila said. She dumped the rest of her coffee into the sink, then put the dirty mug in the dishwasher. "Frankly, I don't think he'll give it much thought. He's open year-round, so he'll be fairly busy up until January."

"So, we'll be two lonely people stuck on an island all winter," Kat said. "Who knows what could happen."

"You? And Roy?" Lila said, shrugging her shoulders. "Maybe." Even though it was clear Lila knew Kat was joking, Kat sensed the thought of Roy being alone all winter except for a few customers bothered her.

Kat held a phantom phone to her ear. "Roy? I can't move this heavy couch. Could you come over and help? I'm ever so helpless without a big, strong man like you," Kat said, having fun with her aunt. "And why don't you stay for supper. I'm so-o-o lonely."

"Joke's not that funny," Lila said in a singsong voice tinged with just the tiniest bit of irritation. "Besides, Roy's not supposed to lift anything heavier than fifty pounds for another few weeks."

"A woman sure gets lonely on this island, Roy."

"If you think you're bothering me, you're not."

Kat laughed. "I am bothering you so much you could spit."

"And here I was feeling sorry for you," Lila said.

The fun was suddenly gone.

"I'm sorry, honey; that was thoughtless of me."

Kat shook her head. "I'm real good at dishing it out, but I can't take it. Obviously. Larry dumping me really knocked me down good. But I feel better today. I can see a light at the end of the long, dark, dank tunnel."

"Good," Lila said, giving Kat a hug. "And you'll be okay when I'm gone?"

"I'll have Roy," Kat said, and Lila gave her a look of mock anger.

"I wish I had Roy," Lila said, surprising Kat. "But I think it's best I go home. He'll still be here when I come back next summer."

Kat thought of the long string of summers to come and felt even more depressed when she should have been excited by the prospect of running the B&B. For the hundredth time, she wondered if she was being the selfish one, the uncompromising one, to want children above the man she loved.

"Did you ever want kids?" she asked, and Lila went still.

"We tried, Carl and I. He felt and acted so young, I think he thought he just might live to a hundred. I know I did. And so we tried for a year. Then we both went through every test under the sun, and it turned out I was the infertile one. He was sure it was him, and every time I got my period, he'd apologize. God, it killed me. Then we got the news that the only hope for us was *in vitro*. By that time, Carl was beginning to get sick, and we decided not to go ahead."

"I'm so sorry, Lila. I had no idea."

Lila smiled sadly. "I wish every day that we'd gone ahead and tried. I never really had a burning desire to have kids until I found out I couldn't. Every month that passed, I'd feel like I was somehow failing. And of course, it seemed like every woman I saw was either carrying a baby or was pregnant. For a while, I thought I was losing my mind." Lila looked blindly out the window at the house next door. "But I'm still young. There's still hope."

"Would you ever marry a man who didn't want kids?"

"No," she said without hesitation. "I know plenty of couples who decide not to have kids, and that's fine for them if that's what they want. But I know now that I want children. If I have to adopt, I will. I've even looked into it."

"Really?"

"Sure."

Kat let out a sigh. "I know I made the right decision, but I can't help but wonder if everything would have worked out once we were married."

"No, honey, don't think that way. You would have gotten married and maybe gotten pregnant—

against his wishes, and I guarantee that would not be a good home for a child. And don't think you could be happy either. It would always be there, that need to have a baby."

"I don't know. I don't have a baby now, and I'm pretty happy. Except for the broken heart and all."

Lila turned from the window and gave Kat a hard look. "You have to make up your own mind about Lawrence. But I'd hate to see you make a mistake that would make you miserable in a few years."

Kat left her aunt in the kitchen to sit on the front porch. As if God were sending her a message, a woman walked by holding hands with a little girl about three years old. The two were talking and giggling and were so clearly happy Kat's throat burned with unshed tears. That little hand holding her mother's was what did her in. She stared at that connection, little fingers, wrist still baby-chubby, holding on to her mother's hand with complete trust and love.

"Damn," she said softly, forcing herself to look away. "Why couldn't it have been a screaming little brat with a harried mother walking by?"

Lila joined her on the porch a few minutes later.

"I made the right decision," Kat said firmly.

"I think so. And I think going back to California is the right decision for me."

Roy liked his life just fine. He liked running his business the way he wanted to, liked dictating his free time, liked being alone sometimes.

And he liked lying to himself.

He knew Lila was thinking about going back to California, and he told himself a hundred times a day that it would be a good thing for both of them. They hadn't spent any real time together. Lila hadn't seen the man he was, the vibrant, funny, healthy man because he'd gotten sick so soon after she'd arrived. She'd fallen for the old man lying in a hospital bed. Well, that just wasn't him.

Each day out of the hospital, he felt better and better, almost back to where he was before the heart attack. He'd been going for three-mile walks every day for the past two weeks and was probably in better shape than he'd been in two months ago.

And he was horny as hell.

Lila would come waltzing into his house completely oblivious to the fact he wanted to throw her down on the nearest flat surface and show her just how strong and fit he was. Or maybe she wasn't so oblivious. Maybe she just wasn't interested.

She'd been spending less and less time over at his house, and he couldn't say he blamed her. He was acting like an ass, though he didn't really know why. At night, he'd look at his dead wife's picture and ask her what the hell was wrong with him. It had been so long since he'd been truly interested in a woman he wasn't sure how to go about it all. Up until three years ago, he'd had a mistress of sorts, but she'd moved off island to live with her son. They'd never had much more to their relationship than occasional sex, and he hadn't been heartbroken when she'd left.

But the thought of Lila going back to California left him feeling madder than hell.

He heard a delicate tap at his private door, let out a sigh, and let Lila in.

"Good morning," she said in her light, singsong voice.

"Morning. Coffee?"

"No, thanks. I had enough caffeine already."

She was wearing a white cable sweater that hugged her body in a way that made a man either want to stare forever or to look away. Roy stared. "Nice sweater," he said finally, knowing he had been caught ogling her.

"It's chilly this morning, almost like fall." Some women might fold their arms over their chests when a man was caught openly staring at their breasts, but Lila arched her back slightly, just enough to make his blood run hot. Goddamn if he couldn't see the outline of her nipples. Guess it was cold outside.

"Getting too cold for this California girl," Lila said, and Roy thought, here it comes, the goodbye. "I'm leaving tomorrow."

"Guess it's about time."

She pressed her lips together. "I guess so."

Roy rolled up the sleeves of his flannel shirt as if he was about to go out and do some work.

"You'll be okay? If you need help, Kat's next door."

"I'm fine," he said. "I haven't felt this good in years."

"I'll be back in the summer. Probably stay a few weeks."

"Stop by if you want."

Lila let out a sigh of impatience. "Roy, you are the most hardheaded man I've ever had the displeasure of meeting."

"Well, you don't have to stop by if you don't want to," he said, knowing he was being an idiot but not knowing how to stop himself. How the hell had he ever gotten a beautiful woman like Sara to fall in love with him and agree to marry him. Had he really changed so much? Had he completely forgotten how to talk to a woman?

"Take care of yourself, Roy."

He clenched his jaw, trying not to do anything foolish like drag her into his arms and kiss the living daylights out of her. He wondered briefly what she'd do, if she'd somehow guess that he'd been foolish enough to fall in love with a woman he had no business loving.

Lila touched his cheek, and for one weak moment, he closed his eyes as if her touch was just too much for him to take.

"Roy?"

He pulled her to him and kissed her the way he'd been fantasizing about since the day he saw her wiggling down Sea View Avenue pulling along her ridiculous mutt. Lila melted against him, invited his tongue in, moved her hands to his shoulders, and hung on for dear life. She felt wonderful against him, soft and sexy, a woman full of curves designed to drive a man insane with lust.

But she was leaving, and somehow he remembered that and slowly stopped kissing her, pressing his forehead down against hers.

"How was that for a goodbye kiss?" he asked, chuckling slightly.

"I wish it wasn't goodbye," she said softly, then pushed away and left him standing in his kitchen wondering what the hell she'd just meant by that.

Roy didn't get a chance to ask her, and the next day when he went over to her cottage to give her another goodbye kiss, he found out she was already gone.

Two weeks after Lila left, Kat walked outside to find Roy nailing plywood to his windows. "Are you expecting a hurricane I haven't heard about?" Kat asked, looking at the piercingly blue late September sky.

"Closing up for the winter," he said. And when he didn't offer an explanation, Kat walked on over to him.

"I thought you stayed open year-round?" she said as he pounded in another nail. Already, the wind off the Atlantic felt cold and damp, so she could imagine winters here would be harsh and long without the snow that made New Hampshire so pretty. She couldn't imagine too many people would want to vacation on the island between November and May.

"Thought it was time for a change," he said, climbing down the ladder and heaving up another piece of plywood. Kat noticed the wood was prefabricated to hook on to the house, and all Roy had to do was nail it securely. Kat would have asked to help if he'd shown even the slightest bit of weakness, but he handled the large planks with seeming ease as if he'd done it a hundred times.

"Heading to Florida like the rest of the summer residents?" she asked, not that she could picture Roy in Florida with a bunch of retirees.

"Nope. Thought I'd check out California."

"He's sad," Laura said, watching the distant figure of her brother-in-law as he walked around the property. That's all he'd been doing for weeks—walking about, sleeping late, staying up late.

"Well, he just broke up with a girl," John said, rustling the newspaper to show his wife he didn't want to talk about his brother. Again. Then Laura laid her hand on his wrist, and he reluctantly put the paper down.

"I've known your brother for years. Even when all that happened at the hospital and that little girl died, he wasn't like this. Admit it."

"Fine. I'll admit it freely. But what precisely do you want me to do about it?"

Laura made a helpless gesture. "I don't know. Talk to him."

"I don't know what that would accomplish. He loves her. She loves him. He doesn't want children. She does. It's very simple and quite unsolvable."

Laura looked at Lawrence and shook her head. "That's what I don't understand. He seems to adore children. Look at all the time he spends with our kids. He doesn't have to, you know. They don't even really bother him into it. But he plays chess with Maybelle almost every night, and he reads stories to Sophie. And Donald and he go to the fish pond daily. He spends more time with our children than you do." Laura smiled when John took affront. "If you won't talk to him, I will."

John grabbed up the paper. "You can try, but I don't know what you can say to change things. The man is torturing himself already." John took a long look at his younger brother. "Hell, if you can help him, do it. Can't stand too much more of him moping around here."

"John."

"Well, just look at him. He's a mess."

"He's in love," Laura said wistfully.

"If you're implying that I don't love you, you're wrong. I'd probably be moping about here just like him if something was to happen between us."

Laura smiled and gave her husband a peck on the cheek. "I know," she said, then headed off to talk to Lawrence. Then she called back, "But it is nice to hear."

Laura knew when Lawrence spotted her because he stopped and waited for her to catch up. He didn't look all that happy to see her coming, likely sensing from her serious expression what he was in for. He'd looked so worn out lately, deep circles beneath his eyes and a kind of weariness that only comes from deep mourning. And yet he still found time to play with the children every day. When she reached him, she continued walking in the direction he'd been taking, not waiting to see if he followed.

"I'd like to tell you something that no one in your family knows," she started as if telling him a story. "When your brother and I were first married, we started trying to have children immediately. It was all I could think of. Me more than John. I just couldn't wait to hold a little baby in my arms."

He made a noise as if he didn't want to hear the rest of what she had to say, but she stopped him. "Let me finish, please. Almost immediately, I got pregnant."

Lawrence looked slightly puzzled because he knew his brother and sister-in-law had waited several years before they began having children.

"I miscarried early, long before we felt it was safe to tell anyone. Over the next four years, I miscarried five times. Five little babies, all dead."

"God, Laura, I didn't know."

"No one did. It was our own private hell. My doctor tried several things, but nothing worked. He couldn't tell us why we were losing the babies. I wanted to keep trying. I desperately wanted children, you see. John did, too. But watching me suffer was becoming too much for him. I think my pain was worse for him than the actual miscarriages. Every time I got pregnant, I thought, 'This is the one. This is the baby I'll get to keep.'" She stopped and gazed back at the house where John still read the paper. "I was four months along once. Started to show even, but we didn't tell a soul. And I lost it." She shook her head as if she still couldn't believe all that had happened. "That was it for your brother. No more. Enough. 'We can't have children,' he said. He was devastated by that last one. Of course, I was too. And so we said, no more. He scheduled a vasectomy."

Lawrence watched as her sadness disappeared, as her face, which he'd never thought was particularly attractive, became almost pretty. "And then I got pregnant again quite by accident. John was horrified. Didn't want to discuss it, didn't even want to know when I lost it." Her smile grew. "But this time, I didn't lose the baby. And that's how we got Maybelle." She shrugged. "After that, it was as if my body finally figured it all out, and look at us now. A family of five."

"I feel terrible that you went through that," Lawrence said cautiously, knowing that somewhere in that tragedy, his sister-in-law was trying to smack some sense into him.

"Bad things happen. Terrible things. But when God gives you a gift, you take it and say, 'Thank you, Sir.'

What if we had just given up completely? What if John had gotten that vasectomy? Maybelle, Donald, and Sophie wouldn't be here. It would just be the two of us, and I suppose that would be fine. But our lives are so much richer with our children. I can't imagine a world without them."

Lawrence was silent even though he knew Laura expected him to say something. If she wanted him to experience some sort of epiphany and declare he wanted children now, she was going to be very disappointed.

"You don't dislike children, Lawrence. You're scared to death of them. There's a vast difference. If you didn't like children, I wouldn't be standing here right now trying to convince you to take the next flight to the States."

He smiled. "Is that what you're doing?"

"Yes. You love this girl. Don't be an idiot about this. It's simple fear, Lawrence. You can overcome a fear."

Lawrence wasn't sure he could, but God, how he wanted to.

"You're so unhappy," Laura said, and her eyes welled up with tears.

At least he could agree with her there. He'd never felt quite so devastated in his life. He hadn't imagined how difficult it would be to say goodbye to Katherine. He'd thought by now he would have moved on, gotten over her, gotten back to his life. But the thought of going back to what he had been doing was almost distasteful, and he was beginning to wonder if he'd ever be the same. He missed her so much he was physically ill with it, and he kept saying each night he went to bed without her in his arms that he'd feel better tomorrow.

But he never did.

Chapter 26

The carousel had shut down for the summer, and a cool, sharp wind slammed the coast with an early nor'easter storm. Kat watched as the last ferry of the day was about to dock, knowing it wouldn't be the one containing her new stove and water heater. All ferry traffic had been suspended because of the storm. Welcome to island life, she thought, looking out over the violent Atlantic. The waves crashed over the wall along the boardwalk in a way she'd never seen before. Once in a while, someone in a bright yellow slicker would walk by, a bit of bright color against the dark gray day.

She was beginning to get a taste of what loneliness meant. Other than Roy, Kat knew no one on the island. They were a tight-knit group, these souls who lived on the island year-round. Most probably didn't even know she was staying at the cottage. When she went to the supermarket, she got a few curious stares, but for the most part, Kat was completely and utterly alone.

For the first time, she wondered if she was really cut out for living on an island. Kat found an excuse to call her mother daily, sometimes more than that. She'd called Lila, too, only to get her answering machine. Finally, Lila called from Bermuda on her honeymoon with Roy, joking that the two of them might open up a small inn on that island because the weather was so nice. Given the impulsiveness of her aunt, Kat wouldn't put it past her. Kat had been thrilled for Lila, but she couldn't help but wonder when it was her turn to find a man who wouldn't run away from her.

Brian cheated on her, then married the other woman almost immediately after dumping her. Larry claimed to love her but dumped her anyway.

Rain began spattering the windows, making the scene in front of her blurry. At the ferry landing, she watched the ghostlike images of people disembarking. There were far fewer than in the summer months, mostly locals coming home after a visit to the mainland. Cars and trucks streamed out, windshield wipers slapping at the rain.

This was Kat's excitement for the day. She looked at the television, but at two in the afternoon, the only thing on was lousy soap operas. She didn't have a good book to read because her Amazon order hadn't come in yet, and the book she wanted to read wasn't in the Edgartown bookstore. As good as the bookstore was, it wasn't one of those megastores that carried every book under the sun.

The workers didn't come today because it was Saturday, and she found herself missing the noise of them, the mere physical presence of other human beings in her house. Other than her mother, Kat hadn't had a significant conversation with another human being in days. That left her way, way too much time to brood about Larry and the decisions they'd both made. Her inner debate on having children was still waging even though she knew, knew, *knew* she'd made the right decision. She just couldn't seem to convince her heart of that fact.

Kat stepped away from the window and decided to go the third floor and look out at the ocean. At least watching the violence of the Atlantic was exciting. She could picture some captain's wife trudging up the stairs, lifting her skirts to get to the tower room so she could gaze out at the ocean where her husband's ship would soon be seen over the horizon. Kat got halfway up when someone banged on her front door. Probably someone who wanted to stay at Roy's B&B and hadn't bothered calling ahead. That had happened twice since Roy had left, and she'd told him so. He hadn't seemed to care and sounded almost giddy in his lack of interest in his business.

Kat gave a quick look in the mirror, knowing she didn't look her best on days when she knew she wasn't going to see another soul. At least she was showered, and her hair was clean. These days, that was a plus.

Kat grabbed the phone number and directions to the nearest open B&B and one of her business cards so the poor person on the other side of the door would hopefully pick her B&B next season. Roy's deserting the Vineyard might work out well for her if he stayed away long enough, she thought and smiled as she opened the door.

"Hullo, Katherine."

Kat's heart slammed to her throat and stuck there.

"May I come in?" he asked, apparently amused by her shock.

"Sure," she said, stepping back. "Are you desperate to see me or just need a place to stay since Roy's is closed?"

"Where is Roy?" he asked, avoiding her first and most important question. His hair was wet and plastered to his head, his clothes hung damply to him, and he held a plaid Burberry umbrella that the wind had turned inside out.

"This isn't London rain," Kat said, eyeing what she assumed was a ridiculously expensive umbrella.

"Not quite."

"Roy is honeymooning with Lila in Bermuda. They are disgustingly in love. Make Thomas and Jocelyn seem like they didn't care for one another."

Larry smiled broadly, and Kat's heart hurt. He was so beautiful standing there dripping in her foyer. "Good for them," he said. "Must have been something in the air around here this summer."

Kat turned away, making a pretense of leading him further into the house. His blithe comment had hurt her, as if their falling in love was something insignificant that they could joke about now.

"What are you doing here?" Kat said, trying to harden her heart against this man who she'd thought about a hundred times a day since he left.

"Let me . . ." He took off his dripping trench coat with the same plaid lining as the umbrella and hung it on the foyer's coat tree. Then he smoothed back his hair ineffectually. "Right. Why I'm here."

Kat folded her arms across her chest and waited.

Lawrence stared at her, loving every inch of her five-foot, four-inch frame. She was better than his memories, more beautiful and certainly far angrier, and he wondered if he should delay his little speech until she was in a better mood. He wanted to kiss away that frown that was marring her lovely mouth. He wanted her eyes to close in passion instead of staring at him as if he was some unwanted stranger barging into her home.

"Here's the rub," he started, and she shifted impatiently. "I've missed you. Desperately." She relaxed just slightly, just enough to give him the courage to continue.

"Go on," she said, softly and with the smallest hint of hope.

That's what did it to him, what made him turn from the strong, confident man standing in front of her to the man who crumpled to one knee, his eyes filling with ridiculous tears.

"I have this," he said, and she stood there looking down at him, her eyes wide. He presented the ring, and she took it slowly, felt its weight in her hands, and then, thank God, she smiled and got down on her knees.

"It's beautiful," she said, holding it in her palm, a battered brass ring from the Flying Horse Carousel. Then she flung herself into his arms, crying and laughing. She felt so good, so right there, and he knew he'd do anything, face anything to keep her there forever.

"Of course, you know this isn't it," she said once they'd both calmed down and wiped the tears from their eyes.

"Yes, I know. We have to talk." He said it as if announcing he was having a root canal.

"Children?"

"No more than three."

She stared at him with open hostility. "If this is just because you miss me, I want you to walk right out that door." She pointed her finger fiercely, but Larry just smiled.

"I realized, with the help of my family, that I don't dislike children; I'm afraid of them. I don't like them getting hurt. I don't like them dying. I don't particularly like the idea of them growing up and moving away."

"Ah."

"But," he said, slapping his knees, "it seems as if that's what having children is all about. I do like them. When they're not crying and carrying on and such."

Kat wanted to take this cautiously. "So what you're saying is—"

"That I want children."

If Larry thought she'd jump up and down for joy, he was going to be disappointed. "Are you sure?"

"Absolutely. I've actually given this quite a lot of thought. Nearly a month of daily misery."

Kat smiled. "You are very brave," she said. "Now. Where will we live?"

He looked at her as if she'd gone daft. "Here, of course. I can write anywhere, and this is actually quite near New York. It will do nicely."

"Final question," Kat said, all business. She held up the brass ring. "When do I get my free ride?"

Larry smiled and drew her into his arms. "I think now is as good a time as any."

By Best-selling Author
Fern Michaels

Weekend Warriors	0-8217-7589-8	$6.99US/$9.99CAN
Listen to Your Heart	0-8217-7463-8	$6.99US/$9.99CAN
The Future Scrolls	0-8217-7586-3	$6.99US/$9.99CAN
About Face	0-8217-7020-9	$7.99US/$10.99CAN
Kentucky Sunrise	0-8217-7462-X	$7.99US/$10.99CAN
Kentucky Rich	0-8217-7234-1	$7.99US/$10.99CAN
Kentucky Heat	0-8217-7368-2	$7.99US/$10.99CAN
Plain Jane	0-8217-6927-8	$7.99US/$10.99CAN
Wish List	0-8217-7363-1	$7.50US/$10.50CAN
Yesterday	0-8217-6785-2	$7.50US/$10.50CAN
The Guest List	0-8217-6657-0	$7.50US/$10.50CAN
Finders Keepers	0-8217-7364-X	$7.50US/$10.50CAN
Annie's Rainbow	0-8217-7366-6	$7.50US/$10.50CAN
Dear Emily	0-8217-7316-X	$7.50US/$10.50CAN
Sara's Song	0-8217-7480-8	$7.50US/$10.50CAN
Celebration	0-8217-7434-4	$7.50US/$10.50CAN
Vegas Heat	0-8217-7207-4	$7.50US/$10.50CAN
Vegas Rich	0-8217-7206-6	$7.50US/$10.50CAN
Vegas Sunrise	0-8217-7208-2	$7.50US/$10.50CAN
What You Wish For	0-8217-6828-X	$7.99US/$10.99CAN
Charming Lily	0-8217-7019-5	$7.99US/$10.99CAN

Available Wherever Books Are Sold!

BOOK YOUR PLACE ON OUR WEBSITE
AND MAKE THE
READING CONNECTION!

We've created a customized website just for our very special readers, where you can get the inside scoop on everything that's going on with Zebra, Pinnacle and Kensington books.

When you come online, you'll have the exciting opportunity to:

- View covers of upcoming books
- Read sample chapters
- Learn about our future publishing schedule (listed by publication month *and author*)
- Find out when your favorite authors will be visiting a city near you
- Search for and order backlist books from our online catalog
- Check out author bios and background information
- Send e-mail to your favorite authors
- Meet the Kensington staff online
- Join us in weekly chats with authors, readers and other guests
- Get writing guidelines
- AND MUCH MORE!

**Visit our website at
http://www.kensingtonbooks.com**